Smith's
MONTHLY

Every Month Original
Novels, Stories, and Articles

USA Today Bestselling Writer
Dean Wesley Smith

TABLE OF CONTENTS

Smith's Monthly Issue #7

Introduction
The Origin
of Yet Another Novel

LAST MONTH I WROTE about how I came up with the novel *Kill Game*.

This month the novel *The Slots of Saturn* in this issue has an even stranger story. And that's going some.

Back about 14 or so years ago I came up with a character by the name of Poker Boy. Poker Boy started in a Christmas challenge with professional writer Nina Kiriki Hoffman.

She and I both liked to write four or five short stories in six days, go down to a local copy shop and make fifty copies and give the little numbered and signed chapbooks to our friends for Christmas.

We had fun and entertained our friends with Christmas stories. And then we often sold the stories to major markets. In fact, the Christmas challenge the

year before I sold a story out of the little chapbook to *Ellery Queen's Mystery Magazine*. The year I started Poker Boy, I wrote four stories from his point of view, all focused around Christmas Eve, which was the topic of the chapbook challenge that year.

I liked the character of Poker Boy so much when I was finished, I kept writing more and more of his stories, selling them to various anthologies. Then a year or so later, on a lark, I wrote a Poker Boy novel called *The Slots of Saturn*.

In the old days of publishing, I had an agent and she didn't much like the idea of a humorous superhero by the name of Poker Boy. She convinced me to write a novel called *Dead Money* instead. (Part of that history is in last month's introduction.)

On my own, I think I sent Poker Boy out to a few editors and then soon forgot about the novel as I have a wont to do at times. I tend to always look forward with my writing, so things that are done I tend to forget or ignore.

Thanks for the Support

Dean Wesley Smith

But along the way I let a few people read the novel, once in a workshop here at the coast. The novel had some issues that a few people pointed out, but they overall liked it. And honestly, so did I. I just didn't want to spend the time to go over it again. I had new things to write.

So into the drawer it went where it was forgotten.

And now, years later, along comes this magazine you hold in your hands or are reading on your device.

Over the years, Kris and others who read the book and who like Poker Boy have been after me to get *The Slots of Saturn* into print, so I decided last month to just take a stab at getting the book under control. It had characters and other aspects of Poker Boy that in thirty-plus short stories I had changed.

Plus *The Slots of Saturn* is the origin story for the team around Poker Boy. I wanted to make that story right.

But as I was thinking of going into the book, I was given an assignment to write a twenty thousand word story for the *Fiction River* anthology series. So I decided to write the sequel to *The Slots of Saturn* as a twenty-thousand word story. But to do that, I needed to put the novel back in my head.

So over a period of six days or so, I worked my way through the novel, updating the Poker Boy information and cutting the novel from 80,000 words to the 55,000 words. Then I wrote the sequel to *The Slots of Saturn* for *Fiction River*. That story is called "They're Back!"

So the novel in this issue was fourteen years in the making. And, of course, I had to add in a brand new Poker Boy story in this issue as well to lead off.

So when someone asks me how long it took me to write *The Slots of Saturn* I can honestly say fourteen years. I just won't tell them I wrote fifty or so other novels in that time as well.

I think the secret is safe with us, don't you?

I hope you enjoy the first Poker Boy novel. I'm fairly certain it won't be the last.

Dean Wesley Smith
March 8, 2014,
Lincoln City, Oregon

Coming Next Issue in Smith's Monthly
Captain Brian Saber's first novel!
The first Earth Protection League novel.

USA TODAY BESTSELLING AUTHOR

DEAN WESLEY SMITH

A DESERT SHOT

A POKER BOY SHORT STORY

Poker Boy and his boss, Stan the God of Poker, find themselves, without warning, in the desert staring at a very dead golfer. Only problem: No golf course within miles.

If not strange enough, the self-proclaimed "Worlds Greatest Detective" joins them to ask for help solving the crime.

As far as Poker Boy feels, how golfers dress constitutes the only crime. But the body smells and the detective could annoy a cactus, so something needs to be done.

A DESERT SHOT
A Poker Boy Story

One

STRANGELY ENOUGH, as a superhero, I seldom see a body. It happens, sure, but rarely. If someone gets to the body state, I figured I failed in my Poker Boy super-hero duties.

The body on the hard desert dirt in front of me hadn't been anyone I had known. The body had been out in the hot sun long enough that it had started to get ripe-smelling. I had a hunch the ripe odor would turn real sour real quick if this guy didn't get moved out of the sun sooner rather than later.

The body had on a light tan golf shirt, golf shoes, matching tan golf slacks, and a tan golf glove. The tan sort of washed out his already really white skin. Not a good choice of color for his last day on the planet.

Of course, I had on my black leather jacket and black fedora-like hat standing in the hot desert sun, so I wasn't one to give fashion advice.

From what I could figure, the dead guy had been about forty with a slight gut and about forty extra pounds. No telling what killed him. No blood stained the bland clothing in any place I could see.

And I sure wasn't touching the body to move it. That would be up to the police.

However, I did find it odd that there wasn't a golf course within ten miles of this spot to the north of Las Vegas. In fact, there wasn't much of anything near this spot but sagebrush and rocks and more than likely a large herd of rattlesnakes. Or bunch of rattlesnakes, or group, or whatever a mass of nasty, mean, and deadly snakes are called.

About a mile to the east, I could hear faint freeway noise of trucks and cars with no mufflers, but otherwise the desert blanketed the dead guy with silence and a lot of heat.

Way too much heat for a leather jacket.

Stan, the God of Poker, had brought me to this spot next to this dead guy with the balding head and blank, dead stare in dark eyes. So I turned to Stan who stood there in his dark slacks, tan button-down sweater, and loafers and asked the most logical question I could think to ask after being surprised by teleporting from a comfortable diner booth in my office to a spot next to a body.

"Think maybe we should call the police?"

Stan took us out of time, which had the effect of cutting off the freeway sounds and wind that was keeping the guy's ripening smell away. He motioned that I should follow him and we moved about fifty steps away from the bland dead guy, staying inside the time bubble the entire time.

"Thank you," I said. "So what are we doing here? And who's the dead guy?"

"Not a clue," Stan said. "And I honestly don't know why we're here."

Now that made me turn my attention from the now distant dead body and look directly at my boss, the God of Poker.

He shrugged, actually looking puzzled. "So you didn't pluck me from that hamburger and vanilla shake in my office?"

"I did not," he said, shaking his head.

"Now I'm worried," I said.

"Yeah," my boss said, agreeing.

"Stop fretting," a voice said from behind us. "I brought you here."

Stan and I both spun around to look down at a short man in dark brown golf slacks, a white golf shirt, a golf hat with a Dunes logo on it, and a brown golf glove. His face was almost round and clearly he had spent far, far too much time in the sun without enough sunscreen. I could barely see his green eyes through the bright red folds of skin on his cheeks that threatened to crawl up and cover his bushy eyebrows at any moment.

I glanced at Stan who had dropped all pretenses of a poker face and was looking as puzzled as I felt. The guy clearly had a lot of magic since he had walked right into the time bubble Stan had around us.

"Laverne," Stan said. "A little help?"

Lady Luck herself appeared next to Stan facing the little golfer.

She frowned.

I can say clearly as a poker player that when Lady Luck frowns, bad things happen.

She glanced over at the body lying on the hard ground of the desert, then back at Stan and me.

The little golfer bowed slightly to her, the smile on his face making the sunburn seem brighter. With the smile, his eyes sunk farther into the rolls of red flesh.

"Work with him," she said to Stan, shaking her head. "He obviously needs your help. You too, Poker Boy. Shouldn't take too long."

She looked at me and I nodded, damn near the only thing a sane person could do when commanded to do something by Lady Luck herself.

Then she vanished.

"I love her," the little golfer said, smiling at me. "Don't you just love her? A little brisk at times, but still a real charmer. Don't you think?"

I said nothing. There wasn't enough money on the planet to get me to say a word about Lady Luck.

"So who are you and what do you want?" Stan asked, his voice cold and low.

The little golfer smiled and bowed slightly, tipping his golf hat just a slight touch. "I'm Benny Douglas, the world's greatest detective, at your service."

I had no idea who he was. Not clue one. Or what area he was a god in.

But Stan seemed to know him and he sighed and nodded. "Your reputation precedes you."

"I hope like the sweet smell of a dozen roses for a beautiful woman on a first date," Benny said.

"Whatever," Stan said.

Oh, wow, Stan didn't much like this guy and was not bothering to hide the fact.

"So what do you need us for?" I asked.

"To help me solve poor Dan's murder, of course," Benny said, indicating the body that wasn't decaying or smelling at the moment because Stan was holding us in a time bubble outside of the flow of time.

I decided right then that I didn't much like this short little golfer who called himself a detective. So I figured a really, really stupid question might just get under his skin a little.

"So who killed Dan?" I asked, expecting him to give me nothing more than a dirty look.

Benny actually sighed at my seemingly stupid question. "Sadly, I think I might have. But I need you both to help me prove that I didn't. And find out what really killed him."

I stared at the short detective. That was not at all the answer I had expected.

Two

"TIME TO CALL THE POLICE," I said, turning to my boss. "Let them figure it out."

"Almost starting to agree with you," Stan said, staring at Benny.

Around us the silence in the time bubble seemed to almost match the look of the empty desert.

Benny held up his hands for us to stop. "Look, let me explain what happened and we can go from there, all right? I trust you two, heard you've helped a lot of people, figured you could help me some on this. And remember Laverne told you to help me and don't you both work for that fine lady?"

I stood there, saying nothing. I wanted to say, "Asking for help would have been nice." But I said nothing instead.

Stan did the same.

After a moment Benny caught the clue and started talking even faster than before, which I was surprised was possible.

"Me and Dan there were on the third hole and we were partnered up in a match against Goldenburg and his assistant Tammy. She's a sweet one, that Tammy, fills out those golf shorts real nice if you get my drift, and can hit a driver farther than the rest of us without even messing up her long brown hair."

"Are you talking about Goldenburg, the God of Magic and Illusion?" Stan asked.

Benny nodded like his chin was on a spring on his chest and some kid had ahold of the string and was pulling it. "Sure, who else?"

Stan just stared at Benny.

I decided to just keep quiet and ask who Goldenburg was when I really needed to know.

"So which team was winning?" Stan asked.

"We were," Benny said. "Two up and about to take the third hole as well. Goldenburg can't hit an iron to save his life, and Tammy, bless those tight shorts, can't putt, but it sure is fun to watch her try, if you get my drift."

"The bet?" Stan asked.

"We win," Benny said, "Tammy works for me for a month trying to get a hundred years of paperwork in my office filed," Benny said. "You know how it goes, a fella gets behind and then there's never enough time to get all the basic stuff done and besides, watching Tammy around the office for a month sure couldn't hurt a guy, if you get my drift."

I bit my lip to not say anything. I bit it hard. Patty Ledgerwood, my girlfriend and sidekick says I look cute when I do that. But cute or not, at least it kept me from spouting out something that would derail Stan's questions.

"If you lose?" Stan asked.

"I wash dishes in Dan's restaurant down off The Strip for a month to help pay for a month's worth of dinners Goldenburg and Tammy were going to eat there."

Benny shook his head and looked over at Dan's body. "We weren't going to lose, no way. Until this."

"So how did you kill your own golfing partner?" I asked.

Benny just shook his head. "He missed his second shot on the third hole and I might have made some comment about him being a dead weight or something like that and when I got done putting my club back in my bag he was gone."

"And then what happened?" Stan asked

Benny shrugged. "We looked for him all over, but after five minutes Goldenburg said we had looked long enough and the rules of golf said we had to move on."

"Pretty sure that rule applies to lost golf balls, not partners," Stan said.

I again kept my mouth shut since I knew nothing at all about golf. It wouldn't have surprised me, though, to know that there was a rule that you could only look for a lost partner for five minutes before moving on. Golf seemed that odd to me.

"I told them to keep going and I would search for Dan," Benny said. "I traced him here and that's when I got you two because, honestly, I didn't know what to think and all this seems just odd to me, being a detective and all, but I sure can't trust my own gut on this one."

"So what's your gut telling you?" I asked Benny.

"That this is some sort of Goldenburg trick on me to get free dinners for a month at Dan's place and I wouldn't be surprised that even with Dan dead, Goldenburg will still collect after he wins."

Suddenly something that had been dinging in the back of my mind sort of dinged again, only slightly louder, like a timer on a microwave going off.

"What did Dan get if you two won?"

Benny looked at me and opened his mouth and then shut it. The little golfer detective was speechless for the first time since he pulled us to this body.

Stan laughed. "Seems like Dan only won with you washing dishes for a month."

"So you saying him dying is a trick to get me to wash dishes at his place? I mean, not a very logical plan for a long-term business model."

"Is he really dead?" I asked Benny. I hadn't been able to get much of a read on Benny up until that question. I seldom did on the more powerful gods, but suddenly I could feel Benny being very uncertain and confused.

"Smelled dead," Benny said.

"How about you go check him out to be sure," Stan said, releasing the time bubble.

The wind snapped against my skin once again and the distant sounds of trucks on the freeway echoed over the sagebrush.

Benny shook his head slowly back and forth. "Never touched a dead body before and you know, maybe you're right, maybe we should be calling the police and all that."

"Go roll him over, see if he really is dead," Stan said, his boss voice in full command.

I had a hunch that Dan was far from dead.

Benny took a deep breath and then in his brown golf shoes headed across the hard desert ground toward the body.

If nothing else, this was going to be entertaining watching him sneak up on his dead golfing partner.

USA Today *bestselling writer Dean Wesley Smith returns with a second novel to the world of* Dust and Kisses *from the first issue of* Smith's Monthly.

Together, Callie and Fisher work to discover the secrets of a galaxy that have been hidden in plain sight, even from the powerful humans who had rescued millions. And in the process, they just might change everything.

Now Available
from all your favorite booksellers
in trade paper and electronic editions.

Three

BENNY FINALLY reached the body and I could tell he had been holding his breath the entire time since he swayed slightly like he was about to pass out.

He gently reached down to roll Dan over and the body vanished, leaving only the carcass of a very dead coyote that clearly had been picked over by birds and other desert animals and was the source of the ripe smell.

Dan's body had been only an illusion, made very real by the smell.

Nice trick.

A good illusion is always in the details and smell was the detail that made this one.

Benny jumped back and instantly teleported to a spot back in front of us. His face was bright red, his green eyes intense and clearly angry.

"Where the hell did Dan's body go? Did you two do that? Did Laverne? Who would take Dan's body? We need to go to the police. Body theft is a serious crime."

"As if murder isn't," I said, shaking my head.

"There was no body," Stan said.

I was having trouble understanding that Stan needed to even explain that to Benny.

"No body, no murder?" Benny asked, clearly puzzled.

The little golfer who claimed to be the world's best detective wasn't really carrying a full bag of clubs when it came to deductive reasoning.

"An illusion," I said. "You said Goldenburg was the God of Magic, right?"

Benny nodded, slowly starting to understand.

I turned to Stan. "To project an illusion like that, wouldn't Dan have to be involved?"

"More than likely," Stan said. "At least at some point. Don't blame Dan, though, since he only got something if they lost."

"So, Benny," I asked our little golfing detective, "what hole are they on and is Dan with them?"

Benny seemed to stare off into the distance for a moment, then grow even redder in his face, something I didn't think was possible.

"They are on the sixth hole and Dan's as healthy as he gets, which isn't going very far since last year he had two bypass surgeries and has a blood sugar level that would kill a honey bee."

Benny kept staring off into the distance. "I bet we're now two holes down because I was gone and Dan can't play a lick of golf and more than likely has fallen down a few times staring at Tammy's shorts, not that I blame him for that, if you get my drift."

Benny glanced up at me and then at Stan. "So you two are telling me that I didn't accidently kill Dan, that's really him playing golf with Goldenburg?"

Stan and I both nodded.

"And that Dan was helping Goldenburg trick me so that they could win the match and I would end up doing dishes for a month in his place?"

Stan and I again both nodded.

"Wow, you guys are as good as everyone says you are," Benny said. "I never would have figured that out on my own."

I almost said that I had guessed that, but again did the cute thing and bit my lip.

"What are you going to do when you rejoin them?" Stan asked.

"Nothing," Benny said. "Just going on as if nothing had happened and win the match and get Tammy and those great shorts of hers to help me get my office straightened out. I really should have hired someone fifty years ago, but you know how it goes when a fella gets busy."

Stan and I both stood there in the wind of the desert and said nothing. Lady Luck had been right. This hadn't taken very long at all.

"I owe you two," Benny said, smiling, his green eyes lost in the rolls of red flesh on his cheeks. "You solved the murder and saved my life."

"There was no murder, Benny," Stan said.

"Yeah, whatever," Benny said and tipped his golf hat and vanished.

I turned to Stan. "How about I buy you lunch and you tell me who that guy really is."

"The world's greatest detective," Stan said, keeping a perfect poker face. "He told you."

"If he's the world's greatest detective, then I'm Sherlock Holmes."

"You can't be," Stan said.

"And why not?"

"Because Sherlock Holmes is a fictional character."

"And Benny isn't fictional, at least in his own mind?"

"No, he's the world's greatest detective as he said."

"It's going to be one of those lunchtime conversations, isn't it?" I asked.

Stan just smiled and jumped us away from the dead coyote and hot sun and sagebrush and back to my office.

I never did find out if Benny ended up winning the services of Tammy for a month. And the first time I used the phrase "...if you get my drift" around Patty, she made me swear to never use it again.

It seemed she also had met Benny at some point in the past.

DEAN WESLEY
SMITH

A BUBBLE FOR A MINUTE

**She Found Love
and the World Changed**

Mike Resnick asked me one fine day to write an alternate history story for an anthology about Wallis Simpson. I asked, "Who's he?"

Mike laughed, said I had some research to do, and hung up.

Since at that point in time I had been playing with how music and time travel sort of go hand-in-hand, I did my research and wrote this story for him. I was very proud of it and Mike liked it as well. (He seemed surprised I could learn so much about Wallis Simpson so quickly.)

The anthology called By Any Other Fame *edited by Mike Resnick and Martin H. Greenberg appeared and vanished, almost without a trace in 1994. I liked the story a great deal and was bummed, but that was the nature of traditional publishing in those days.*

So in a continuing effort to bring some of my favorite stories back to a wider audience at times in this magazine and then later in book form and in collections, here is the story again. Even after twenty years, it's still one of my favorites.

I hope you enjoy it as well.

A BUBBLE FOR A MINUTE

One

THE LAST NOTES of the old song, Paper Moon, faded into the thick antiseptic smell of the small nursing home room and the needle on the record made an impatient clicking, demanding that someone stop it.

In the wheelchair beside the bed, the old woman named Wallis Simpson nodded, almost in time to the clicking needle. She had a faint smile and distant haze in her eyes that gave her ninety-eight year old face a peaceful look. Seventeen-year-old Gary Sullivan studied that face for a moment, shaking his head at the incredible story she had just told him. A story of her youth and her marriages. A story identical to the stories she had told him every day for the last week. Identical, that is, right up until the story reached 1932. Right up until she stopped and asked him to put on the long-playing record of Paper Moon.

Gary pulled back the sleeve on his sweatshirt and leaned forward in his chair over the old-fashioned phonograph. Carefully he picked up the arm and put it back on its holder. It was amazing something this old still worked and even more amazing that the old record hadn't been worn into dust since she listened to it so much.

He clicked off the machine and the small tape recorder on the nightstand beside it, then faced Mrs. Simpson. "Would you mind if I came back again tomorrow?" It was the same thing he had asked for the past two weeks.

She took a moment to come back from whatever time she had been inside her own head, then smiled at him. "Of course not." Her voice was soft and almost hoarse after the workout she had given it telling him her story today. But her voice still had a tremendous power and aliveness that he had admired since the first day he had interviewed her.

"Besides," she said. A light smile slowly filled her face and smoothed out some of the wrinkles. "Who else would I have to talk to? Who else would believe in me?"

"Great," he said, with as much enthusiasm as he could muster, even though he had no idea what she meant by believing in her. It was just part of that song she loved so much.

He stood and, for the first time in the last half hour, noticed just how hot and closed-in this modern little room was. It felt like a prison and suddenly all he wanted to do was run for the door, escape, see what had changed.

What had changed seemed to be his constant question. Today, her story had ended with her marrying a business man by the name of Harvey. With him she had two children. Gary had no idea what that would do to the world outside. But he doubted it would be enough to help his dad. So far, in two weeks of trying, none of her stories had been enough. But somehow he knew that if she just kept telling stories, in one his dad would still be with him and his mother.

Mrs. Simpson turned her wheelchair slightly to face where Gary stood. "You know," she said. "This little experiment of yours has made me the envy of the wing. No one ever comes to talk to most of these folks, except on holidays and the like."

He took a deep breath of the hot air and forced himself to smile. He didn't have the heart to tell her that his little experiment, as she called it, had started out as nothing more than a history paper for a senior high class. A simple assignment that had been done and turned in two weeks before. But he had kept coming back because at first he didn't understand why she kept changing the last part of her stories.

And then, after a few days, he needed her to keep changing the stories until she came to the right story. The exact right story that would bring his dad back home.

"Well," Gary said, "how about same time tomorrow afternoon? You know how important reputation is to high school students."

She laughed. "Thanks for believing in me," she said again. She said that at least once every day and it was starting to give him the creeps. He just nodded and turned into the hall. The name beside her door now said Mrs. Harvey. It had been the twelfth time her name had changed, yet he still thought of her as Wallis Simpson, the name she had been the first time he asked her to tell a story.

Gary forced himself to walk slowly and carefully to the front door, smiling at the nurses at the nurses' station and taking slow, deep breaths of the thick antiseptic and death-filled air. The front door was only a few yards ahead.

He wondered what world he would find beyond it this time.

Two

THE ASSIGNMENT had been given by Coach Kinser, the heavy-set ex-jock who taught Gary's third period. He was also Gary's football coach, which made getting a good grade even more important. "Go to a nursing home," Coach Kinser said, "ask permission to talk to a resident, and interview that resident about his or her past."

The entire class had groaned and the Coach had just smiled. "History is an oral tradition," he had said. "You will enjoy it."

Gary, of course, had waited until a few days before it was due and then found Mrs. Simpson. "Wallis," as she said she liked to be called. Her room was the standard modern nursing home room, just like the one Gary's grandmother had died in. There was a bed with metal rails, a small desk, a small nightstand, and a television across from a rocking chair. Nothing else decorated her room and the place instantly made him feel like he was being smothered.

His first thought was to make the interview fast and get it over with. But Wallis Simpson was a good storyteller and, as Mr. Kinser had said, Gary enjoyed listening to her.

It took over an hour the first day and filled a tape.

That first day she told him about her early years. She was from Baltimore and had been married twice. Her first marriage was to a naval officer by the name of Earl Spencer, whom she divorced in 1927. Her second marriage was to a Washington D.C. businessman named Ernest Simpson.

From the way she talked it was clear that she loved Ernest and everything he gave to her. She talked about how much they traveled and how she met kings and presidents while at his side.

On a business trip to England she and Ernest had become fast friends with the Prince of Wales, who later became King Edward. She said she had many wonderful stories about trips with the Prince and parties at his castle.

But when her story reached the summer of 1932 and the party she and Ernest attended at the White House, everything suddenly changed.

The Prince of Wales had gotten them an invitation to the party to meet the new American President. It was at the mention of the party that she asked Gary to put the long-playing record of Paper Moon on her old phonograph.

He did as she asked and while that record played, she told him about the party and meeting President Roosevelt and the First Lady and then about how Ernest was killed in London and how she returned to the states and never remarried. Her story ended with the record and Gary thanked her and went home, thinking he had more than enough information for his paper.

But it turned out he didn't.

He actually wanted more about the White House party and the young President Roosevelt, figuring that would make the most interesting paper for the

Coach, since the Coach had a thing for the Roosevelts.

So the next afternoon Gary stopped by the nursing home again to see Mrs. Simpson. She seemed happy to see him and again she went over the same story of her life, right up until the party at the White House.

And again, when she mentioned that White House summer party, she asked him to put on the record.

This time she told him much more about the party and about how she and Ernest had taken a limousine from the hotel. Then she went on to tell him about how she had fallen for the limousine driver. Two years after the party she went back to Washington, leaving Ernest in London, and got a divorce. She married the limousine driver, a man by the name of Barkley. He died five years ago and she was now all alone.

At first Gary had wanted to ask her about her change in her story, but then just shrugged it off to senility. And he was so startled by the change in story that he forgot to ask her more about President Roosevelt.

She thanked him for believing in her and, as he left the room, he noticed the nametag on the door. It now read Mrs. Barkley, where the day before he was sure it had read Simpson.

As a lark, and with the same excuse that he needed more information about President Roosevelt, he went back the next day. In that day's story she met a businessman at the White House party and married him three years later. Not only had her name again changed on her door, but on the way home that afternoon his mom's favorite grocery store, DANNY'S, was gone, replaced by a small shopping mall.

He asked his mom about the store, but she just gave him a blank look and shook her head. And there was no store by that name listed anywhere in the phone book.

The next day DANNY'S Grocery was back after Mrs. Simpson told him a story about how she and Ernest traveled to Africa, where he died in a hunting accident.

By this point Gary had figured out what seemed to be impossible: that her stories were somehow changing the world.

And he had also figured out that maybe, if he got to the right story, his dad would come back. His dad who had left him and his mother when he was five. A dad who his mother would never talk about and who he had dreamed about for as long as he could remember.

So he kept going back every day, listening to Mrs. Simpson, or whatever her name was that day, tell the same story right up to the hot summer of 1932, right up to the White House party.

Then he would listen to her change the world around them.

Three

ON GARY'S seventeenth visit to Mrs. Simpson he finally got his wish. His dad came back.

Her story the day before had left her with two children and today, for some reason, there was a vase of fresh flowers on her nightstand. She looked happier and healthier than he had seen her and he commented about it.

She thanked him and they started into the same routine. She told him about her early life, her uncle and her grandmother, both of her marriages, and all the traveling she did. Gary had this part memorized and it never varied. And as always, when she reached the summer party at the White House, she asked him to put on the record of Paper Moon.

"Why Paper Moon?" he asked her as he placed the record in place.

She smiled, her mind obviously a long way back in time, remembering. "It was the song the big band at the White House played three times. I danced and danced that night, feeling like a princess gone to the ball. I remember wanting the song and the night to last forever."

She smiled at him. "So I bought the record. And besides, didn't you know that music has magic in it? With music, the world can be more than just make-believe."

Gary just nodded as the shivers ran up and down his back. With his hand shaking he carefully started the record.

"He was so handsome," she said, her eyes glazed as she looked off into the past, "standing there beside Eleanor, greeting his guests." She paused and looked at me. "You know he couldn't walk, don't you?"

"President Roosevelt?"

She nodded. "They had his braces locked in place so he could stand and greet his guests. He told me later that hurt him, which was why he didn't give many parties."

Gary had a sinking feeling that he didn't want to know where this was heading, but he just nodded and she went on.

"After dancing a few times, I got this message that the President would like to talk to me. He told me I danced beautifully and wished he could join me." She smiled, remembering an obviously joyful event.

"He was sitting in a large overstuffed chair and when he said that, he reached down and knocked on his braces through

his pants. 'Not much chance of that,' he said and then laughed as if it were funny. I laughed with him."

She swayed back and forth in time with the music as she talked. "I remember I was hot from the dancing and the humid evening, so I sat on the footstool in front of him and we talked for the next hour between interruptions of other guests and business from his advisors."

She looked up at Gary as the song continued. "You know it was that hour that I think I fell in love with him. I know that seems hard to believe, but it only took an hour. After that evening Ernest and I went back to England, but Franklin and I kept in touch and I saw him three or four times a year for the next few years.

In 1936 I went back to Washington and divorced Ernest. Franklin and I saw each other much more during his second term, usually meeting in the home I owned in Maryland. Even though the people wanted him to, he decided to not run for a third term in 1940. He divorced Eleanor in 1941 and we were married the next year."

Suddenly she seemed to age and her face turned pale. "I'm sure you know he was executed right after the invasion of fifty-two. I've been alone ever since."

The last note of the song ended and faded into the dingy-looking room. Gary took a few deep breaths trying to calm the panic filling his stomach. Oh-God-oh-God-oh-God. What had he done? He picked up the arm of the record player and stopped the clicking.

Invasion of '52?

What was that?

What had happened?

Slowly, he looked around the room. The flowers were gone and the bed had become a wooden frame with nothing more than a stained mattress and a rumpled sheet on it. This was the first time that the changes in her story had actually come into her room. He had no memory of when they had happened, even though he had been sitting here the entire time. In her other stories he had always remembered what had changed, but had never been near anything when the change took place.

Mrs. Simpson, or he would assume now, Mrs. Roosevelt, looked to be almost in a coma.

Her eyes were glassy and she seemed about to collapse. Only the belt strapping her to the wheelchair held her upright.

He patted her hand and thanked her, but she paid no attention. He stood and turned for the door. His legs felt weak and his stomach twisted as if he had just been caught with his pants down in front of the entire school.

"Tomorrow?" he asked as he reached her door, not really wanting to go beyond it. But again she didn't notice his question.

Even though it was still mid-afternoon, the hall was almost dark, with only a few bare bulbs in the ceiling fixtures. The smell was of a musty attic, and the floor was stained and unwashed. Very, very different from the modern nursing home he had entered less than an hour before.

This felt more like a jail for the elderly.

At the end of the hall, near the entrance hung a huge sign in a foreign language Gary didn't recognize. All he had taken in school was French and he hadn't really paid much attention to that. Behind an old wood desk where the nurses station had been when he came in was an old guard wearing a black uniform and reading a tattered paperback novel.

As Gary took a deep breath and started toward the front door he remembered.

He remembered what life had been like before she told her story and what life was now like for him in this world. Memories like clear plastic, one over the other, flooded into his mind.

This time he remembered his dad. In this world he had a father who had not disappeared when he was five. In this world Germany had joined with Russia and won World War Two. Japan controlled the West coast of what had been the United States and Maryland was now nothing more than a German satellite state.

And in this world his dad was a drunk who beat him and his mother. His dad never worked and blamed his mother for almost everything that was wrong in the world. He was an ugly, sadistic man who hated everything and everyone around him. Nothing like the dream father Gary had imagined him to be.

Gary staggered against the wall out of sight of the guard and forced himself to take deep breaths like the Coach had taught him to do in pressure games. How did Roosevelt not running for President in 1940 cause America to lose the war?

How could one woman change the world so much?

It wasn't possible, yet Gary knew it was.

And how could his father hit him?

Gary looked down at his arm where the angry red bruise had appeared.

He looked quickly in both directions down the hall. His memory of the clean, modern nursing home overlaid the prison-like feel of this old building.

But his memories of the world before were quickly fading. He would have to get Mrs. Simpson to switch it all back, to tell a new story. But what if her new story was worse than even this? What would happen if in the next world he hadn't even been born?

Then what would happen?

He wanted to pound his fists against the wall and scream. Why hadn't he thought of that before now? How could he have been so stupid, hoping that he could find a world where he would know his dad? Well, it had worked and he had real vivid memories of his father now. Real vivid memories bruises and beatings and of wishing his father were dead, night after night, over and over again.

He eased back into Mrs. Simpson's room. She still sat beside the old phonograph, her eyes glazed.

"Mrs. Simpson, I mean Mrs. Roosevelt?" Gary said, sitting down across from her and keeping his voice low. "Would you mind telling me a story about your life?"

Nothing. She didn't move and Gary passed a hand in front of her unseeing eyes. No blink.

Nothing.

As far as he knew she might have been like this for years in this world. Maybe there was no going back. He took a few more deep breaths to fight off the panic, but this time it didn't seem to help. "Mrs. Roosevelt. Can you hear me? Please talk to me."

He shook her shoulders, slowly at first, and then harder, but her blank stare went right through him.

He stood and paced back and forth in front of the door. He had enough memories of this new world to know that if he was caught in here, he would be in trouble.

Big trouble.

Carefully he poked his head out and looked toward the guard. The old guy was still reading and except for a low moaning coming from a room down the hall, everything was the same. No movement.

Nothing.

Gary went back and shook Mrs. Roosevelt one more time without luck. She was dead to this world. And now he was stuck here.

Footsteps came from down the hall and Gary quickly darted in behind the open door. The guard passed by, walked to the end of the hall, and went into a room there, letting the door bang closed behind him. The banging echoed down the hall and Gary turned to see if Mrs. Roosevelt had noticed.

She still sat there blankly staring over the old record player. And for a minute Gary stared at it, too, remembering what she had said and remembering the words of the song she loved so much.

That just might do the trick.

Gary quickly stuck his head out the door to check on where the guard had gone, then went over to the old machine. It was still on and still had the record of Paper Moon in place. Maybe that would take her back to the party and both of them out of this nightmare.

He listened for a moment to make sure the guard had not come back out of the room, then put the needle in place and started the record. As the first few notes filled the room he wanted to stop it. It sounded so loud, far loud enough to bring the guard.

He went to the door quickly and checked the hall. The opening of the song seemed to be amplified in the stark hallway. It could be heard all over the building, he was sure.

He went back over to Mrs. Roosevelt and again shook her shoulders. "Wake up! Please? "I'm playing your song for you."

Slowly, he felt some life come back into her shoulders where he held her.

He let go and sat down. After a few bars Mrs. Roosevelt's eyes flickered and she smiled faintly.

"Tell me about the party," Gray said, trying to keep his voice under control and not panic filled. "Tell me who you met there at the White House. Please?" He glanced at the door and then back to her.

"Why," she said, her voice gaining strength and power with each word. "I met the President and the First Lady and lots of others. It was a wonderful party and I danced and danced all night. You know, after Edward and I were married I thanked him for getting me invited to that party by taking him on a tour of Washington D.C. It was such a sweet thing for him to do, don't you think?"

"Edward?" Gary asked. "Who was Edward?"

Mrs. Roosevelt laughed, a strong, hearty laugh. "You are teasing me, aren't you? Why, he was the Prince of Wales and then the King of England. After his abdication we were married. I am the Duchess of Windsor."

She reached over and patted Gary's hand. "A young man like you should study his history more."

Gary only nodded in agreement and glanced around at the room. The air shimmered like a heat wave had hit it and the layers of the dark prison-like room faded away, replaced with a modern nursing home room.

And the old record player was also shimmering and fading, as was Mrs. Simpson. In her place sat an elderly gentleman named Harrison and he was finishing a story about how he fought in the Pacific and how the kids of today just didn't understand how important history was and how smart it was for Gary's history teacher to have them do this assignment.

Gary agreed, quickly thanked the man, and headed for the front door.

The relief washed over Gary as he went down the hall.

He felt light, almost like dancing. He could still remember his dad from the other world, but it was fading into the background like remembering a bad nightmare, pushed into the corners by the warm sun and the smiles of the nurses. He doubted if he would ever again wish for a father he didn't have.

And for one final time, faintly from down the hall, he thought he heard Wallis Simpson say, "Thanks for believing in me."

~

Poems by DEAN WESLEY SMITH

Time's Window

Angie Bennett, at ninety-three, could no longer smell
her own soiled diapers, the thick sour smell
of disinfectant the nursing home used,
the fresh daises or roses that sat on her nightstand every day.

Angie Bennett, at ninety-four, could no longer talk,
laugh at her son's bad jokes,
or even make goggle-goggle noises to her great-grandchild.
The stroke had taken that ability as well.

Angie Bennett, at ninety-five, had a body that had failed her,
but a mind as strong as ever, trapped in her head,
waiting to be released with the comfort of death.
No one outside her body knew this. She couldn't tell them.

Angie Bennett, at ninety-six, watched the nurse every morning
open the blinds on her window.
Through that glass Angie stared at first
into the happy moments of her past.

Angie Bennett, at ninety-seven, wondered why her grandson
instead of her son came to see her every Wednesday.
Then she saw through her window that her son had died,
saw her grandchild become a United States Senator.

Angie Bennett, at ninety-eight, watched the future
unfold for her though her window, all the marvels,
all the bad events, all the accomplishments
of her family and the human race.

Angie Bennett, at ninety-nine, could have saved millions
of lives if someone would have figured a way to talk to her,
ask her about her life, about the window into the future.
If someone would have cared enough to bother.

Angie Bennett, on her one-hundredth birthday, died,
taking with her the knowledge of her family, of the country,
of the world, of the human race.
A part of history, a part of the future, died with her.

USA *Today* Bestselling Writer

DEAN WESLEY SMITH

THE LIFE AND TIMES OF BUFFALO JIMMY

Chapters 19-21

What Came Before...

Nineteen-year-old Boston native Jimmy Gray had been traveling with his parents and older brother, Luke, headed west to find a new home and new riches. Before even reaching Independence, they were attacked and robbed by Jake Benson and his gang. Jimmy's parents were killed, his brother wounded.

In one of the wildest towns in all of American history, Jimmy Gray, a sheltered, educated son of a banker from Boston, suddenly finds himself very, very much alone. But then through some luck, he finds other young men about his age and down on their luck who might be able to help him.

Together, the five of them head west after Benson.

They end up hunting buffalo as he always dreamed of doing, but then they are hit with a massive flash flood and Jimmy is left alone, his friends more than likely dead. Luckily, they all meet up again and are all safe. So they continue west, knowing that Benson is just ahead of them.

Suddenly they come upon Benson and his men killing a farm family. They manage to get one of the men separated from the others, but in a fall he accidently dies. So they scatter to meet up later at a camp.

THE LIFE AND TIMES OF BUFFALO JIMMY

Part Nineteen
BACK TOGETHER

THEY HAD ALL ARRIVED IN CAMP SAFELY, with Long coming in last because he had wanted to make sure where Benson had gone. Long had the ability, because he was part Indian, to move silently and get amazingly close to things without ever being seen.

He told them that Benson and the other two killers had waited for their man for a while at the homestead, poked around a bit, then finally started down the trail at a good speed, clearly trying to put distance between them and the burning homestead.

Long said that there had been a lot of swearing and that Benson thought their "friend" had taken the horses and headed back up the trial, leaving them.

Or maybe the Indians had gotten him.

Good news to Jimmy. They did not suspect they were behind them.

Jimmy still posted three guards that night, and they hadn't built a fire. They didn't dare let Benson find them, not after what Benson had done to that family.

Jimmy hadn't slept much at all, and the only time he managed to fall asleep, he had a nightmare of the dead killer and the family standing and politely applauding. It was a horrid nightmare that woke him up sweating and made him take over guard duty an hour sooner than he was supposed to.

He couldn't believe he had killed a man. Even as an accident, did that make him as bad as Benson? He tried to push that thought away, but it kept coming back over and over all night long.

The next morning, Long scouted ahead and finally found Benson and his two remaining men moving west down the California Trail. They seemed to be pacing behind a small wagon company.

An hour later, they headed back and arrived back at the homestead and slowly dismounted. The building was still smoldering, sending a thin line of smoke into the clear blue sky.

"We need to bury these folks," Zach said, picking up the shovel the boy had been carrying when he was shot in the back.

Jimmy nodded and looked around. The ridge where he and the others had watched yesterday would be perfect. "Up there, where they can stand watch for all time over their homestead."

Silently, all six boys went looking for what it was going to take to dig three graves, get the bodies up the hill, and get this done.

Two long hours later, they were all hot and sweating, but they had the family in the ground with crosses over each grave. It reminded Jimmy far too much of when he and his brother had buried his parents.

Benson had to be stopped.

"I wish we knew their names," C. J. said.

"The Goose Creek family," Josh said. "As long as we remember them, they will live on."

Some Classic Jukebox Stories
Available at your favorite booksellers.

"No way to forget this," Truitt said. "I'm going to be having nightmares for months."

"Yeah, me too," both Jimmy and Zach said at the same time.

"Should we do anything about him?" Zach asked, pointing to the trees where the body of the killer was.

"Let the animals have him," Long said, disgusted.

"He was a human," C.J. said, taking his glasses off his face and wiping sweat from his forehead. "He deserves something."

"He killed this family," Zach said, pointing up the hill at the graves they had just dug. "He doesn't deserve anything."

"We'll put some rocks on him," Jimmy said, staring up into the trees.

He was having enough trouble with the death of the killer. He couldn't have the thought of animals getting the man in his mind.

"I'll help you," Truitt said.

All six boys helped, and in fifteen minutes they had the man under a cairn of rocks. They didn't mark the grave.

As they came out of the trees toward the barn, a stage came into sight from the west, pulled by a team of six horses.

During the trip west, they had passed a number of large wagons and stages going east. All of the stages had been Butterfield Stages, carrying mostly letters and a few passengers who didn't mind getting tossed around inside a stagecoach for a few thousand miles.

The stage pulled up in a wide area just off the trail and the boys went down to meet it.

"What happened?" the driver asked, his hand on his gun. His co-driver had his rifle up and ready.

Jimmy understood their fear. The house had been burned down, and these two men had no idea that Jimmy and his friends hadn't done it.

Jimmy told them what they had found, and then who had done it. He didn't care for going over the story again and not a one of them said a word about what they had done to Benson's man yesterday.

"We buried the family up on the hill," Jimmy said.

"There are three men tucked in a few miles behind a wagon company about a half day up the trail," the driver said, clearly relaxing, taking his hand off his gun. "Not much we can do."

"Out here, there's not much anyone can do," Zach said.

"Ain't that the truth," the driver said.

Jimmy described Benson and the driver nodded. "That was the man. It's too bad, too. The Bennetts were good people. Thanks for burying them. You boys stay away from those three."

"We will," Jimmy said to the driver, even though he knew they wouldn't.

Josh and C.J. got the Bennett's full names from the driver. Josh wrote them down carefully, then the two of them went back up the hill to put the names on the crosses.

Jimmy asked the driver if he could send a letter along to someone in Independence and the driver said sure. Jimmy wrote a quick note to his brother Luke, care of Doc Davis, and gave it to the driver. He offered to pay for the letter's delivery, but the driver just tucked it in his pocket. "You've paid for the letter by burying our friends."

The stage left and they all paid their last respects to the family on the hill. Then, as they were back near the barn silently getting ready to mount back up, Long held up his hand. "Do you hear that?"

Jimmy strained to hear something besides the wind in the trees and the distant sound of some fast water in the creek. Nothing, but Jimmy had come to accept that Long could hear and see things that none of the rest of them could. It was an amazing special ability.

Long handed his horse lead to Zach and went back toward the smoldering house, quickly and silently.

Finally, Jimmy heard what Long had heard.

A faint whimper.

Something was alive back there.

But how could that be possible?

Long and Jimmy went to the right of the cabin, Zach with his gun out went to the left. C.J. had his rock sling out and was right behind Jimmy.

On the other side of the burnt-out building, they all stopped.

Jimmy held his breath, listening to the sound of the stream and the faint wind in the leaves of the trees.

Then the sound came again.

A whimper.

Long turned and moved around behind a few trees. There, he pulled open what looked like a sod-covered door on a root cellar that none of them had noticed tucked behind a tree next to the hill.

Inside, sitting on the stairs, was a young boy, about seven years of age.

He blinked at the bright light, then covered his head and started crying.

It took an hour or so for the boys to get the child calmed down and some water and food in him. He said between sobs that his name was Arthur.

Jimmy knew they certainly couldn't take Arthur with them, but they also couldn't just leave him either.

Jimmy pulled Zach aside. "We need to get the kid back to Fort Hall."

"That's a hundred miles back," Zach said. "I can do it."

"Or find someone in a wagon company who will take him," Jimmy said. He didn't much like the idea of Zach not being at his side. There had to be a better choice.

"A wagon train is unlikely," Zach said. "Fort Hall with the military is his best bet. Unless we can catch up to that Butterfield Stage." He didn't sound hopeful, and Jimmy doubted they could. Those stages moved fast, and kept going, changing horses all the time.

Jimmy stood thinking for a moment, staring at the three crosses on the hill above them. He knew that Zach was right, and he was the best person to do the ride because he was the most responsible of all of them.

"Take along the two horses that we rescued," Jimmy said. "They belong to the kid now anyhow. They might help him get a home. And give him the killer's saddle and gear. Truitt can go with you."

Zach nodded.

"If you don't catch us by Virginia City," Jimmy said, "we'll wait for you there." Virginia City was on the other side of Nevada from where they were, up against the Sierras and the final mountain passes over into California. At a good speed, they were still three weeks away from there, but with Benson moving slowly ahead of them, Jimmy doubted they would be moving very fast at all.

Zach nodded. "If we ride solid, it won't take anywhere near that long. We should be back with you by the time you are down on the Humboldt. Maybe ten days."

"That's what I was figuring," Jimmy said.

Twenty minutes later, Zach and Truitt headed back east with the young boy saddled up on one of his horses.

The other four Wild Boys continued west, using the killer's horse as a packhorse. They still had three killers to track and try to stop.

Part Twenty
ON A KILLER'S TRAIL

THE NEXT DAY, Jimmy, Long, Josh, and C.J. caught up with Benson and his men again just after the trail crested over a slight range of hills and dropped down onto Dead Horse Creek.

The hills were covered in sparse dry grass and sagebrush. Only the areas along the creek were green.

This area felt a lot more like a desert to Jimmy than anything they had come through, giving them almost no protection from the hot sun. The rock bluffs along the stream were brown, and sometimes towered a good hundred feet into the air above the shallow creek.

The coach driver had been right, Benson and his three men were following a few miles behind a small wagon company with only eight wagons. Only having eight wagons was just asking for problems. Usually the companies were far larger when they left Independence.

More than likely, this was just part of a larger company that had slowly split apart over the long months of travel.

Long scouted ahead, watching Benson and his men, as the rest of them stayed back and out of sight. Jimmy was convinced that Benson planned on robbing the train at some point. The questions were when and where.

And more importantly, how could Jimmy and the rest of them do something to stop it? This time, he didn't want to kill any of them. The accidental killing of one of Benson's gang bothered Jimmy a lot. He wasn't about to let his friends become like Benson and his gang.

That evening, the train made camp up against a tall rock bluff, with the wagons in a loose circle to protect the middle of the camp. Benson and his men camped back a few miles near a bend in the stream in some small trees.

Jimmy had the boys get off the trail and make camp on top of the bluffs above the wagons and far enough away from the company that their fire wouldn't be seen.

"So, how are we going to stop Benson from robbing that wagon train?" Jimmy asked after they had a fire going. The sun was still an hour from setting and Jimmy figured they had just about that much time to do something.

Josh held up some weeds. "This might do it," he said.

C.J. pushed his glasses down his nose and stared at the weeds in Josh's hands. "You want to poison them? That's called Loco-Weed and it drives cattle crazy."

Jimmy had never seen anything like it, and he was surprised that both Josh and C.J. knew what it was. It had been along the trail for miles.

"My people use it in special ceremonies," Long said. "It makes you see things that cannot be seen. It will not kill taken in small amounts."

Jimmy laughed, then stared at Long. "Think you can get some of that into Benson's and his men's food if we gave you a diversion? That ought to keep them from robbing anyone tonight."

Long nodded. "They are cooking beans and coffee they took from the homestead."

"What do you need for a diversion?"

Long moved over toward the rocks without saying a word, then moving faster than Jimmy could see, he grabbed into a hole and picked up something. When he turned around, Jimmy could see it was a very angry, very large rattlesnake. The rattle on the end of its tail was making an intense noise. "There horses will not like this," Long said, holding up the huge snake he held behind the head.

"I don't like it," C.J. said, backing away.

Long held the snake with one hand while he watched Josh chop up some of the weeds into tiny bits, then smash them between two rocks until he had a fine powder. Long held out his empty hand and Josh brushed the powder into his hand.

"Follow me," Long said. "I will show you where you can watch their camp."

A few minutes later, Jimmy, C.J., and Josh were hiding behind rocks as Long worked his way down toward the killer's camp. The three were sitting around the fire, clearly getting ready to eat. Their three horses were tied up in the trees about thirty paces from their fire.

Long got close, tossed the snake into the middle of the horses, then ducked down behind a large rock near the three men. Jimmy would have been scared to death getting that close to those three killers like that, but clearly Long had very little fear of them.

Their horses went crazy, rearing back against their ties, trying to get away from the angry rattlesnake.

All three killers reacted as one, jumping up and running for the horses.

Almost like a ghost, Long appeared near their food and drink and put powder in both, then vanished back behind a rock.

It was everything Jimmy and Josh and C.J. could do to not laugh. They ducked down to make sure they weren't seen, and after a few minutes, Long joined them.

The four boys watched the killers eat. At first, nothing seemed to be happening.

They cleaned up their camp, put out their fire, and got ready to ride out as it started to get dark. Clearly, they were still planning on robbing the wagon company.

Then Jimmy noticed that one of the killers tried to get on his horse and missed, falling into the dirt. The other two laughed and pointed and laughed.

"The plan seems to be working," Josh said.

"But not enough," Jimmy said as the three rode laughing toward the wagon company.

Part Twenty-one
ONE MORE PLAN

"CAN WE GET TO A PLACE above the wagons without being seen?" Jimmy asked as the three killers rode off. He couldn't let Benson and his men kill more innocent people. He just couldn't.

"What are you thinking?" Josh asked, looking worried.

"No plans yet," Jimmy said. "But I'm open for all kinds of ideas. We can't let those monsters kill an entire company of people."

"I agree," C.J. said, patting his sling. "I just wish Zach had left the rifle."

Jimmy felt his stomach clamp at that. They were unarmed against three armed killers.

"This way," Long said, vanishing back into the darkness.

It took them a good thirty minutes on foot to get to the bluff over the wagons. By that point, there had been shots and women screaming.

The sound had made Jimmy' blood go cold and his heart race. This couldn't be happening again.

Not again.

A half-dozen cook fires lit up the area under them, making it seem like a bright day among the wagons. Benson had killed what must have been the train's leader, and two of the killers were holding two women with guns to their heads. The rest of the families were standing helpless, just watching. The killers were weaving back and forth like they were drunk, and laughing at anything.

There had to be twenty men and women in that train, plus another ten children.

Jimmy knew that most of them were going to die unless they did something, and did it fast.

Jimmy signaled that they should move back from the edge, then turned to C. J. and Josh, the two smartest of the Wild Boys. "Any ideas?"

"We have surprise on our side," Josh said. "They don't know we're here."

"And we have the darkness to help us," C. J. said. "We can spook them into running since they have so much Loco weed in them."

"I can do a very frightening Bannock war cry," Long said. "If I ride through the shadows near their horse making the cry, they might think they are surrounded by Bannock."

Jimmy nodded. "Especially if we are pelting them with rocks at the same time."

C.J. laughed and whipped out his homemade sling. "They won't even know what hit them."

Three boys with rocks against three men with guns.

Jimmy had no doubt they were going to have to be very lucky to get away with this attack.

Very lucky if they lived, actually.

He couldn't believe that for the second time in three days he was going to attack Benson and his men. It was crazy.

"Long, when we hear you coming, we'll start throwing," Jimmy said.

"Five minutes," Long said, nodding and then vanishing silently into the darkness back toward their camp and their horses.

Jimmy went on. "C.J., you take the younger killer, Josh, you take the other one. "I'll take Benson. Make sure you are in a sheltered place with a lot of rocks to throw when they start shooting. And if your man leaves the light, we all run."

Long and C.J. nodded.

"This is going to be fun," C.J. said, laughing.

Josh just shook his head.

Jimmy would have never called this fun. Crazy, yes, deadly, yes, but never fun.

They all spread out along the top of the cliff, picking up fist-sized rocks as they went.

Jimmy found at least a dozen and put himself behind a large rock that allowed him shelter, but if he leaned out and forward, he could clearly see the camp below.

His heart was beating so hard, he was sure Benson could hear it.

"Okay," he said softly to himself. "Make each throw deadly."

At that moment, an echoing Bannock war cry filled the air, sending shivers down Jimmy's back. It seemed to hang in the night air, echoing off the rocks like there was more than one call.

Long was right, that was something that would frighten enemies and friends alike.

Long came flashing into the light, past the fire, and back into the darkness. All three killers spun around, guns aimed into the darkness, but they had so much Loco-weed in them, they barely stood up.

Jimmy took a deep breath, stood and threw the rock at Benson as hard as he could.

Benson was standing in the middle of the camp, near a fire, staring after the ghost-like image of Long.

The rock fell a few feet short, bounced once and slammed into Benson's shin.

Benson snapped forward and grabbed his leg, swearing and clearly in pain.

In all his life, Jimmy had never felt such a thrill as that moment. Maybe C.J. was right.

Maybe this would be fun.

An echoing Bannock war cry again filled the air, sending more shivers down Jimmy's back. The people in the wagon company dove for cover under the wagons as the three killers stood their ground under the rocks from above.

All three killers started firing up at the cliff face, but their aim was random and far off target.

Long flashed past the camp again, coming in closer behind the men, screaming out his war cry.

Jimmy missed with his second rock, but his third throw hit Benson squarely in the chest and knocked him to his back in the dirt.

Before he could get up, Jimmy hit him with another rock, this time in the back, sending him back to the ground.

The gunfire had stopped.

The two killers came running toward Benson, heading past him at a mad dash for their horses. They were clearly as scared as a grown man could get.

Long's war cry again filled the night air.

Jimmy was throwing as hard and as fast as he could, letting his anger at Benson power his arm.

A rock from C.J.'s sling caught the youngest of Benson's men in the arm, clearly breaking it. The other man was bleeding from a head wound and limping from the attack that Josh had waged on him.

Jimmy kept throwing, fast and hard, not letting the man who had killed his parents a moment's rest.

To the men below, it must have seemed as if the dark night sky had opened up and just dumped rocks at them.

Long screamed out the Bannock war cry again.

It made Jimmy shiver, and even Benson's horses reared up at the sound.

Jimmy's aim was getting better. He hit Benson squarely in the shoulder as he climbed to his feet, spinning the man around and forcing him to drop his gun.

Benson scrambled on all fours for his gun as Jimmy hit him in the back with another rock, sending him to his stomach.

Finally, Benson scrambled up, turned and limped behind his men for his horse.

Jimmy managed to hit him one more time in the back of his leg before Benson got mounted and rode at full speed west, out of the camp, following his two men down the California Trail.

There was silence in the wagon camp.

Jimmy knew that Long would follow the killers for a distance, terrorizing them, making sure they didn't turn back on the wagon company.

Below them, the stunned people of the wagon company scrambled for their weapons and got ready to defend themselves as well. It was going to take a little explaining as to why they wouldn't have to.

"Well," C.J. said from somewhere in the darkness. "Shall we go down and say hello?"

"I don't see why not," Jimmy said, laughing, feeling better than he had felt in a long, long time. They had beat Benson once more.

Now Jimmy knew they could somehow do it again.

And again.

Until the killer was finally brought to justice.

Jimmy looked down at the stunned people staring upward into the darkness, waiting for more rocks to come flying, then laughed again. "It seems they might owe us a dinner."

Continued next month…

USA Today Bestselling Author

DEAN WESLEY SMITH

GODS AREN'T FUNNY

A Poker Boy Novel

In the Poker Boy novel in this issue (which is the origin story for Poker Boy and his team), Poker Boy's boss mentions something that happened earlier, before the novel.

This story details that event, written as the third Poker Boy story I ever wrote and never published anywhere but in a fun little chapbook that Nina Kiriki Hoffman and I did and gave to about twenty friends.

I figured since Stan, the God of Poker, mentions this event a few times in the novel, I had better let everyone read the story first.

Poker Boy, still a freshly-minted superhero just learning the ropes at the time of this story, runs smack into the charms of someone who knows his secret name, knows who he is. And won't let him use his superpowers.

As a red-blooded young man with needs and hormones, Poker Boy must face those challenges in an epic battle of perfect skin, stunning looks, and a hormone-clouded mind.

GODS AREN'T FUNNY
A Poker Boy Story

I WAS STARTING to really dread Christmas Eve.

I mean, do you blame me? Two Christmas Eves ago my old girlfriend, Julie Downer, came to me for help. Then she didn't like my suggestions about what to do, even though I offered to pay for her new boob job.

Eventually she ended up getting her breasts sucked out through her ass by the Silicon Suckers, which needless to say, killed her.

Makes me shudder just to think about it.

And then last year short Bob showed up in the poker room, knowing he was going to die in the morning, and wanting to leave with ten thousand so that he could go out of the world exactly as he had come in: Dead Even.

As a poker player, I understood his desire, but his poker playing ability sucked, right along with his bad temper. I ended up just giving him the ten big ones on a sham bet. He died right when he said he would.

So do you blame me for being a little spooked about this third Christmas Eve? Two years in a row someone who had come to me for help on Christmas Eve had died. And neither of them I could have done anything about, even though during the last year I had wondered if I could have.

Guilt trips are often my strong suit, which I understand from other superheroes, is one of our professional hazards. We help fifty people, but it's the one we can't help that haunts us. I had two on two successive Christmas Eves that I couldn't save. I was in guilt trip heaven.

Now, it was Christmas Eve morning again. So far no one had shown up, and I was determined to forget Bob and Julie and just have my normal Christmas Eve.

The day dawned bright, the air crisp, the light snow not bothering anyone getting to Spirit Winds Casino.

My plan for this Christmas Eve was the same as I had done for the last dozen or so holidays, at least the ones people didn't die around me.

I would go over to the Casino in the early evening, and get into a poker game with the rest of the non-family poker players. Many poker players don't have family, and many of us like it that way, so I had little worries that there wouldn't be a game.

I would play until some time in the morning, go home and get some sleep, and be back in the poker room after a turkey dinner in the buffet. If I timed it right, I would be there for the really good games that always started later Christmas Day.

An aside. A really good game to a professional poker player like myself is when there are a bunch of people with a lot of money and very little skill. Those kinds of players were there to have fun, and I bless them for their goals. I did everything in my power to have fun right along with them as I took their money.

Late Christmas Day seemed to have an extra number of these types showing up, done with their family obligations and ready to have some fun.

I loved my holiday schedule, I loved the sameness of it year after year, I loved not having to put up a tree or buy anyone presents or hang stupid lights on my gutters. I just did my thing and enjoyed it. So even though I was a superhero, sworn to help those I could help, I didn't want anyone to come asking for help this Christmas Eve. My track record just wasn't good on this day.

I'd even lost a dog the first year, and that was the only time in my memory of being Poker Boy, superhero who helps people and saves dogs, that I had ever lost a dog. Other people had died when they didn't take my advice, which wasn't my fault. And there really hadn't been anything I could have done to stop Bob's massive heart attack last year. I could sort of live with that, but I hated not being able to save dogs.

I had almost made it to the poker room when I saw her.

She was sitting on a bench near the front door of the casino, her back to the window, her posture straight, her eyes focused on the people who went past, watching every move, clearly searching for something or someone.

She had longish blonde hair, a body that looked tanned and in good shape, and she definitely had her proportions in order. She was also at least fifteen years younger than me.

So sue me, I'm human underneath all the superhero stuff. I can look at a good-looking woman, even though a woman like the one sitting there never looked back.

Then she looked up at me, directly at me, actually seeing me, and I was struck by her deep, blue eyes.

She smiled and I was pulled by her wonderful, friendly smile.

She patted the bench beside her and I knew at once I was hooked, not by the woman's charms, or good looks, or great, perfectly proportioned body, but by some power even greater than my Poker Boy casino-fed powers.

I moved over, walking like a stiff-legged zombie in a bad movie, and sat beside her as if I didn't have an ounce of control over my body. And when a superhero loses control of his body, that's a very bad sign.

> *I moved over, walking like a stiff-legged zombie in a bad movie, and sat beside her as if I didn't have an ounce of control over my body.*

An aside. I have been with my share of beautiful women over the years who have made me lose control of all, or part, of my body, and that is not what had just happened. This was no little head controlling the big head. This was magic or superpower or something besides womanly charms, although I must admit, womanly charms often act like a superpower on me.

Just not this time.

When I was seated, I felt the control over whatever had made me do the monster walk loosen, and then vanish, like heat coming from an oven when you open the door and try to look in too fast.

My eyes fogged for an instant, I felt flush, and then it was gone.

"Wow, that was pretty good," I said. "You use that power for helping others, or just making people walk funny?"

She laughed, the sound high and just a trifle shrill, but she was so good-looking, and had such perfect skin on her perfectly proportioned body, I didn't much care about a slightly-off laugh.

"No," she said, "I'm no superhero like you, Poker Boy."

My instant reaction was *Shit! She knew my name!*

But she went on talking before those words came out of my mouth.

"Dave gave me that power," she said, "to make sure I got your attention when I found you. I could only use it the one time."

"Dave?" I asked, actually getting the word out of my suddenly dry mouth. My stomach was twisting like I had just had two big polish dogs and forgot to take an antacid. There was only one Dave I knew who could give superpowers away like they were quarters.

"Dave," she said, nodding. "I was sitting in his office just yesterday."

For a moment the word "Dave" echoed a little around the lobby of the casino like she had shouted it into a deep canyon.

An aside. In my world there are a number of what are called Gambling Gods. My superpower as Poker Boy, I am sure, comes directly from the Gambling Gods. Now these gods are more like what I would have imagined the old Greek gods were like.

And there is a very clear hierarchy in the Gambling Gods' world.

The hierarchy is set up just like a casino management. In fact, there's a major discussion about whether the gods just recently patterned their world on how super casinos were run, or if casinos patterned their management after how the gods have always been.

I actually think the Gambling Gods have always had the same management system, and modern super casinos just followed along naturally. Or not so naturally, but that's only my opinion, and I really don't know for sure.

Near the top of this system is the General Manager, one of the many Gods working right under Lady Luck herself. The General Manager is one of the most powerful, can stomp on other gods like they were ants, and pretty much controls the nature of the world behind the normal world that most people see in the gaming and hotel worlds.

Below the General Manager comes the Head of Casino Operations, then the Head of Hotel Operations. Below them are all the directors, such as Director of Security, Director of Food and Beverage, Director of Entertainment, and so on. And below that group are the regular gods, such as the Keno God and the God of Poker.

The gods below those, if there were that many, didn't much count, and I figured I had as much power as Poker Boy as many of the lower level gods, like Pit Bosses and Shift Supervisors. But they are still considered gods in the realm of things, and I am only a superhero, so what do I know. I certainly have no plan on putting my powers up against any of them.

Now this woman had just finished telling me she had talked to Dave, had been in Dave's office, and had gotten the power trick to get me to sit down from Dave.

To say I was stunned would be an understatement. Dave was the General Manager.

You didn't bow to Dave, or worship him, but you certainly didn't mess with Dave, or make him angry. I honestly hoped I would never even meet Dave. I figured it was just safer that way.

And no way in hell did I ever want to meet Lady Luck.

Now Dave had sent this good-looking woman to me.

Up until this moment, I wasn't even sure if the General Manager of everything even knew I existed.

I desperately wanted to ask her what Dave's office looked like, what Dave looked like for that matter, but somehow I refrained from being a god geek and asked the most intelligent question I could think of.

"Dave sent you to me, huh? It must be really important."

Duh. Dumb-ass question. This was not getting off to a good start.

"I think it is," she said. "My name is Audrey Koch. Can I buy you a drink and tell you about it?"

Here was a beautiful woman asking to buy me a drink on Christmas Eve, and I was scared more than I have been in years.

"Buy me a Diet Coke" I said, keeping my voice level and my poker face on. Thank god I was a poker player and I could do that under stressful situations. "I'll be glad to listen."

"Great," she said, standing up quickly like the bench had an ejection button.

I got up a little more slowly, making sure that all the *Come-and-sit-beside-me* spell was gone. It was, and two minutes later we were in the bar.

The place had twenty tables and a big screen t.v. Only one other couple sat against the far wall, so we took a table in front of the window looking out at the people headed from the hotel to the casino.

Audrey ordered an eggnog drink that sounded like it could cause diabetes all by itself, and I stuck with my original plan. I didn't want any alcohol because I still held out hope of getting to the poker table tonight. But with Dave sticking his all-powerful nose into my Christmas Eve, that hope was fading quickly.

"Here's my problem," Audrey said, getting right to the point. She looked me right in the eye and with the most serious of expressions on her face said, "I need to get laid. And it has to happen in the next four hours and ten minutes."

She actually looked at her watch as she said that second sentence.

I glanced at my watch as well. Seven-fifty. Four hours and ten minutes until Christmas.

She wanted to get laid on Christmas Eve. Why?

I must have heard her wrong. That couldn't be the big problem. The General Manager of the Big Casino couldn't be pimping me to some woman. It wasn't possible.

Besides, this woman could get just about any man she blinked at.

"Would you repeat that?" I asked.

She laughed, the sound echoing through the almost empty bar. Again the laugh was just a little off, but the wonderful blue eyes and the perfect smile made me not care at all.

"I need to have sex before midnight with a superhero. And Dave thought you would be the best choice for me."

"Oh, Dave thought I would, huh?"

She nodded, smiling. "And I agree. You're older than I usually like in men, but you're cute."

Okay, I'm a poker player, a guy who is usually in complete control of his emotions, yet right at that moment I didn't have a clue if I should feel angry, excited, flattered, or insulted. I was being pimped by the big guy in the Executive Suite to a young, very attractive woman. There

had to be something I was missing, and I needed to resort to my superpowers to find out.

I turned on my Tell-Me-No-Lies Superpower and stared directly at her.

An aside. I used to call this power my Empathy Superpower, but that never seemed to fit, so this year I finally renamed it.

"Why do you need to sleep with a superhero before Christmas Day?" I asked, directing all my power at her.

No person could resist me.

She resisted.

But no person could resist me.

She still resisted, bouncing my superpower away like it was water on a freshly waxed car.

Then she blushed.

"Dave said you might try to get the truth out of me," she said. "He's blocked all your powers from working on me."

Then she shrugged and smiled. "Sorry."

I stopped focusing my useless power and sat back. What good was a superhero with his superpowers not working? I pushed that thought away, and all thoughts of feeling sorry for myself, and directed my attention to her.

"You're not going to tell me why you want to sleep with me inside this time frame, are you?"

"I can't," she said, the look on her face deadly serious.

I sat there thinking while the waitress served our drinks and took Audrey's money. I could only come up with a couple of reasons for this strange request.

First, the General Manager was rewarding me for all my good deeds over the years. But that didn't seem to be

Dave's style. And this kind of reward certainly wasn't mine either.

Second, this was a bet. Bets in the Gambling God's world were everyday things. Someone might have bet I would sleep with this woman before Christmas Day, giving up my evening of poker for sex. And Dave was in on the bet in some fashion.

I could think of no other reason this woman needed to sleep with a superhero this evening, before midnight.

None.

And if there was a reason, she should be able to tell me. Only things like bets made silly rules like not telling.

So it had to be a bet.

And I was just a pawn in the bet. Nothing more. But did I want to play poker tonight and let one side win the bet, or sleep with a beautiful, young woman, and let the other side win?

Actually, that was a tough choice for a professional poker player at my age. At twenty-nine, there would be no thought. The little head would have controlled the decision and thirty minutes later I'd be looking at this young woman's nude body.

But at my slightly older age, sleeping with a woman always brought many side effects. I don't mean this to sound like I don't have relationships. I do. Just not ones that started in Dave's office and brought me into the picture doing a zombie walk. Thinking back, not one of my long-term relationships with women has started that way, and I doubted this would either.

My little voice told me there was still something I was missing.

An aside. My little voice isn't a superpower, but it saves me more often than my powers do.

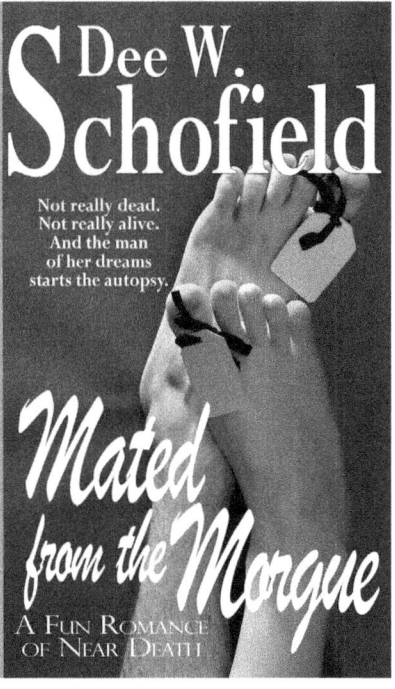

"Okay," I said, facing her as she sipped on her sugar-drink. "You want to sleep with a superhero before midnight, but you're not going to tell me why. Am I right?"

She nodded, her beautiful eyes staring at me.

"And I'm the superhero that Dave sort of picked out of a hat for you, right?"

This time she nodded a little slower. From what I could tell, that wasn't the complete truth, but I was getting close.

"You didn't even know I existed before Dave mentioned my name, did you?"

She shook her head this time, still saying nothing.

So I was just a convenient superhero, doing nothing on Christmas Eve but playing poker. This was making me a little angry, I had to admit.

"And I assume this is what you really look like, that you don't have AIDs, and you don't want to get pregnant."

"This is what I really look like," she said, spreading her arms, which gave me a clear view of her assets just above the table, "No magic, no nothing. I don't have any diseases, and I will never have kids."

"Yet right now you want to check into a hotel room and have sex with me?"

"I already have a room," she said, smiling at me.

Damn, if this woman was just a half-an-ounce less beautiful, had a fraction less fantastic smile, and didn't have such perfect skin, I wouldn't be having any problem. I'd be telling her it was nice meeting her and move on to the poker room.

But it was hard for any mortal man, superhero or not, to turn down an offer of sex from a goddess-like woman.

Then I realized what word had gone through my head.

Goddess.

No wonder she had access to Dave. This woman was one of the Gambling Gods.

Oh, shit! Now what should I do?

Sleeping with a Gambling God can only cause trouble. I've heard that a dozen times over the years.

But not sleeping with a Gambling God in this situation could cause even more troubles. Again I needed more information.

And I had always felt the best way to get information was directly.

"Can you tell me more about yourself?" I asked, sipping on my diet coke. "For example, I know you're one of the gods. Which position do you hold?"

Her face turned white and she tried to cover it quickly by bending forward and taking another sip of her drink. I'm a poker player. I can read expressions like other people read books. I knew for a fact I had hit the right answer with my little fishing question.

Finally she looked up at me. "How did you know? And without your superpowers?"

"You're dealing with a poker player. How would I not know?"

She nodded, taking that in. Finally she said, "I guess I can tell you. I'm the Keno Manager."

"So Audrey isn't your real name," I said. "You're Betty."

I had made it a habit of following all the main and lower gods, and who left, who got moved, who moved up or down, and so on. I was a poker player and a superhero. It was just part of my superhero job.

I reached across the table, hand extended. She took my hand and I shook hers, saying, "Nice meeting you, Betty."

"Nice to meet you as well, Poker Boy," she said, smiling, those teeth perfect in the bar light.

So now that I knew who she really was, there were only two options available as to why she was doing what she was doing. First, it was a bet as I had figured before.

But the second reason felt to be the more likely prospect. Betty wanted to move either up, or sideways, in her job status in the Gambling God Big Casino.

Suddenly I knew the answer. Dave was involved, therefore this wasn't a bet. This was an audition.

Betty was trying to move over to Poker Room manager and take Stan's job.

And Dave must have figured that if she understood a major poker player enough to get him to sleep with her instead of playing poker, she might get the job.

Now twice over the last few years since he hired me and told me I was a superhero, I had talked with Stan, both times in the middle of adventures. Usually the Gambling Gods didn't get involved in my adventures, and I doubted they even paid much attention most of the time.

But I liked Stan. He treated me fairly. I wasn't so sure yet that I liked Betty. Granted, any normal, heterosexual man would want to sleep with her, but that aside, I didn't have a good feeling about her.

And she had clearly let me surprise her as well. No one surprised Stan. And he seemed to understand poker players.

Betty clearly understood sex. And since Keno had the worst odds of any game in a casino except the Big Wheel, she understood suckers. And she was playing me as one during this entire exchange.

Some Classic Dean Wesley Smith Stories
Available at your favorite booksellers.

Poker players hated being played as suckers, even though the payout was sex with a goddess. It still wasn't worth it.

I took a sip out of my drink and leaned forward over the table. "Betty, you are a stunningly beautiful goddess."

"Well, thank you," she said, beaming that beaming smile at me.

"And I think you will make great middle management in the Big Casino."

"I hear a but coming," she said, her smile now gone.

"But I don't think you'd make a good Poker Room Manager. You're going to have to find another way to move up."

She sat there staring at me for a moment, her mouth slightly open. Clearly I had hit the nail right on the head. I had read her reasons and motives like I read a mid-level poker player.

"Dave told me I wouldn't be able to fool you," she said. "But I don't understand how you knew without your superpowers. Did Stan tell you?"

"No one told me," I said. "I'm a poker player. Knowing people and understanding why they do what they do is my job, and how I make my living. And I'm very good at my job."

She nodded. "Dave told me that if I didn't understand poker players, I could never have the job. Clearly I don't. At least not yet. You want to give me a private lesson?"

She smiled such a seductive smile, I thought the glass in my hand might melt. Yet somehow I managed to hold on.

"Sorry," I said. "I hope you don't hold this against me." Actually, I hoped that a lot, but I figured that since I helped Stan keep his job, Stan was going to help me as well if I needed protection from Betty.

"No hard feelings," she said, still smiling, only with the seductive part dropped. "But tell me, how would I have gotten you into bed if I had known poker players."

"Just play good cards," I said, giving her the same advice I gave any beginning poker player. "And never get in the way of a big game."

She nodded. "And tonight's a big game for you?"

"It is," I said. I had really been looking forward to my Christmas poker ritual, especially after the last two years.

She laughed softly, and stood, extending her beautiful, perfect-skinned hand. "Well, Poker Boy, it certainly has been an education meeting you. I'm sorry we're not going to have that roll in the sheets."

"Not half as sorry as I am," I said, taking her hand and holding it.

Her off-kilter laugh echoed through the mostly empty restaurant as she faded away, leaving me with my hand extended into mid-air.

I turned and headed for the poker room.

No one had died on me yet on this Christmas Eve. And I kept Stan's job for him, which had to be worth a little.

So far, so good.

And I hadn't even played a hand of cards yet.

~

Now Available
from all your favorite booksellers
in trade paper and electronic editions.

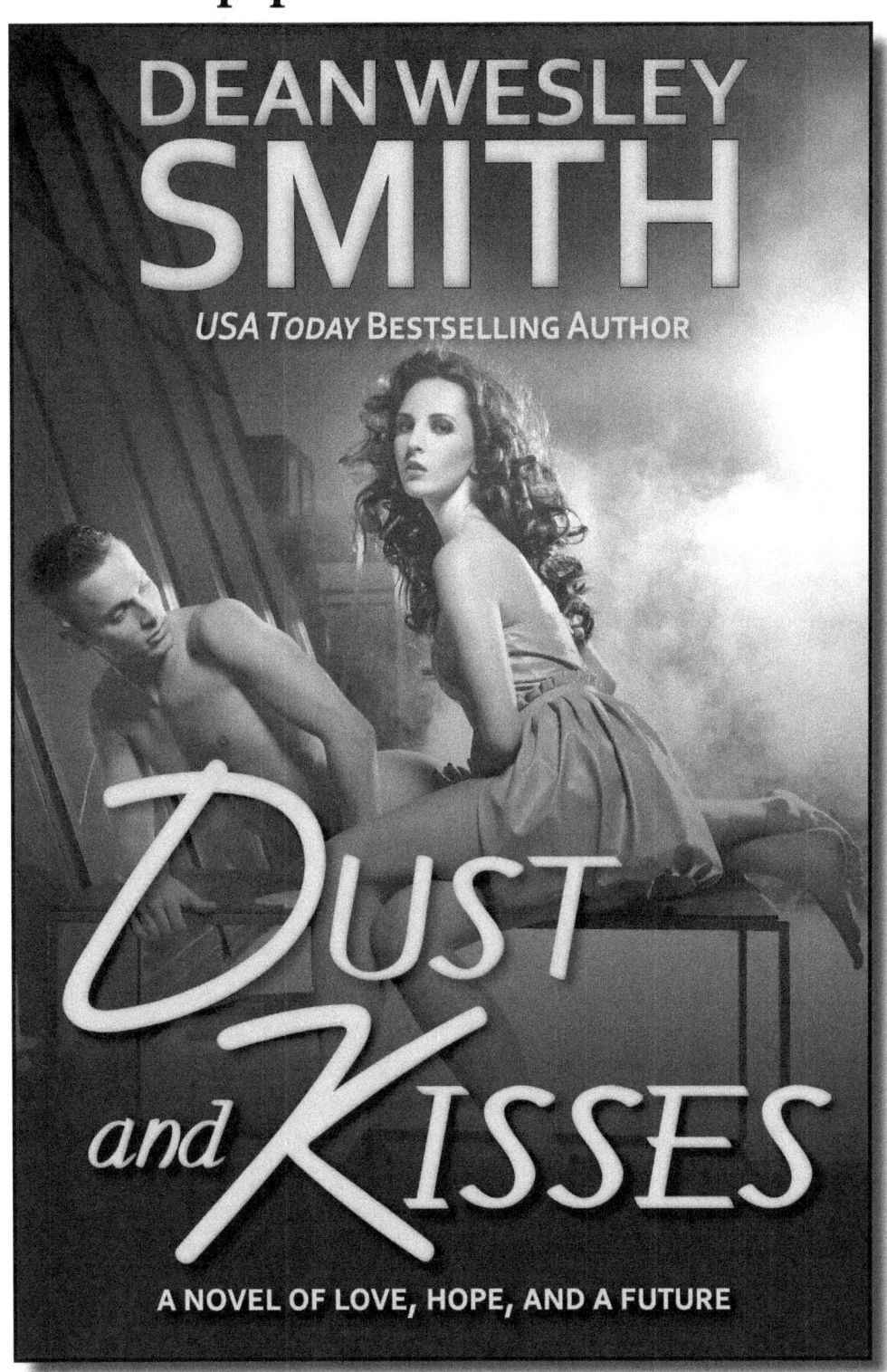

DEAN WESLEY SMITH

THE ADVENTURES OF HAWK

Chapters 19-21

What Came Before...

Nineteen-year-old Danny Hawk, his uncle, and his best friend Craig, were in Cairo to look for his missing father. Danny had witnessed the death of his only contact in Cairo, Professor Davis, because the professor had Danny's father's journals.

Danny knows that the men who had killed the professor were now after him and the journals. Danny finds the journals and gets his uncle and friend to safety in an airport hotel where he tells them what happened. They decide to keep searching for Danny's father and try to rescue him.

Along the way, Danny and Craig find some help from a street kid named Bud and twins from South Africa who had worked with Danny's father.

They managed to escape the men chasing them twice so far, Danny wasn't sure their luck would hold a third time.

And it barely did. They finally decided to head out of Cairo.

THE ADVENTURES OF HAWK

CHAPTER NINETEEN

September 1, 1970
Upper Lake Nasser, Sudan.

THE FIRST PART OF THE TRIP up the Nile had been fantastic, at least from a tourist perspective.

They had somehow managed to get out of Cairo without being seen and book a boat going south up the river. They had slept the first night on the wood plank floor of one small cabin, taking turns because there was only room for three to sleep. For Danny, that felt better anyway, since the two who weren't sleeping stood guard.

At every major port, they got off the ship and hid, then changed ships and kept going, sometimes booking a nice tourist ship, other times catching rides on fishing boats.

With every face that looked their way, Danny imagined it might be one of the Hydra League.

Or one of the brown-shirted men who had chased them out of Ed and Ernie's apartment.

From Cairo, for the first 400 miles, between Abu Roash and El Kula, there seemed to be a mountain range of pyramids along the west bank. Many times, Danny wished he and the others were there to sightsee, but they weren't. Even the slightest halt at this point might be enough to get them killed.

When they had crossed out of Egypt and into Sudan on a ferry on the great Lake Nasser behind the Aswan Dam, they had been asked for their passports, but were paid no attention to after that.

Danny had been surprised that Bud even had a passport. Later, Bud told him he had found it in the street a few years back and just kept it. The kid's name on the passport was Anthony Penn, and it was British, which fit Bud's accent.

Both of the twins also had British passports, but Danny didn't want to ask them how they got those. He was just relieved to have no further trouble. It looked like they had made a clean escape.

But that night, as the ferry pulled into Wadi Halfa, Sudan, two men climbed on board. It was just after midnight, but the air was still hot. The night sky was full of stars, brighter than any night sky Danny could remember seeing.

Danny, who was standing guard at the time, knew at once that they had been found. It was the same two men who had killed Professor Davis back in Cairo. He would recognize those two men anywhere, especially with the distinctive snake-rising-out-of-water tattoo on their right hands.

Hydra League.

Danny wanted to be sick. They were six hundred miles up the Nile River, yet these two men had found them.

How was that possible?

"They found us," Danny whispered to the others, waking them. They were on the top deck of the three level ferry, near the rear. "Hydra League men."

"How?" Craig asked, shocked. "Are they human?"

"I would not bet on it," Bud said.

Below, the two men split up, one going toward the bow, the other toward the stern.

Danny looked at the lit dock and the large Sudan village beyond. It seemed impossible to reach without being seen. The ferry was about to pull out, and clearly the two men planned on riding along. Once the ferry was into the middle of the huge Aswan Lake, the boys would have no chance of escape.

"We need to get down to the next level," Danny whispered.

"Then what?" Ernie asked, looking panicked in the faint light.

"We're trapped," Ed said.

"When the two come up the stairs to the second level," Danny said, "we go over the side to the first level. We'll have to be quick. We'll only have a few seconds."

"We'll need to wait there until just as the ferry is pulling out," Bud said, nodding. "Then make a jump for it."

"Exactly," Danny said, trying to breathe evenly to slow his heart from pounding right out of his chest.

They made a dash for the second deck, moving as silently as they all could on the wooden stairs. On the second level, Bud went on down the stairs to the first level to see where the men were while Danny,

Craig, and the twins moved quickly to a place in the middle of the ship away from both staircases.

A moment later Bud came running back. "Get over the side," he said as he went past Danny and flipped himself over the railing, sliding down a support pole to the first deck.

All four of them followed Bud, with Danny going last. As he slid down, he caught a glimpse of one of the Hydra League killers coming up the stairs near the front of the ferry.

At that moment, a signal sounded, echoing through the night air. The ferry was going to pull out. The engines got louder and the ferry lurched into motion.

"We jump at the last minute," Danny said, running along the edge of the ferry's lowest deck. He got to a point near the stern, swung himself over the railing, his backpack on his shoulder, then waited for the dock to come sliding past.

The other four were in the same position beside him on the outside of the rail. He would be the first to jump, and the dock looked like it was getting farther and farther away from the ferry.

He had to wait.

Time it right.

Too soon and he would hit the water, too late and he would do the same on the other side of the dock.

The ferry had really gained speed as he finally said, "Now!"

He jumped with all his strength.

The blackness of the water between the ferry and the dock seemed to be a vast expanse, but somehow, he cleared it, hitting the dock with a few running steps before stopping.

The others did the same. Craig, the last one off, actually hit and rolled, but came up all right.

On the boat, one of the men standing on the second deck yelled something in Arabic at them that Danny didn't completely understand, since most of it was swearing.

Danny waved at the man like he was a relative going on a cruise.

"Now, that's not nice," Craig said, laughing. "You really shouldn't tease the big man with a gun."

"True," Danny said, turning and heading for the city of Wadi Halfa as the ferry vanished into the darkness of the big lake. "But what's he going to do? Kill me twice?"

CHAPTER TWENTY

September 11, 1970
Upper Lake Nasser, Sudan.

DANNY FIGURED the two men would circle back by land to the city to look for them, so they took another ferry an hour behind the last one and for the rest of the trip up the river didn't see anyone following them. It took another full week, making good speed, before they had reached Lake Albert. It wasn't the headwaters of the Nile exactly, but it was close. The river that led to Lake Victoria fed off of Lake Albert.

They stopped on the Republic of Congo side of the lake because of a conversation Ernie had had with a boat pilot a few hundred miles back. It seemed what was called "the path of elephants" by the natives was from the bank of Lake Albert, over a range of mountains and into the deep jungle of the Congo.

The elephants had been using the same path for thousands of years.

Danny had been stunned. There really was a "path of elephants."

"The area is haunted," Ernie had told them. "It's never really been explored. The pilot said it goes through what is called the Land of the Dead. None of the native tribes go near the area."

Bud had laughed. "Well, at least we won't have that problem. But we're going to need someone to guide us."

Ernie had nodded. "The Captain gave me a name of a guide who would take us along the elephant path to the Land of the Dead."

In the small village of Bumia, ten miles inland along a mud road from the lake, they had found their guide, a skinny, older man with long grey hair and rotted teeth named Hassett.

At first, Danny wasn't sure the old man could help them, but then after watching him move around his hut-like home, it was clear the man was still in great physical shape.

Danny had told him what they wanted and his answer had been to laugh. When none of them laughed with him, he had asked simply. "Why would I take you five into the jungle?"

"I'm in search of my father," Danny said. "And our only clue is to walk the path of the elephants."

"Path of the elephants?" Hasset asked. "What do you know about that?"

"Nothing," Danny said. "That's why we want to hire you to walk it." Danny had made no mention of the Hydra League or anything else. Hassett had finally agreed and Bud had helped him with the negotiations for Hassett's fee and buying the supplies they would need.

Twenty-two days and nights of travel after leaving Cairo, they started off into the jungle.

In all his life, Danny had never been so scared. He was leading an expedition into an area of the world that had never been explored.

And he had no idea what he was looking for.

CHAPTER TWENTY-ONE

September 15, 1970
Deep in the jungle, Republic of Congo

WALKING THE PATH of elephants had actually turned out to be fairly easy, considering the thick underbrush of the jungle that bordered the half-mile-wide band of brush and trees trampled down by the passage of thousands of elephants twice a year. Danny couldn't imagine even trying to walk through that jungle. It looked like a two-story green wall on both sides.

Except for watching for the mounds of what Craig called elephant chips, they made good time. And the dried elephant chips made great fuel for fires at night.

They never saw an elephant, either, but did see a few scattered remains of ones, rotting and smelling in the hot, humid air.

Hassett had warned them that if they felt the ground shaking, get off into the jungle fast. Elephants mostly moved along this path slowly, but at times they moved a lot faster, and then they were real dangerous.

At first, the bugs that seemed to be everywhere had driven them all crazy, but as Hassett had said would happen, they all got used to them, and from what Danny could tell, as soon as they did, the bugs seemed to almost stop bothering them.

After five days of hiking, mostly uphill toward what Hassett called Elephant Pass, Danny was getting frustrated. He and the others had no idea what they were looking for. The only clue was the words "teeming masses" in the Hydra Journal entry #3. And in this jungle, it sure didn't look like they would find any teeming masses of anything except insects.

"When do we enter the Land of the Dead?" Danny asked Hassett just after they started out on the fifth morning.

Hassett laughed, a sort of choking sound that Danny still wasn't used to. "Son, we've been in it for a day now."

"Can we stop and talk for a minute?" Danny asked.

Hassett shrugged and pointed to some shade to one side.

With the pack off his back, Danny told the twins that they were all in the Land of the Dead, and what Hassett had said.

"Are there any ruins in this area?" Ed asked Hassett.

"I wouldn't know," Hassett said. "Never been off this trail. Never had any reason to go bushwhacking out in that stuff." He pointed to the high wall of what looked to be solid green that bordered the path of elephants.

"Any high place we could look over the Land of the Dead area?" Ernie asked.

"Sure," Hassett said. "Later today we'll reach Elephant Pass. To the right there's Ishango Peak."

"Ishango?" both Ernie and Ed said at the same time.

Hassett nodded, surprised.

"Ishango is the name of an ancient people," Ernie said.

"Rumored to exist before the first Pharaohs," Ed said.

"Can you get us to that peak where we can look out over the Land of the Dead?" Danny asked Hassett.

"Sure," he said. "but before I do that, you are going to have to tell me the truth."

He looked around slowly at each of them, but no one said a word, so he kept going. "Two men have been following us for days, staying behind us, pacing us. What kind of trouble are you boys in?"

Danny thought his heart was going to stop. Craig dropped to the ground and just sat there shaking his head. Clearly, they had been found yet again.

Danny looked at Hassett, then at the twins, who both nodded that they should tell Hassett everything.

"How familiar are you with archeology?" Ed asked.

Hassett did his laugh, then said, "I have a degree in it from Oxford, back before any of you were born."

Now Danny was even more shocked.

Ed smiled. "You're Dr. Steven Hassett. Expert in pre-Egyptian empires. Discredited for your beliefs that at one time an advanced civilization had spread around the world on the equator."

Hassett bowed in acknowledgement.

Ed pointed at Danny. "We are looking for his father, Professor Kenneth Hawk. He was taken by the Hydra League."

Now it was Hassett's turn to be shocked. His face went white and he had to swallow before he spoke. "Ken was taken? Then he must have found the third Hydra Journal entry?"

"He did," Danny said, surprised that Hassett had known his father. "And I have his notebooks well hidden. We are after the fourth entry in the assumption that the only way to find my father is to follow the Hydra Journals."

"And that means those two men who have been following us are Hydra League," Hassett said, clearly suddenly very afraid. Now he too sat down, so Danny and the rest did as well.

"Have I said before how screwed we are?" Craig asked, shaking his head.

"I know these Hydra League men on sight," Danny said. "If you can take me back close enough so that I can see them, I will tell you for sure."

Hassett shook his head. "They have been pacing us very carefully. They are not hunters, and are clearly out of their element here in the jungle. They are after you, and clearly hope you will lead them somewhere, and I will not take you to the old city if they are following."

"Old city?" both Ed and Ernie asked at the same time.

Hassett nodded. "Why do you think I've been living here, pretending to be a guide? This is called the *Land of the Dead* because of a city buried by the jungle centuries ago." He pointed to the right off the trail. "I have worked it, explored it, for twenty years now."

"We will give you the first three Hydra Journal entries if you take us to the city," Danny said.

Hassett stared at Danny for a moment, then nodded and stood. "I have the first two, but I need the third. You have a deal. But first we got to make sure we're not followed."

He turned and started up the path, moving at a good pace.

"Where are we going?" Danny asked, scrambling to get his pack on his back and follow.

"We're going to hide your friends," Hassett said. "then you and I are going to get rid of the men behind us."

Continued next issue…

Now Available
from all your favorite booksellers
in trade paper and electronic editions.

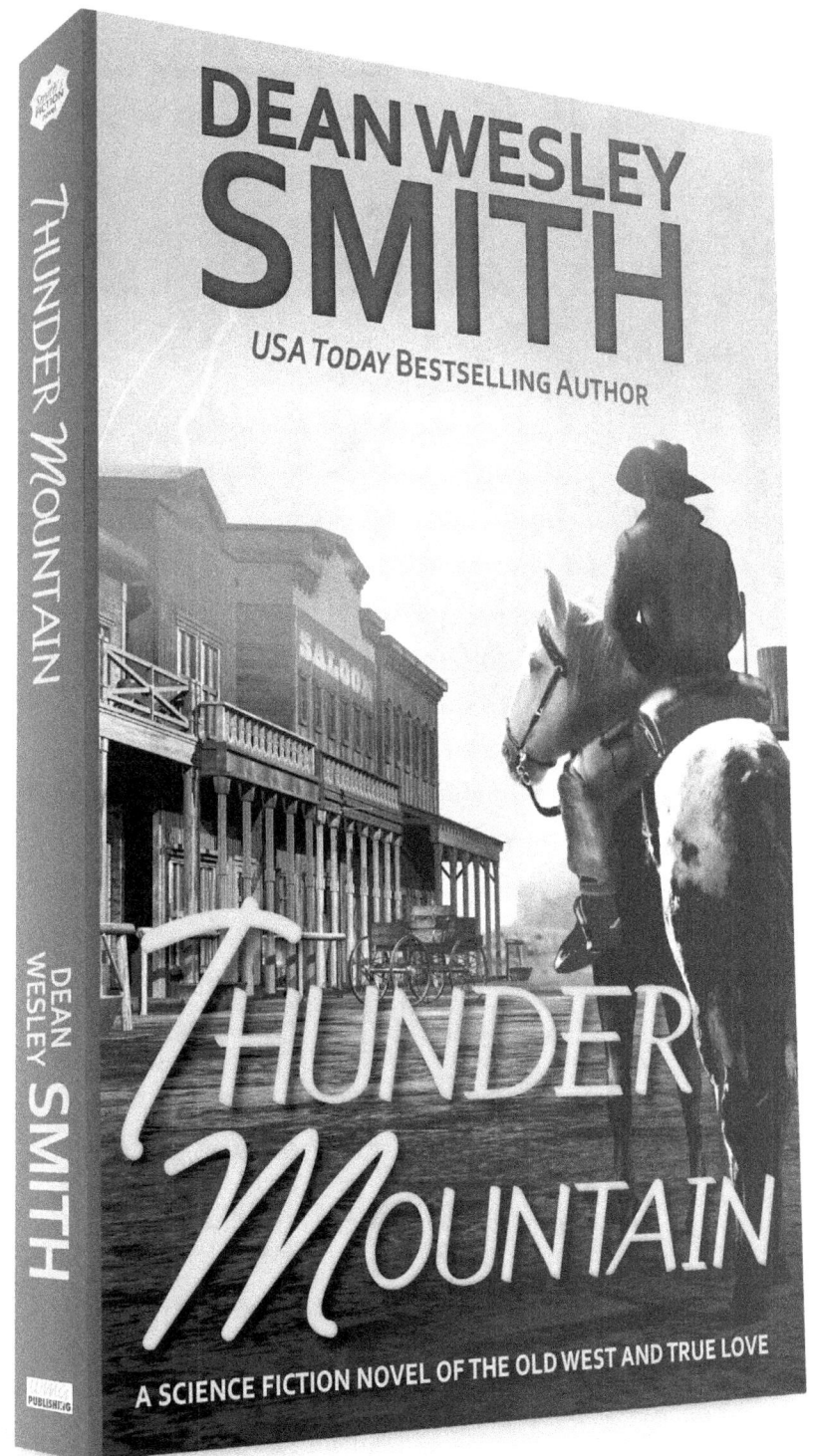

DEAN WESLEY SMITH

WAITING FOR THE COIN TO DROP

USA Today bestselling writer Dean Wesley Smith has two major ways to approach time travel. First is the alternate timeline approach, where any change in history starts a new timeline. His entire series of Jukebox stories and Thunder Mountain series of stories works that way.

Then he has the theory that time is tied to mass and energy, with anything physical having a complete tie to an instant of time and energy. And if something is changed in the past, it resets the next instant.

He developed a series of stories that are space opera starring Captain Brian Saber around this second approach to time and mass. This story approaches another side of time being tied to mass and energy.

A slightly ugly side.

This story first appeared in Fiction River: Timestreams *in the summer of 2013.*

WAITING
FOR THE COIN TO DROP

NICK STARED AT THE SIGN on the antique gumball machine near the door in Donna Hayman's living room and sighed.

Wait for the Coin to Drop.

If he waited for a coin to drop in that machine, he would never live long enough. Sometimes he really wished mechanical things would work here. Anything. But nothing mechanical did work, nothing electrical, nothing that required a moving part, even down to simple door hinges.

Just to get into Donna's apartment, he had had to use a sledgehammer and smash open the door. It took a crowbar to open a refrigerator, and that was after removing the screws on the hinges.

Now, after almost a year of living in this apartment building, he had almost every apartment open so he could come and go with ease. Counting Donna's, there were only six more apartments on the top floor left to open, six more hidden lives to explore, six more adventures to take before his research was finally finished and he could go home.

He stopped inside the door and glanced around at Donna's apartment. He could almost smell the uncut Canadian bacon and pepperoni pizza on the coffee table. He knew that wasn't possible, since he needed special implants and a breathing device to even breathe or walk or see light through the air of this time period. Air molecules that didn't move were as hard as steel. And since nothing moved, no smell could move to his nose either. Without the special implants, he would have died instantly on arriving in this moment in time.

Outside the clean window, the city of New York spread out, the deep canyons of the buildings tightening down in the distance. No sound came from the city, since it too was frozen in this moment, this instant of time, as was everything else around him.

He shook his head. It still smelled like pepperoni pizza in this apartment. He hadn't had a bite of pizza for almost a year. It hadn't occurred to him to bring any with him, or program it into his food replicator. No wonder he was imagining the smell. But he did remember to bring along his fine cigars and best whiskey. And after each day he allowed himself a few sips and a cigar, so life without pizza hadn't been all bad.

He had no idea if Donna Hayman was home at this very instant in time, but it sure looked like she was. He hoped she was. If nothing more than to give himself another beautiful woman to look at for his last few weeks in the building and in this time period. He knew, from his files that

he had brought with him from the future, that Donna had been good looking at one point in her life.

He doubted she would be as good as Betty in apartment 310, or Sandra in 241, or Kitty in 608, whom he had found in the shower, her head thrown back, her naked body frozen in a moment of showering, her almost perfect body covered in a silvered sheen of water.

He had to admit, he had spent far, far too much time in that bathroom, staring at her, a woman long dead as far as he was concerned. Kitty would never realize that for a fraction of a fraction of an instant in time, she had had a visitor from the future staring at her in a very private moment.

At first it made him feel a little perverted. But his job here was to study the people and he had decided there was nothing at all wrong with admiring a perfect human form.

After a time, he thought he had actually fallen in love with her. An impossible romance, since the only way a person from his time could travel back to another time was inside an instant, a fraction of a second too small to even measure, where nothing moved, and the laws of conservation of mass and energy wouldn't allow anything to be changed from one instant to another.

That fact, that reality, solved all time paradoxes.

And that allowed for middle-aged writers like him, with far too much time on their hands, to go back in time for a year to study the people who lived in a crowded apartment building in New York and write a book about their long-dead lives of 2015.

Granted, studying people in the past was nothing really new or original. But that wasn't his focus. He had decided that for his book, he would put a special spin on the idea of ordinary people's lives.

He would study their secrets. He would learn their hidden desires, their fetishes, their affairs, and their faults.

Every person, either in 2015 or 2259 had secrets. And a lot of people loved reading about other people's secrets. His challenge to research his book called "The Secrets of Lexington Avenue" was to look into everyone's lives in this building, and then through historical documents, if possible, learn how ten of these people fared with their secrets.

So, for almost one year now, he had lived in a special time bubble set up in the lobby area. And every day he left that time bubble and broke open people's doors and cabinets and everything else they kept secret and closed off and hidden from their neighbors.

Of course, in the next fraction of an instant of real time for this building and these people, the universe would reset everything as if he had never been here, broken down a door, or even existed in this moment.

It was impossible for him to do any real harm in this time.

And to him, all these people were long dead, including Kitty in 608. And to Kitty and everyone else in this building, he was below notice.

He had been surprised that living alone in a city of frozen, uncaring people had bothered him for the first few months. But eventually he got used to it.

And now, after almost a year, he had come to like the people of this building, for the most part. He hadn't expected that. He had expected them to just be statistics in his research. But by looking for their secrets, looking through their hidden lives, they had become more than frozen flesh and data. They had become human to him.

USA Today *bestselling writer Dean Wesley Smith returns with a second novel in the world of* Thunder Mountain *from the second issue of* Smith's Monthly.

Historical interior designer April Buckley and architect Ryan Knott are hired to design and furnish a huge lodge to the year 1900 standards. The two that hire them are Bonnie and Duster Kendal, two of the world's great mathmaticians.

Only problem: The lodge can't be built. It can't exist. Yet somehow it does because they built it. And fell in love in the process.

And he had no doubt that was going to make his book a much stronger book.

Of course, there were a half-dozen he had also come to hate when he discovered who they actually were. So far he had found two child molesters living in the building. Even though they would never notice, he had cut off their hands. It made him feel better, even though in the next instant of time, everything would reset and the monsters would continue on in their own time.

But screw it, it made him feel better doing that.

Even more surprising to him was that over a quarter of the people in the building had very few, if any, secrets. They simply lived their lives, many of them very sad and dull lives.

Just as life treated them, he was sure he would go home and just forget them. They would live on as nothing more than a few notes in his research. He had come to realize that in many cases a person without secrets, without desires, without courage, was not worth studying.

Or remembering, for that matter.

However, a large number of people in the building lived interesting lives, had fascinating secrets, and often varied sex lives. He knew his readers would be interested in that, so for each person he tried to determine what their sexual desires and secrets were.

There were twelve gay couples in the building and at least sixteen men and a dozen women who liked to look at pornography on their computers. Eight others were heavily into different aspects of bondage. Some had pornographic pictures in hidden boxes or in the back of drawers, often of themselves with some unknown partner.

Fifty people in the building played musical instruments and another dozen were travel freaks, people who seemed to live to do nothing but leave town and see the world beyond the confines of New York City.

Six were working on novels and from what he could tell, none of them were any good. And three were working on plays, none of which were ever produced that he could discover.

Almost half of the people in the building were having money trouble of one sort or another.

He had no doubt he would have trouble focusing on just ten people in this building for his book.

Maybe Donna would end up being one of those top ten most interesting. He could call her the "pizza woman" since that pizza really seemed to have invaded his imagination.

Nothing could smell or feel hot or cold in this instant of time. And if not for his specially contained living bubble that sucked energy from his own time period and allowed him to live in his real time, he wouldn't even be able to shower or eat.

He had once tried a bite of a steak in one of the first apartments he had broken into. It had tasted like sawdust and his special implants had warned him away from such action by instantly causing him to throw it all back up all over the plate of the apartment occupant.

Nick ignored the imagined smell of the pizza and forced himself to really look at the apartment around him. He needed to find out just how human Donna Hayman of apartment 719 really was, and what her secrets were.

Just as he was doing now, living in the past, Donna clearly also had lived in the past in her life. Every detail screamed out another era long before 2015. From the old gumball machine with its strange sign telling someone to wait for the coin to drop to a huge mural on one wall with the pictures of *Gone with the Wind* stars taken at the opening of the famous picture in Atlanta.

The furniture was of the 1940s, overstuffed and comfortable-looking. A Shirley Temple doll sat on one chair and a game of Monopoly with metal pieces and wood houses covered an end table, looking like it was half-played.

The room looked lived in, with the pizza on the coffee table and Coke in an old bottle beside it. His stomach rumbled as he got nearer the pizza. He was going to have to call the day early and head back to his time bubble to get some dinner.

"You want a piece?" a woman asked from behind him.

He spun, his heart threatening to explode out of his chest. It had been almost a year since he had heard another

person's voice, even though he had talked to the frozen residents all the time.

Facing him was a woman with a very nasty-looking knife held casually in her hand like she was used to using one in all different ways, including cutting pizza.

Not possible.

She was moving and breathing and blinking and doing everything a live person would do.

Not possible. He was inside an instant of time, a random instant. No one else could be here at this moment.

His mind just wouldn't believe what he was seeing. Then finally he caught his breath and realized that the live person he was staring at wasn't Donna Hayman, the resident of this apartment.

"How?" he asked, which was just about all he could manage to get out.

He lowered his hand slowly and let it hover over his emergency recall button covered with a protective cap on his belt. He had thought about hitting that button that would send him back to his normal time a great deal during those first lonely days, but after three months, he had sworn to himself he wouldn't give up on this idea or this book.

The woman smiled at him and her face seemed even more attractive in a classical model way, except for the fact that the smile didn't reach her green eyes. She had on a knit yellow sweater and shorts that allowed her beautiful, thin legs to stand out. She was barefoot and her long, blonde hair was pulled back into a ponytail.

Damn, she was the best-looking woman in the building.

He was dreaming. This wasn't real. It simply couldn't be real.

"Don't bother to hit your recall button," she said, her voice low and husky.

"You're inside my bubble now and it won't work."

He shook his head. His mind was reeling. This could not be happening. It was against all the laws of physics that he understood, and he had spent some time studying them before he was allowed to take this research trip. And this was really, really against the laws of time travel.

"You sort of stunned me," she said, again smiling at him, "when you started banging on my door with that ax."

He watched as she twisted the knife in her hands. Crap, he had left the ax out in the hallway.

She went on. "Clearly, you're from some point in the future. What year is it where you came from?"

"2259." His voice sounded high and he swallowed the dryness.

"What month and day is it for you now?"

He had to think for a moment and do a little calculation, since he hadn't thought of what day it was back in the future, in his real time, for a while. "August twenty-first."

That time he managed to keep his voice normal and level, even though he was having an impossible conversation with a woman twisting a knife in her hands.

She nodded. "Two more years and twelve days. That's what I figured."

"Until what?"

"Until I get out of this jail," she said, waving the knife around at the apartment. "I've been here for six years, 353 days. Nine-year sentence in this instant in time, living in this stupid apartment that a woman by the name of Donna created."

Suddenly Nick understood exactly what had happened. He had broken into a prison cell.

After time travel had been discovered and the realization that nothing could be affected in the past, society had started dumping criminals into the past, letting them live in contained time bubbles in an instant in time, isolated, unable to hurt anything or anyone until their sentence was up.

It was fantastically cheaper than prisons. He had read studies on it. No guards, self-replicating food, and no need to even bother with keeping track of the prisoners. Their locations and instants of times in the past were always kept a secret, thus they would be impossible to find.

This woman was a criminal and this was her cell.

Somehow, when he had traveled back in time, he had ended up in the same instant of time she was in. Against all odds, but more than likely the time travel machines used a bunch of the same settings and that's how they had both ended up in this same instant in the same area.

The thinking went that there was so much room in the past, there was no real reason to spread out the criminals over too wide a number of time moments.

The woman stared at him for a moment, clearly shocked at his stunned reaction. "You weren't looking for me, were you? You stumbled in here by accident, didn't you?"

He nodded.

She shook her head, clearly sad about something. Then she brightened. "Well, this is one for the record books."

Again, all he could do was nod. More than likely this little accident would help the sales of his book, but at the moment

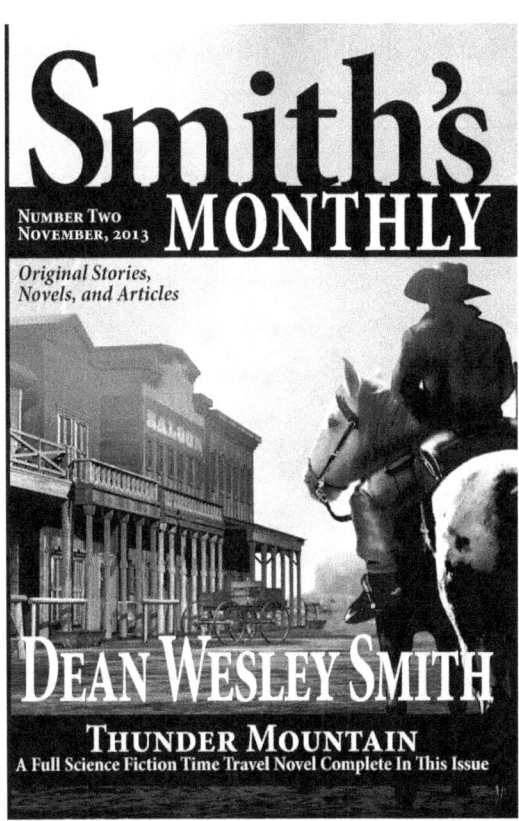

that was the least of his worries. The knife in her hand bothered him a lot more.

"So, you want some pizza or not?" she asked, moving with the knife toward the couch. "I think it's still warm."

"So, what did you do?" he asked, trying his best to make his voice stay level and his tone conversational, like he was asking her the time of day.

"Stabbed a man," she said, smiling as she held up the knife.

This time the smile got to her eyes and he knew she was kidding.

She laughed and then said, "Drugs. Smuggling the most recent designer drug from a modeling assignment into the wrong country. Stupid."

The realization hit him as to who he was looking at. Her name was Nancy. Nancy Robinson, a supermodel convicted and sentenced back when he was still working on his third novel. Her face had been all over the world net, and they had even filmed her disappearing back into time to serve her sentence.

Now, after the six years, she had aged slightly, but was still a stunning beauty.

"So, who are you and what the hell are you doing here?" she asked, picking up a piece of pizza.

She bit into the pizza, watching him with her intense, green eyes.

"My name's Nick," he said. "I'm a writer here researching a new book on the secrets of people living in this building. Including Donna Hayman, the woman who was supposed to be living in this apartment at this point in time."

"Welcome to her apartment," Nancy said, looking disgusted. "Trust me, she's not home and she has no real secrets, unless you call dying her hair and being behind on her credit cards a secret."

Then she laughed, the sound husky and odd in a weird way. She indicated that he should sit down and have some

pizza. "Might as well get comfortable. It does look like you stumbled on a really big secret in this apartment."

He smiled and let himself relax a little. "It does, doesn't it?"

He took the offered piece of rich-smelling pizza and carefully bit into it. It tasted even better than it smelled, if that was possible.

For the next thirty minutes, while they finished off the pizza, they talked and laughed about all sorts of things, and he got the short version of the events that put her in this jail cell.

All he kept thinking was how fantastically beautiful she was, how lucky he was to have found her, and how much more enjoyable the last few weeks of his research trip was going to be. He should have started at the top floor instead of the bottom floor. He would have found her ten months ago.

After he told her about a few of the other residents in the building, she smiled and sighed. "I like you, Nick. It's going to be good to have company for the last two years of my sentence."

"I only wish," he said, laughing. "I've only got two weeks left on my research time, although I might be able to extend a month or two before hitting my recall button."

The emergency recall button, and the main one in his time bubble in the lobby, were the only way anyone from his present could track him to this moment and bring him back. He had been warned that if something happened to those two buttons, there would be no finding him.

She looked at him, a puzzled frown wrinkling her wonderful face. Then sadly she shook her head. "You don't understand, do you?"

She pointed to the door. "Your recall button is blocked in here. Go ahead, try to leave."

He stared at her, again trying to absorb her words. He then glanced back at the shattered wooden door that he had stepped through and the hallway beyond. There were two other shattered doors he had gone into earlier in the week.

"This is a prison, remember," she said, softly. "No one leaves here until they call me back when my time is up. It is why I never crashed through that door and explored the city."

"You don't have the special implants to do so," he said, pushing the panic he was feeling down. Suddenly the pizza wasn't settling so well in his stomach. "You would not have been able to move through the air out there."

"Of course I have them," she said, sadness filling her eyes. "Every prisoner has them just in case something goes wrong with the bubble. We also have special recall buttons that will only go through the bubble when our time is served."

He shook his head and stood and headed for the shattered front door to the apartment. She couldn't be right. She was just pulling some sort of sick joke on him.

As he reached the door, he started to step through the opening and his leg banged into what felt like a very hard surface. Pain shot up his leg and he grabbed his knee for a moment. There didn't seem to be anything in his way, yet there was something there.

"Force field around the bubble," she said from behind him, her voice soft. "A prison far more effective than any cell invented. And it will remain in place for just over two more years."

"Sorry, got to go," he said, his voice again high and showing the panic he felt.

He pushed his emergency recall button and waited for the tingling feeling of the time travel kicking in.

Nothing.

He just stood there, with a former supermodel staring sadly at him. He clearly wasn't going anywhere, at least for two years and twelve days.

But at least he had a beautiful supermodel to keep him company.

***

Six months later, he was still sleeping on the couch.

Day after day of those six months he had stared at that stupid sign on the gumball machine.

Wait for the Coin to Drop.

He had come to find the secrets of the residents of an apartment building. And he had done just that.

It seemed the resident he had ended up trapped with had enough secrets to fill a dozen books. To start off with, she was bulimic, with no desire at all to help herself do anything else. In the small three-room apartment, the sounds of her forcing herself to throw up after every meal soon went from worrisome to completely revolting.

She had told him, on the second night, when he made a pass at her, that she had once been a man, had had the operation, and now hated everything to do with men. In fact, during the second month of his time with her, she had told him that he disgusted her.

It seemed that everything about her was fake. She took off her small breasts every night and hung them with her blonde wig on the wall beside her bed.

Worst of all, she was the most shallow human being he could have ever imagined in even a horror novel. The only topic of conversation that was allowed was her looks and her career and if she could save her career when she returned. She wondered if the world will have forgiven her "little mistake" as she called it.

She had quit school in the tenth grade and seemed proud of that fact. She had brought nothing to read and claimed that she had never read a book, ever, in her entire adult life. And there wasn't a thing he could use to write on in the entire prison cell. What little bit of writing he managed to do was to fill the last of his notes in the pad he kept with him each day before it ran out of power.

Every day Nancy spent hours and hours and hours in the bathroom, staring at herself in the mirror.

Three small rooms filled with secrets. They had become impossibly small within the first week and downright tiny by the end of the first month. Plus he had no clothes to wear besides what he had been wearing, so his main chore was to cook himself something to eat twice a day and do laundry every third day.

The rest of the time he just lay on the couch and stared at the sign on the gumball machine sitting beside the open door that promised his freedom, yet never brought it.

The gumball machine became the symbol of his life.

Wait for the Coin to Drop.

He was trapped in a moment in time with the secrets he had uncovered, the same type of moment that existed when a child waited for the coin to drop in the gumball machine to deliver the promised reward.

~

Coming Next Issue in Smith's Monthly
The first ever Captain Brian Saber novel

Smith's
MONTHLY

NUMBER EIGHT
MAY, 2014

*Original Stories,
Novels, and Articles*

DEAN WESLEY SMITH

LIFE OF A DREAM
A Full Earth Protection League Novel

USA TODAY BESTSELLING AUTHOR

DEAN WESLEY
SMITH

THE SLOTS OF SATURN

A POKER BOY NOVEL

USA Today bestselling writer, Dean Wesley Smith, takes you into his first full-length novel featuring his most popular character, Poker Boy.

Set in 2004, the last year the World Series of Poker *took place at Binions Horseshoe Casino in downtown Las Vegas, Poker Boy meets the love of his life and forms the team of superheroes and gods that will save the world many times over in the coming years.*

But first, he and his new team must save all of gambling and over fifty lives, from the evil ghost slots. And not get killed in the process.

The Slots of Saturn
A Poker Boy Novel

Note to the readers:
This novel is the origin of Poker Boy's team. The year is 2004
and Poker Boy has only been a superhero for less than four years.

Chapter One

A Superhero Arrives

I LOVE CASINOS. Always have.

I mean I truly love them, like some people enjoy sitting beside a calm mountain lake. Walking into a casino, it feels like I have stepped on an ocean beach on a warm evening with no wind, combined with the at-home feel of sitting by a fire, under a nice reading light, with a warm drink and a good book.

I admit, casinos are loud, with both machine and people noises, and are designed by experts to take a person's money. Yet every time I step through the door into a casino, either in Vegas, Atlantic City, or in timbuck-six North Dakota, I know I am home, that I am safe, that I am in control of my surroundings.

As Poker Boy, when I am in a casino, I also have my superpowers. I have to be honest that I love that feeling as well.

My superpowers, which are needed by definition to be a superhero, are varied. I have still not explored them all. Sometimes even I am surprised at what I can do.

As I stepped through the side door of Binion's Horseshoe Casino and Hotel in downtown Las Vegas, I walked right into the center of at least forty poker tables. I knew I had once again found my own little slice of heaven. I could feel the power flowing through me. My muscles, tense and tight from the long cab ride, relaxed as if rubbed by a Swedish hot-rub expert.

And trust me, Heidi, my Swedish hot-rub expert from two Vegas trips back, could relax the man of steel down into a pool of metal. Those fingers of hers were secret weapons and, I know for a fact and from wonderful memory, that she turned Poker Boy into Go Fish Man in two minutes.

I stopped and just took a deep breath of the smoke-tainted air of the old casino, filling my lungs with the poisons that killed others, but gave me strength.

Stopping just inside a casino front door was a habit of mine. Every time I went into a new casino, or an old one like the Horseshoe, I would just stop inside the door and look around, giving myself a few seconds to enjoy the feel. As Poker Boy, I get a lot of good feelings, especially when I have helped someone, but there are never enough of those good feelings in life, so I take my joys where I can get them. And stopping inside a casino door and just looking around was one of my joys in life.

Today, everything around me looked like a standard day in casino world.

On my right were some of the live poker games, on my left the overflow part of the tournament area, now with all the tables empty. The main desk for the hotel was beyond all the tables, and I had to get there by sort of following the yellow brick road of the pattern on the carpet, through the tables, down between the railings along the poker tables, and then through the ropes in the open area in front of the hotel desk.

Those ropes that guard the front desks of most hotels always made me feel like a cow being herded to the guy with the hammer who would hit me, put me out of my misery, and turn my body into prime rib and flank steaks. Some hotels had almost done that to me in the past.

There wasn't even anyone waiting in line to check in. Maybe I could avoid the ropes altogether and just go for the hammer.

I put my head down and moved toward the front desk, following the pattern on the carpet, hoping I could get checked in and to my room before anyone knew I was here. Even superheroes needed time to unwind from the traveling and the cab ride from the airport.

Actually, I was looking forward to taking a nap.

I somehow made it all the way to the front desk without being recognized. Granted, I am really not that famous, in a strict sense of the word. But I am often recognized across a crowded casino by someone who wants my help, like a dog in need to pee spotting a tree. I was the tree, and thankfully, at the moment, there were no dogs.

"Good afternoon, sir," the nice-looking woman behind the front desk said as I stepped up to the polished wood counter.

I had cut inside the ropes like I knew what I was doing, and was actually feeling a little proud of myself at that moment. Avoiding front desk rope lines, combined with the flowing power of a casino around me, could sometimes be a heady experience. I savored the moment, then looked up at the woman who had greeted me.

Her smile actually included her eyes as she leaned forward a little. And what eyes they were. I had an out-of-body experience as I studied them.

Brown, large, and round, with the light over the front desk giving them a little twinkle. I could stare into those eyes forever, but I knew I shouldn't.

Yet I wanted to.

I knew I shouldn't.

Stare.

I shouldn't.

I floated there, arguing with myself, until I finally returned to my body and somehow managed to look at the rest of her.

She had long brown hair pulled back into a flowing ponytail, a smile that showed perfect teeth, and skin that was pleasantly tan. She wore the Horseshoe employee brown jacket and white blouse in such a way as to somehow make the dull outfit look sexy.

Of course, a woman with those eyes and that smile could make burlap look sexy as far as I was concerned, so my astute powers of perception on her uniform was more than likely skewed by my own interests.

"Checking in," I managed to say, even though my throat was suddenly dry.

"Here for the tournament?" she asked, her smile not fading.

"I am," I said. "That obvious?"

"Poker players do have a look about them," she said, laughing.

Her laugh was so fine, so perfectly tuned that it matched her smile, her eyes, her sexy look. The Horseshoe sure had a way of greeting a poker player. I wanted to stand on the counter, shout "Poker Boy is here to save you!" and jump her right there.

I refrained, but I had no doubt I was in love.

Actually, more accurately, lust.

I was in lust with Miss Brown-eyes behind the front desk. Nothing unusual, but very enjoyable.

It was good to be back in a casino.

"Your name, sir?" the beautiful woman—who I shall forever think of as Brown-eyes until I learned her name—asked.

She stood in a non-threatening manner behind the front desk of the Horseshoe Casino and Hotel, her fingers poised over the keyboard of her computer. I would have much rather had those fingers poised over me, but since she was about to type my name with those wonderful hands, I couldn't complain too much.

"Conway Moore," I said, giving her one of the fake names I had been using since I had become Poker Boy.

Her fingers stroked my name into her computer, her head nodding slightly.

I watched, mesmerized as her hands worked.

I often got mesmerized by a woman's hands. It only becomes a problem when a woman is playing with her chips in a poker game. I then have to force myself to stare down at my own chips at that point, or into the eyes of the other players to break the spell.

I would have loved to have told this woman behind the desk that my name was Poker Boy, but Poker Boy wasn't the name I had made the reservation under, so it would have just confused the issue.

Poker Boy was my superhero name, and Conway Moore was the other part of my superhero name, used when I needed to do regular world things like check into a hotel, sign into a poker tournament, rent a car, that sort of thing.

Actually, Conway Moore wasn't the name I was born with. I had known Poker Boy was going to need a secret identity to get by in the world. Conway seemed like a good name. Conway was also a character thought up by James Hilton in his novel *Lost Horizons*. I liked the book, so I borrowed the name for my secret identity.

At first, I thought about just using Conway as both my first and last names, then the last name of Moore came from a poker game like a hundred dollar bill laying in the parking lot.

Shortly after I became Poker Boy, some guy in a ten-twenty hold-em game accused me of never getting enough of his money. I don't remember what casino I was in, but I do remember that he said that all I wanted was more and more. I had to agree, since he was one of the worst poker players ever to flash a large roll of bills in front of me. As long as he sat there at the table and pulled out more bills, I sat there and took his money. Thus was the nature of poker.

And besides, a superhero had to eat.

On the way back to my room hours later, I kept thinking about how he just repeated "More and more and more." I decided that would be my last name. I changed the spelling of "more" to Moore to make it seem name-like. And thus, my secret identity of Conway Moore was born, both from the heart of a literary novel and the sweat of a poker game.

Perfect secret identity for Poker Boy.

"Here is your key, Mr. Moore," the woman said, sliding the paper packet with the plastic key toward me. I reached for it and her hand brushed mine.

I saw stars!

I saw the gambling gods!

I saw a royal flush against four aces, all in that order.

"I hope you have a good stay," she said. "And good luck in the tournaments."

Her smile was in full force, her wonderful eyes controlling me like a well-trained seal that could bark and balance a ball on its nose on command.

"Thank you," I managed to say without barking or balancing a ball.

Then I turned and tripped over my luggage.

Somehow, I managed to miss getting tangled in the front desk rope maze as I fell.

That floor may have been carpeted, and I may be a superhero, but it was still hard, and it still hurt.

"Are you all right, Mr. Moore?" she asked, a frown of worry crossing her beautiful face, making it beautiful in a different way. She leaned over the desk and looked down at me like an angel, the light behind her head giving her a halo.

I thought of lying there, staring at her until she floated over to help me up, then I thought better of it.

I sprang to my feet.

"I'm fine," I said, pretending to laugh it off.

I had heard that superheroes always spring back to their feet when knocked down, and I sure didn't want to be an exception to the rule in the superhero world, even when the fall was caused by my inability to not be consumed by a pretty woman.

That, and poorly placed luggage.

Every superhero has his weak spot. Superman has Krytonite, Poker Boy has pretty women. Especially pretty women with big, brown eyes who can make a plain hotel uniform look sexy.

Luckily, I took the fall while in my secret identity of Conway Moore. Conway Moore had far less to lose than Poker Boy.

The pretty woman behind the desk watched me, trying not to laugh, as I rounded up my kicked luggage.

"Thanks," I said, finally getting myself together.

"You're welcome," she said.

Her smile was different than the one she had greeted me with. I might have been only imagining it, which was very possible, but I think I felt in that smile amusement, maybe attached to a little fondness.

I turned and headed for the elevator. If I knew what was good for me, Poker Boy and his alter ego, Conway Moore, would stay very far away from that front desk area.

Yeah, right. And that was going to happen.

Chapter Two

A Beautiful Woman and Trouble is Found

I HAD LEFT MY LUGGAGE in my room, taken a quick nap, and then headed upstairs to get a great steak dinner. Now I was on the way to the tournament, the World Series of Poker, something I looked forward to every year. I had just gotten off the elevator on the second floor and turned to go to the tournament registration, when I saw my first dog of the trip.

Now, understand, as Poker Boy, I often end up saving dogs as well as people. In fact, it's a rare adventure that I don't save at least one dog.

The dog facing me looked like a mix between a golden retriever and a lab, although I wouldn't swear to either being in there. It was a beautiful dog, clearly well-kept and its longish golden hair was brushed regularly.

It was sitting next to a wall, watching everything around it with big, brown eyes. I was having a brown-eyed sort of day. Brown-eyed woman behind the counter, now a brown-eyed dog.

I didn't take it as a sign, but maybe I should have.

There was one of those seeing-eye walker contraptions on the dog's back, with a handle that was held by a very pretty woman wearing dark glasses. She leaned against the wall as if the wallpaper was giving her strength.

I had heard of stranger things giving people strength, but not many. Actually, I doubted the wallpaper was helping her at all, since it was a floral pattern that had faded over the years.

Since she was wearing dark glasses inside the hotel, it meant she was either a poker player, or blind, and from the looks of the dog sitting beside her, I would bet on her being blind, or at least vision impaired, as they liked to say this last decade or so.

I hesitated in my walk toward the poker tournament and studied her. She was beautiful, in sort of a Midwest, take-her-home-to-meet-the-mother way. Her face was scrubbed, no make-up and her light brown hair was combed and pulled back. She had on black slacks that were well-pressed, and a white blouse which showed just a hint of the white bra under it.

And there was something wrong with her.

I stopped and stepped out of the main flow of traffic in the hallway, letting two of the better known poker columnists walk past me talking about a player I didn't know.

With tournament poker growing so fast, there were a lot of players I didn't know these days.

I studied the woman standing beside her dog. There was something about her that needed help. I would have to use one of Poker Boy's superpowers to find out.

Raising my arm like I was trying to fix something caught in the long hair on my neck, I pulled slightly while staring at her.

Pulling on my own hair was one of my ways of triggering one of my superpowers. That, and focus.

Mostly focus. I really didn't need the hair-pulling part, but it acted like a trigger for me and helped. I was still fairly new at all this and any trick helped.

After a moment of tugging on my hair, the hallway, the carpet, the other people moving about seemed to vanish as everything I could see narrowed down on the woman and my Extra-Vigilant-Vision took over.

I had always wished as a young man to have Superman's X-Ray vision. What teenage boy didn't? What fun it would have been to see into women's locker rooms, see through women's dresses, see through walls to know when your mom was coming so that you could stop masturbating because you were staring into the neighbor's house watching the girl next door take a bath.

Oh, what fun it would have been to have that superpower as a teenaged boy.

So when I grew up and became Poker Boy, I thought I might get lucky and manage X-Ray vision, but instead all I could do was Extra-Vigilant-Vision, which was the ability to look at something very closely. I couldn't see through anything, but as an adult and a poker player, I had come to realize this was almost as good.

Especially at a poker table when I was trying to discover if a player was bluffing. All I had to do was stare at the player and with my Extra-Vigilant Vision I would be able to see clearly if they were worried, or confident, and then make my bet accordingly.

The woman under my special super-power vision gave me a lot of clues quickly that something was very wrong with her. She was breathing faster than normal, her bra pushing up against the fine fabric of her white blouse. I could almost see the pores in her skin, which looked pale, as if not getting enough blood. It was also clear that she might start perspiring at any moment.

Her head moved back and forth, as if trying to listen to everything around her at once. Her hand grasped the dog leader like it was a life-line tossed to someone drowning.

She looked scared and very worried.

Suddenly another superpower kicked in, my Ultra-Intuition Power shouted at me, *She's lost. Or has lost something.*

Actually that power doesn't shout, it sort of echoes, like a deep voice coming up from a canyon into my mind. Imagine the deepest base singer in the Temptations saying to me from a deep, dark hole in the ground. *She's lost-t-t-t-t* and you'll have the idea.

When two of my superpowers start working at the same time, I'm really hard to beat at a poker table. And in real life. This woman and her dog needed my help. That much was clear.

I dropped out of Extra-Vigilant Vision so I could see if anyone else was around, then stepped toward her. She turned, as

> ***Actually that power doesn't shout, it sort of echoes, like a deep voice coming up from a canyon into my mind.***

if she knew I was coming at her, even though my shoes had made no sound on the carpet of the hallway.

When a person was blind, the other senses kicked in, often making up for the lost sense. Since she knew I was coming and I hadn't made a sound, I figured she might have something similar to my Big Nose Super-Sniffing Power. I hadn't needed to use that super-power very often, but twice so far it had saved the day.

"Excuse me," I said before I got very close to her, "you look like you might need some help?"

For an instant panic seemed to flash over her face, then she got herself under control and asked, "Do you work here?"

A logical question under the circumstances.

"Actually, no," I said, stopping far enough away so that I would give no threatening signs to either her, or her dog, who was looking up at me with a worried look in those big, brown eyes.

"I'm just here to play in the tournament. My name's Conway, and I know my way around this old hotel pretty well. It's a confusing maze, even on the best of days. I'd be glad to help you if you need it."

"Actually," she said, smiling at me, her face relaxing a little under her dark glasses, "I know exactly where I am. But thank you."

"Then can I help you find whatever it is that you've lost?" I asked.

I knew my Ultra-Intuition Power had not been wrong. If she knew where she was, then her problem was that she had lost something else.

My question made her jerk, and again her skin paled slightly, even noticeably without my vision super-power in use.

"How did you know I am looking for someone?"

I laughed. "How did you know I was coming toward you when you couldn't hear me?"

She thought for a moment, then laughed with me. "Top sirloin, rare."

I was impressed.

"So I assume," I said, pressing on with her problem, "that you have tried all the regular methods, such as having this person paged? Having an employee check the tournament room? And so on."

Modern casinos, and even old ones like the Horseshoe, are extremely easy to get lost in. And without clocks anywhere, and the focus on money and games, time can seem to vanish. People being lost in a casino is a common problem, and usually not one that would require Poker Boy's help.

But I knew, without a doubt, and from my Ultra-Intuition Power, that this woman needed me.

"I have," she said, nodding. "A number of times, actually. They are starting to think I am nuts."

"Who is missing?" I asked.

Sometimes the best power a superhero has was to simply ask the right questions and then listen very carefully to the answer.

"My husband," she said, a look of caring and concern on her face.

I could tell, by my heightened ability as a poker player and not as Poker Boy, that she really loved her husband. This wasn't the old tired cliché of the married couple coming to Las Vegas and the husband dumping the blind wife and running off with a Keno girl.

No, this guy was really missing.

"When was the last time you were with him?" I asked.

"We were eating lunch at the café downstairs, the one in the basement."

I knew the place well. It too had the feel of an old supper club, but it had been remodeled with the wood posts and low ceilings to look a little like a Carnegie library with tables. The waiters wore short, white aprons over black pants and white shirts and always seemed extra busy, even at times there was almost no one in the place. Every time I ate there I always felt as if I should order something more with my omelet, just to make it worth the waiter's time and energy.

"I've eaten there," I said to her. "So what happened?"

She took a deep breath, clearly blaming herself for what she was about to tell me.

"I wanted to sit and just finish my tea, so Ben, my husband, said he would just go out in front of the restaurant and play the bank of slots there. He said he'd come back in and get me in fifteen minutes."

"He never did," I said.

She nodded. "I sat there for an hour, then paid the bill by charging it to our room. I got a waiter to help me get out of the restaurant and up the stairs to the slot machines, thinking Ben had gotten wrapped up in winning and had forgotten about coming back for me. No one around the top of those stairs remembered seeing him."

My Ultra-Intuition Power was rumbling in the back of my brain, clearly almost ready to echo me a deep-voiced insight.

"I had him paged," she said, "and I had security look for him. About two hours after he vanished I went back to our room and waited until about an hour ago. I don't know what to do, to be honest with you."

"And I know the Vegas police won't help until a certain amount of time has gone by," I said.

Again she nodded. "It took me an hour on the phone to finally get that figured out."

My Ultra-Intuition superpower was still rumbling, but nothing was echoing forth from the depths just yet. I still needed a little more information.

"Did he say which bank of slots he was going up to play?"

She shrugged. "No, but he liked the really old slots. That's why he liked staying downtown instead of out on the strip."

Ghost slots!

My Ultra-Intuition shouted at me, the sound echoing around inside my head like my brain was missing.

"Ghost slots," I said out loud, not really meaning to.

"Ghost slots?" she asked.

"Nothing," I said. "Would you mind walking me down to the restaurant and showing me anything else you might remember."

She cocked her head sideways a little. "I don't even know you, Mr. Conway."

"Actually, the name is Conway Moore," I said. "And I think you do know me. And could use my help."

"Are you the police? Or a detective?"

"Neither," I said. "Just a person who helps when someone needs help."

She reached out slowly and touched my arm, then my shoulder, then ran her hand over my face, noting my black hat, lack of facial hair, and black leather coat that was part of my superhero uniform I always wear.

The hat was a Fedora-style and combined with my coat, it seemed to focus my energy when in a casino.

Then she nodded. "You're right, I do need your help. And I would be willing to pay for it."

I laughed. "Payment is not necessary. I make my money playing poker, and

Some Classic Poker Boy Stories

Available at your favorite booksellers.

that's good enough for me. Just say thank you when we find Ben."

Again she sort of stood there, clearly running all her emotions and senses about me over in her mind. Could she trust me? Should she trust me? Did she have any better options at the moment?

Under normal circumstances, this woman would never accept help from some strange man. But Poker Boy has a way of putting people at ease, making them feel as if they know me, without ever really knowing anything about me. I am convinced it is one of the superpowers that goes along with the job, but I couldn't come up with a decent name for it.

And I had tried. Ultra-Acceptance Power didn't feel right. Come-to-me-for-help Power didn't do it either. For a time I had called it my Trust-Me Superpower, but that sort of went away as any bad name does.

Plus, I couldn't call it up at will. It was sort of just there.

"Okay, Mr. Conway Moore," she said. "I'll thank you now for your help, and after we find Ben."

"Deal," I said. It seemed my un-named, superpower worked even on the blind.

She stuck out her hand and I grasped the warm, firm grip. "Deal," she said. "And by the way, my name is Samantha. And this is Sue."

She bent down slightly and patted the top of the beautiful golden-haired dog.

"Sue and Samantha MacDuff," the woman added.

"Nice meeting you both," I said.

I am convinced we were both glad I didn't ask the obvious question about why anyone would name a dog Sue.

And it took every bit of super will-power I had to not say, when she turned toward the elevator, pulling her dog around, "Lead on MacDuff."

I didn't say it, but I wanted to.

Chapter Three

A Side-Kick Joins the Fun

SAMANTHA, SUE, and I wound our way through the gaming tables and slot machines until we were near the front of the cafe. I maneuvered us into an area out of the way so that Samantha would have a wall to lean against.

As I had expected, there were no older-looking slots anywhere near the front of the restaurant. In fact, I had been watching for older slots since we got to the main casino floor, and hadn't seen any.

"Okay, what does your husband look like?" I asked, just a fraction of a second before I realized I was asking that question of a blind woman. "Oh, sorry."

She laughed and patted my arm. "It's all right. I've only been blind the last eight years of my life. And I was already married to Ben before this happened."

"Okay," I said, again restraining from asking about how she had become blind. Instead I focused on the task at hand. "So anything you can tell me would help. Height, hair color, balding or not? And do you know what he was wearing this morning? That sort of thing."

She nodded, turning her head slightly to listen as a machine half the room away released a flood of coins, one right after the other into a tray, banging as a loud alarm went off. Casinos always wanted to draw attention to any time they gave away money, but never when they took it. Just good business sense. But any customer with any common sense knew they didn't build those multi-billion dollar resorts out on the Strip by giving away too much money.

"Ben stands five-foot-ten," Samantha said, "weighs about one hundred and seventy, and keeps himself in good shape. He has thinning brown hair, with a hairline that has started to recede slightly. He was wearing tan slacks, a brown golf shirt, and deck shoes this morning."

"Perfect," I said. "Will you be all right standing here for a few minutes while I look around?"

"I'll be fine," she said.

I touched her arm lightly, then turned away, heading down the flight of stairs in to the restaurant. I had to check a few things before I went any farther in helping her.

A number of times I have had people come to me for help who were actually in no need of help. I wish I had a superpower that could tell when someone was lying or not. But I didn't, so I had to rely on the old fashioned way, asking questions like a detective would. And even though I had approached her, and everything about her story made sense, I still had to check.

I found the restaurant manager and within a few seconds confirmed the woman's story. She and a guy had been having breakfast, he left her after they had finished, and she seemed to wait for him for an hour before paying and asking to be helped up the stairs.

That was all the information I needed. That, combined with my Ultra-Intuition Power confirmed for me she was telling me the truth.

"Any luck?" she asked me before I got within ten feet of her. Clearly this woman's hearing was fantastic, or the steak I had eaten for dinner was still with me.

"I didn't see him anywhere," I said. "And there are no older slot machines anywhere near here."

"Really?" she asked, seemingly surprised. "When I came up to the top of the stairs after waiting, the manager asked a few of the people in the area if they had seen Ben. I heard one of them tell him they thought they had seen him playing the old Saturn Slots near the stairs."

I glanced at the staircase. No Saturn Slots anywhere to be seen. Just a half dozen video poker games and some newer Monopoly machines. I didn't want to think about the chance those Saturn Slots had been ghost slots.

"Let's go get some more information." I took her gently by the arm and led her, and her dog Sue, through the tight rows of slots, past the gaming tables, and toward the front desk.

I was hoping the woman with the big brown eyes would be behind the main desk, and I was in luck. She looked up at me, smiled fondly, and for an instant I was lost again.

But the feeling only lasted an instant, since I wasn't just Conway Moore checking in, I was Poker Boy, helping a woman and her dog. Superhero duties come first, even over lust.

The woman with brown eyes looked over at the blind woman and frowned, a worried look crossing that beautiful face. "Mrs. MacDuff, have you found your husband yet?"

"I'm afraid not," Samantha said.

Clearly this woman had been involved with the paging that Samantha had done earlier.

"So what can I do to help?" the woman asked, glancing at me.

I knew right then that this brown-eyed employee would be a valuable assistant. I'm not sure which of my powers told me that, but I was convinced.

"I'm hoping we could get your help, or someone's help in the back office," I said, smiling at her and putting on my best Poker Boy charm. "We need to find out where a certain bank of slots are in the casino. Or if they are still here."

"And that would help Mrs. MacDuff find her husband?"

"It might," I said. "It's the only bit of information we have to work with at the moment.

I didn't want to get into my theory that Ben might have been taken by ghost slots. Neither of these women, or Sue the dog for that matter, would believe me. At least not yet. And I didn't want to make myself look like a fool without some proof to back up my theory.

The woman with the brown eyes held my gaze for a long moment, as if she knew what I was thinking, then she nodded. "All right."

She glanced over at a man dressed in the same uniform she was. "Dan, I'm going to help these folks for a few minutes, then head for home."

Dan only nodded and kept typing something into a computer in front of him. Clearly this woman was about to get off for the night. Normally, if I wasn't working on a case, that might have interested me. Now that part of my interest would have to wait for another time.

The woman indicated that we should move to a heavy-looking wood door off one side of the main desk. She led us inside and down a hallway to a room with big desks. I could tell at a glance that this office had been in use for the same function for a lot of years, and had more than likely been missed in the big remodeling back in the eighties and nineties.

In all my years before becoming a superhero, I hadn't managed to get behind the scenes once in a hotel or casino. But since becoming Poker Boy, it seemed I did a lot of wandering around in offices and secure areas that most normal folk didn't even know existed.

The only man in the room stood immediately as we entered. "What's going on, Patty?"

Now I knew the brown-eyed desk clerk's name. It fit her, actually.

"This is Mrs. MacDuff," Patty said, indicating Samantha. "And Mr. Moore. This is our Manager on Duty, Bob Silvers."

Bob's stern look immediately melted when he heard Samantha's name. "No luck finding your husband yet?"

Samantha shook her head. "Mr. Moore is helping me. It's still too early to get the police involved."

"So what can we do to help?" Bob asked, glancing at me, then back at Samantha.

I took the lead, using my nicest, most convincing voice. "Two things, actually," I said. "First off, would it be possible to look up where a bank of slot machines were in this casino?"

Bob sort of jerked, clearly catching my use of past tense. He turned to stare at me. "You don't think that—."

Clearly Bob had heard of ghost slots. It sometimes surprised me how many people in Vegas had. But I didn't want him blurting that out just yet, so I interrupted him.

"I don't know what to think just yet," I said. "But if we know where the slots that Ben MacDuff was seen playing are located, we might be able to find something on a surveillance camera that would tell us what happened."

He glanced at the frowning face of Samantha, and then at the worried face of Patty, and nodded. Without another word, he turned back to his desk and grabbed two badges that said "Guest" on them in big red letters.

"Wear these," Bob said. "Patty will help you look up the information you need. If you don't mind staying a little after your shift, Patty?"

"Not at all," she said, smiling at me as she helped hook Samantha's guest pass on her white blouse.

And with that look, I knew that Poker Boy had found his sidekick. I had no doubt that Patty had her own share of superpowers to bring to the case of the missing MacDuff. With Patty, the fun part was going to be figuring out what those powers might be. I would bet that most of them were hooked into those big, brown eyes.

And the ability to make a hotel uniform look sexy.

Chapter Four

One Office, No Windows, No Escape

PATTY LED ME, Samantha, and her dog, Sue, down a well-lit back hallway of the Horseshoe Hotel and Casino to a large file room.

The place was windowless and had a few library-like tables in the center, with old file cabinets all around the outside of the room. A number of computers filled smaller work desks at different spots around the room, and each computer had a stack of files beside it. There was no one in the room when we got there, which actually relieved me.

Working in a room like this was my worst nightmare. The place smelled of old paper and bad air-conditioning, and I had a hard time imagining working in such a room for eight hours a day.

I had no doubt that if I tried to work regularly in there, even just a few hours a day, the plain painted walls and pictures of old Vegas taken back in the fifties would soon close in, smashing me like a fly between the pages of a book. I would be nothing more than a blood and guts splatter over the file cabinets, my very essence merging with the dull paint and old photos.

Luckily, I had learned how to play poker for a living and became Poker Boy so I didn't have to sit very often in such dull rooms.

"We're trying to get all of the most important old information entered into the computer system," Patty said. "But it's taking time, and with a casino this old it's a difficult task at best. There's a lot of information and people only work on it during slow times."

"And with the World Series of Poker starting up, this isn't a slow time," I said.

"Far from it," Patty said, laughing as she got Samantha seated at a table with Sue sitting at her feet. Then Patty sat down at one of the computers and keyed in the words "Saturn Slots" as I watched over her shoulder, trying to focus on her and what she was doing instead of the room around me.

"Nothing," she said, shaking her wonderful, soft-looking hair as the screen came up blank. "I was afraid of that. These computer records only go back ten years on slots."

"And no Saturn Slots during that time?" I asked. "Or anything with the name Saturn?"

"Nothing," Patty said.

"So we have to go back farther by hand," I said, "if there are records for that."

"There are," Patty said.

I was amazed. Hundreds of thousands of slot machines must have come through this casino over the years. Clearly the state gambling board, or the IRS, made them keep track of all of them. Sometimes all the stupid regulations of "Big Brother" came in handy.

Behind us Samantha said, "But I don't understand why we're looking for slot machines that are that old. Ben just disappeared today."

"I know," I said, "but you did say you overheard someone saying they thought they saw him playing the Saturn Slots. Right?"

She nodded. "But if slots like that haven't been in this casino for ten years, how could he have been playing them. I guess I just don't—"

Patty interrupted. "We're just trying to eliminate some things. It won't take too long, I promise."

Samantha said nothing more, but I could tell she was very confused.

I certainly didn't add in anything. The idea of there being such a thing as ghost slots was crazy, yet Patty and I, without actually saying anything to each other, were both worried that ghost slots had gotten Samantha's husband. We just didn't want to tell Samantha that theory without some proof.

Hell, I didn't even want to talk with Patty about it.

Patty stood and moved across the room to a file cabinet. I followed like a puppy on a leash, enjoying my time close to her. I had picked up a couple of details about Patty since our hike into the back room depths of the Horseshoe Casino. First off, she smelled wonderful, like a raspberry bush in full bloom. Across the front desk I hadn't had a chance to notice that.

Second, she had a mole on her neck that flashed in and out of sight under her hair, sort of teasing me to come closer. I'm not saying I have a thing about moles. There was nothing sexual or kinky about a parasite growing on a human, but that said, I sure hoped me and that mole would get a lot closer over time.

I made myself stop staring at her mole as she pulled open the second drawer of the old metal cabinet and thumbed quickly through some files.

The moment I stopped staring at the mole, the room started to close in again, so I gladly went back to my focus on her neck while she worked.

"Here it is," she said as she pulled out a thin file. "Saturn Slots. There were four of them in one bank." She turned and put the file on the top of the cabinet before opening it for both of us to see.

A colorful ball in the image of Saturn, tipped slightly to one side, dominated the area above the slots. The planet's rings extended even higher into the air and also down, seemingly through a couple of the slot machines. It was a fine piece of old slot craftsmanship.

Most people don't know that the graphics and design that goes into slot machines has become almost an art form over the years. Casinos and slot machine companies have spent millions trying to figure out what attracts a player to a certain slot machine. The design, the playability, the graphics, the colors, the shapes of the box, the payouts, all have to combine to form something that is not only fun, but is easy to play, yet challenging enough to hold interest.

I know I considered slot design an art form, but I doubted we would be seeing slot machines in any art galleries anytime soon, which was a crime. Think about it. A gallery patron could enjoy the art show, and all that caché that went along with being an art snob, while at the same time playing a slot machine, with the art gallery taking a cut of the profits, of course.

I stared at the picture. All four Saturn Slots were the old-fashioned pull handle type, and all four looked old, like they had had some use by the time they reached the Horseshoe. On top of that, they were nickel machines. You didn't see many of those any more that weren't electronic and allowed a person to play twenty nickels at a time.

"Sixteen years," Patty said. One of her beautiful fingers pointed at a date. "We took them out sixteen years ago, after five years of play."

"Who leased them?" I asked, "Or who were they sold to when you got rid of them?"

In Vegas, and in many other places, some slot machines are owned and serviced by companies that are not affiliated with any one casino. Often, the machines are just leased to the casino. This is happening a lot with the new licensing of such media products as *Monopoly Games, The Adams Family*, and so on. I didn't know if the Horseshoe leased or bought their own machines. My hunch was they did both.

"Valley Slots," Patty said, studying the paper in front of her. "We leased them."

"Damn," I said. "Valley Slots has been out of business for a good ten years. I think Standard bought part of their assets."

Patty nodded. "I seem to remember something about that."

"Does it say where these slots were on the floor sixteen years ago?"

"Not from the records," Patty said. She pointed to the picture. "But from the looks of that, they were set up just outside the restaurant."

I looked closer. She was right. The distinctive wooden railing that led down into the basement restaurant was clearly visible to one side of the slots. Luckily, when they had done the remodeling of the casino and restaurants, they had decided to go back to how it had looked. Sometimes retrograde designs saved time and money, and in this case it helped us.

"Well," I said, turning to Samantha, "we found where the slots were."

"Sixteen years ago," Samantha said, her disgust not well hidden in the tone of her voice.

"Would you know exactly what time Ben left the restaurant?" Patty asked.

"Just after one," Samantha said. "We went down for lunch at noon, and they were a little slow. I remember checking my watch and it was one just a few minutes before he left."

Patty moved over to a phone sitting beside the door and dialed a five-digit number.

I sat down beside Samantha at the table and patted her arm. Sue moved around under the edge of the table a little to nudge against my leg, clearly thanking me in dog language. Either that or she wanted to be petted. I knew better than to pet a dog trained for seeing-eye work, so I refrained.

Around me, the room closed in even more. I was sweating and I wanted to take off my Poker Boy leather coat and special hat, but I knew better. We needed to do this research and get out of here before Poker Boy, superhero, lost it and went screaming down the hall.

"Steward, this is Patty in the file room. I need you to pull up the security tape for the area outside the restaurant stairs. From one this afternoon to one-ten. Can you feed it to me in here?"

She listened for a moment, then said, "Yeah, include the stairs. And set it to replay a few times would you? Thanks." Then she hung up.

"We're going to know more in a minute," she said.

"Thank you both for all your help," Samantha said.

"Thank us after we find out what happened to Ben," Patty said. She moved over to a security monitor sitting on the top of a file cabinet against one wall. She clicked it on to show a blank screen.

I patted Samantha's arm and stood to join Patty and her wonderful raspberry smell and attractive mole. The mole wasn't visible at the moment, but the smell lured me closer like a flower's nectar to a bee who couldn't report back to the hive without filling a quota.

"It's going to take Steward a few seconds to get the tape up," Patty said. "Luckily, we upgraded our entire security system this last winter. It's now state of the art."

I could feel my stomach twisting. I had no idea if we were actually going to see, on tape, evidence of ghost slots taking a man. If so, we were going to be the only people to ever see this tape, of that much I was certain. It would be destroyed at once.

There was no casino on the planet that wanted the press release about slot machines kidnapping customers. And besides, even with a tape, who would believe it. If what we thought had happened showed up on this tape, another tape, of say a quiet time ten minutes before, would replace it, all time-coded to look perfect, of course.

And no one would dare say anything different.

That was why the general public didn't know about ghost slot machines, or a dozen other strange things that went on in Las Vegas. It just wasn't good for business. But anyone who was in Vegas for any amount of time, working or playing like I did, heard about these things.

Suddenly the screen flicked to life. It was the image of the stairs down into the restaurant, and the slots around the top of the stairs, all shown from a camera in the ceiling. A time code was running on the bottom.

There was no sign of any Saturn Slots in their old location. The slots that occupied that spot now were newer Monopoly machines.

An older couple came up the stairs, turning and heading for the door out into the heat. A moment later a man started up the stairs.

"That's him," I said.

"You see Ben?" Samantha asked.

"He's on the security tape," I said. "Coming out of the restaurant."

Patty pointed to the area where the Monopoly slots had been a moment before. Now the Saturn Slots sat there, the image of the ringed planet in full neon, the lights blinking.

"Oh, shit," I said softly.

Ben reached the top of the stairs, turned and moved over in front of the bank of Saturn Slots, fishing in his pocket for change as he went. The old machines didn't take bills, but he dug a role of nickels out of his pocket.

Then he sat down into one of the chairs attached to the front of the Saturn Slots, dropped a coin into the slot, and reached for the handle.

As he pulled it he seemed to freeze.

The old wheels on the slots spun, but from the angle of the camera, I couldn't see what they showed.

Ben seemed to shake for a moment, his hand still holding the arm of the machine.

How do you tell someone her husband was kidnapped by a gang of old nickel slot machines?

A moment later the Saturn Slots faded away, taking Ben with them.

I somehow managed to take a deep breath, staring at what were normal, modern slots where the Saturn Slots had been a moment before.

"I never thought I'd ever see it happen," Patty said, her voice hushed.

"What?" Samantha demanded from where she sat at the table.

A moment later the phone rang as the tape cut off, not repeating as Patty had asked.

Patty picked up the phone and listened. Then she said, "I understand."

She hung the phone up slowly before turning off the monitor.

"We never saw that?" I asked.

"We never saw that," she said.

"Would one of you please tell me what just happened?" Samantha demanded. "Do you know where Ben is?"

The silence in the room got so loud I thought the door might burst outward from the pressure.

Patty and I just stood there, staring at the blind woman and her dog, Sue. How do you tell someone her husband was kidnapped by a gang of old nickel slot machines?

How do you tell someone that one of the urban myths of Vegas was true, and had just been caught on film, which was being destroyed as we stood there letting the silence get louder and louder.

How does anyone tell a wife that her husband had been taken by ghost machines, and we had no idea to where, or to when, for that matter?

I knew for a fact there just wasn't an easy way.

So instead, I changed the subject. I have learned over the years that changing the subject with a woman in the middle of a serious discussion often only makes matters worse, but at the moment it was the only thing I could think to do.

I turned to Patty. "Have you had dinner?" I knew this was a strange way to get a first date, but at this point, any date was better than none.

Besides thinking of the date and getting closer to that mole, I had to get us all out of the room, which was more than likely heavily monitored, before we could have any discussion about what we had seen.

And I had to get myself out before I melted into a puddle of Poker Boy fluids that would surely stain the floor. The walls were getting *really* tight.

Patty glanced at me, puzzled. Then she realized what I was doing. Or at least part of what I was doing. I hope she didn't know about my desire to get closer to the mole on her neck.

"No, I haven't. And I'm hungry."

"How about you, Samantha?" I asked.

"I don't think I could eat," she said. "I just want to know what happened to Ben."

"Well, you're going to need to eat," I said, making my voice sound as upbeat as I could without making it sound like a game show host. "To keep your strength up to help us find Ben. We'll talk about all this over food, I promise."

Again the silence filled the room, making the walls close in even faster. This room was bad enough all by itself for me, but silence was making it torture. We needed to get out of here.

Seconds ticked past.

I started sweating. Or more likely I noticed I again that I was sweating.

Patty and I just stood there, Sidekick and Superhero, staring at the woman we were supposed to be trying to help. But we needed to get out of this room, and maybe out of the casino for the coming discussion.

More seconds ticked past as a blind woman faced us with sunglassed-covered eyes.

I thought about putting out my arms and trying to hold the walls back, but I knew that wouldn't work any more than it worked in the first Star Wars movie. I was in the trash-compactor of offices and there was no robot to throw a switch to save me.

More seconds.

Not even the wonderful raspberry smell of Patty kept me from sweating even more. I doubted even a close-up visit to the mole would save me at this point.

The walls really were closing in.

Honest.

Finally, Samantha pushed herself to her feet, moving to get Sue into position. "I suppose I'm not going to find out what you saw while we're in here. So lead me to food."

I barely made it through the door seconds before those walls smashed me into brainless pulp and trapped me in a windowless office, working a filing and data-entry job the rest of my life.

It had been close.

I had almost ended up living my worst nightmare. I was shaking as I went down the hall, forcing myself to not run.

I'm a superhero who helps people, rescues dogs, and plays poker for a living. I never said things didn't scare me.

But it had been worth the risk. We knew what had happened to Ben, and I had a dinner date with Patty.

Chapter Five

Addiction

PATTY SEEMED TO KNOW where she wanted to go, so I followed along as she took Samantha's arm and expertly got her and her dog Sue from the back rooms, through the slots, and out one of the many doors of the Horseshoe Casino and Hotel.

We emerged onto what used to be called "Glitter Gulch" back in the days when train passengers got off the train a few blocks away and faced a street lined with blazing lights and signs.

Vegas Vic, a two-story tall, rail-thin, neon cowboy still looked over Frontier Street, just as he did back in the forties. He had a cigarette hanging from his mouth like a bad movie cliche, and a thumb that pointed toward who knew where.

In the old days, his thumb was meant to direct customers to the Pioneer Club. I suppose a two-story tall cowboy with a butt hanging out of his mouth was an attraction. I never saw him as that. I thought of him more as a landmark of downtown Vegas, a symbol, if you will, of the merging of the cowboy west with the neon lights of gambling, punctuated by the threat of dying from cancer.

A perfect Las Vegas icon.

During the sixties, Glitter Gulch had become more like a classic skid row as the strip casinos miles away became more popular. Back then the bums hung out on the street corners, the casinos didn't have the money to fix much of anything, and only the gamblers who were into grinding out each buck went downtown. Even with the Horseshoe starting the World Series of Poker back in the early seventies, I didn't want to go down there. There was just too much fun to be had out on the strip.

Things for downtown Las Vegas started to change in the early 1980's as the city did everything it could to revive the downtown area. They even went so far as to turn a few blocks of Frontier Street into a pedestrian mall and cover it with a light show that was hard to match. I think I remember hearing there were about two and a half million bulbs in that canopy over those four city blocks, but I could be off by a few hundred thousand either way.

Now, with the casinos around the big downtown mall remodeled as much as the space would allow, the area had at least held steady for a few years. I sort of liked it more now than the strip, actually.

It had a more personal feel about it than the big super casinos.

And it was only a few feet between casinos instead of dozens of football fields. And when you're walking on a hot evening, that's an important consideration.

The heat slapped at me as we stepped outside. Even though the sun was setting on the town that never slept, it was still damn hot. In the middle of the night in the summer it was known to stay above a hundred degrees here. It was too early in the year for that kind of really intense heat, but it was still hot outside.

Too hot for my tastes, but after my close call with office death, it felt good to be out under the darkening blue sky and millions of light bulbs.

Patty quickly got us across the mall area, around a corner, and into the wonderful coolness of a cafe tucked between a casino and the side of an office building. The place had the feel of a fake diner, with bright replicas of things from the fifties plastered all over the walls.

I doubted any place actually looked like this back in the fifties. This was just a twenty-first century version of what people thought diners looked like in 1955. I hope the history books recorded the decade more accurately than diners, or the country's kids were going to be really messed up.

However, what the tacky pictures of Elvis and poodle-skirts on the walls often meant was decent food and large portions. Monster portions, actually. A burger in a place with a bubbling jukebox (always a replica of a real bubblier) was extra big, with more fries than an Idaho potato field.

And God forbid you order a milkshake with your burger. Unless your body had a high tolerance for sugar and milk, don't order a milkshake in a place with fifties memorabilia on the walls. It will be so good you'll have to drink it all, and so big you'll regret doing it. So the safest course is just not order one.

Since I was still full from my wonderful steak, I ordered an iced tea and nothing more from a woman who looked like she might have actually been a waitress since the fifties. Her face had more ravines than the Grand Canyon and her lips were painted bright red, with a gloss that made them seem to extend off her face. Her bright blue eyeliner contrasted with her large black hair and pink waitress uniform with the name Madge clinging to the top of her large right breast.

Madge, chewing gum and without a word, took my drink order, Patty's order of a salad and diet coke, and Samantha's order of a cheese sandwich and coffee. Then she nodded to Sue and spoke for the first time. "I'll bring the dog a dish of water."

With a pop of her gum, she turned and headed for the kitchen.

My gaze followed her for a moment, wishing almost instantly I hadn't. My mind shouted, "Don't look!"

But habit wins, and even if I am a superhero, I am a male. I couldn't help myself, honest. I looked at Madge's ass moving under the tight skirt as she walked away. Her ass was large and sagged in places a woman's ass shouldn't sag. It was also clear that Madge wore bikini underwear under her pink uniform. Even through the uniform it looked like that underwear hurt.

I knew, without a doubt, the image of Marge's ass would haunt me for the rest of the World Series of Poker.

Madge walked past a row of sit-down video poker machines, the type seen ev-erywhere in Nevada and many other states. An elderly woman sat at the second one, her big black purse beside her, her attention focused on the screen, her hand shaking every time she made a play.

She had thinning, gray hair done up in a type of bun, and was wearing an older-style long cloth coat that looked like it had seen better days back when Madge was young and could wear bikini underwear without shocking guys like me.

When you play live poker against other players in a poker room, or home game, skill is everything. You win what the other players and your comparative skill allow you to win. But poker machines are set to pay the house a given amount, called an edge, just like a slot machine. Sure, it might be set loose, meaning it will return to the player ninety-nine out of every one hundred bets made, but it still kept that one bet. And given enough time, those one bets built huge casinos.

Most video poker machines were not set that loose.

On a video poker machine, you could knock that edge down some by making good decisions, but you could never really beat the machines day in and day out, no matter what any book (written by a guy making money from writing a book) told you.

Studies have shown that of all the slot machines, for some reason, video poker was the most addictive. The theory was that it engaged the player more than just yanking on a crank, or pushing a button and watching wheels spin. And that engagement turned into a form of gambling addiction.

As I watched, the old woman reached into her big black purse, pulled out a ten-dollar bill, and fed it to the machine, which yanked it from her trembling fingers.

I had no idea what that woman's story was. She might be very rich and very lonely, and playing that machine was just her way of passing the time.

Or she might be playing a part of her retirement funds with that last bet, allowing herself only ten or twenty or thirty dollars in losses every time she played. She might have that kind of control. Most people did.

Or maybe that was food money she had just put in there.

Or money she had gotten from selling something she had owned for decades. Maybe she was one of the growing numbers of elderly that were addicted to the machines and unable to get away.

Or not want to get away.

For many people, playing the machines gave life reason, and hope, and excitement where there was none. It was a reason to get up in the morning, something to look forward to the next day. The excitement of the big wins made them feel alive for a short time.

Las Vegas (and every casino in the world) was full of men and women like that gray-haired woman sitting at that machine. They all played for their own varied reasons, just like I played live poker for mine.

But it was said that men and women like her created the ghost slots. Or at least so the theory goes. At some point in the past, I was sure that someone had spent weeks, or even years, playing the Saturn Slots, begging them, cussing at them,

talking to them, pleading with them, day in and day out. Those slots had become a person's life, had given them both joy and misery.

Sometimes for months, sometimes for years, a person can pour his or her life force into a slot machine, until finally the time came when not only did the machine have all the person's money, but it held their entire being.

The numbers of people who died every year in Las Vegas playing slot machines was another well-kept secret, but it happened so often no casino thought much about it. There was always another live body to take the cold one's place.

But who were these people who died? No study I had ever seen had looked into it, but I was sure that most were just tourists who had heart attacks. But a few were regulars, local residents, gambling addicts who made one machine a part of their life, and of their death.

And in that death, when some person gave a slot machine everything they had, the theory was that the machine took on a life of its own.

But like any slot machine, it must be fed. Only ghost slots don't need money, they need more life.

I'm a superhero and I have no idea where my powers come from. Half the time I can't even figure out names for the powers I have. As a person given superhero powers to help others, I know that there are many strange things in this world. And having ghost slots was not beyond my belief system.

> ## *For many people, playing the machines gave life reason, and hope, and excitement where there was none.*

But I also understood that a person does not have to be kidnapped by a ghost slot to lose themselves, their lives, and their loved ones to a machine.

It happened all the time, all over the world.

As I watched the old woman with the big black purse, she pulled out another ten-dollar bill and the machine ate it like a hungry animal.

She didn't even seem to notice.

Chapter Six

Another Superhero

IT BECAME CLEAR, in very short order, before Madge even got back with our drinks, that Samantha was not going to believe Patty and me about what happened to her husband.

We tried to tell her, honest we did, but our story sounded wild and far-fetched, even to me. I couldn't blame her for not believing us. She was blind, hadn't seen anything, and now had two people she had just met telling her that they had seen her husband taken away by ghost slot machines, but that the tape they had seen it on had been destroyed.

Yeah, right.

It would be simpler for her to believe we were trying to pull a scam on her than the story we were telling her.

Madge delivered our drinks and turned away. I managed not to look at her ass, but the image of the first look was still with me clearly. And it was when I was trying to push the image of Madge in tight bikini underwear out of my mind that

I realized I knew how to get Samantha to believe Patty and me.

I needed the help of another superhero.

"You have a cell phone?" I asked Patty.

She looked at me with those big brown eyes questioning me, then nodded.

The silence in our booth was cut only by the sound of Elvis singing "Hound Dog" on the jukebox. Patty handed me the phone and I dialed a number I had memorized a few years back.

The voice on the other end said, "Yeah?"

"Screamer," I said. "I need your help."

"Where are you at, Poker Boy?" Screamer asked, recognizing my voice at once and not making me identify myself in front of the women.

"A diner down off the mall on Frontier. Across from the Horseshoe."

"Madge working tonight?" he asked.

"She is," I said.

"Whatever you do," Screamer said, "don't look at her ass."

"Too late," I said.

"No wonder you need my help," he said. "I'll be there in five."

And he hung up.

"Who is Screamer?" Patty asked as Samantha shook her head in clear disgust. I had no doubt that she was about to get up and just leave.

"Screamer is a guy named Toledo Moss. He's been a friend of mine for years."

"Toledo Moss?" Patty said. "The same guy who helps the cops all the time?"

"The same guy," I said. "He does that for free. Mostly, he makes his living working with casinos stopping thefts."

Actually, what I didn't want to tell either one of them, especially Samantha, was that Screamer had a superpower. He could take the image from one person's mind and transfer it into another person's mind. Such a superpower made him a very strong weapon in solving all kinds of cases, especially if there wasn't enough proof, or a body had been hidden.

Screamer could take the image of the crime from the suspected criminal and transfer it into the cop's mind, and then the cop would go out and find the evidence that would stand up in court.

I was sure that taking of thoughts like that had to be protected under the Constitution in some fashion or another, but I doubt the original framers had given superpowers any thought. Just to be safe, though, Screamer never ended up in court on any case he helped solve, and no one really claimed what he said he could do actually worked.

It just did, and the cops and casinos that hired him left that alone.

"So how is this guy going to help find Ben?" Samantha asked.

I didn't answer, or brush off her question, because at that point Madge brought the food. And by the time she had turned to go back into the kitchen, Screamer had pulled a chair up to the table so he was between Patty and Samantha.

Screamer looked to be about forty, had a smile on him that woman said was to die for, and could stop a truck with his intense, green-eyed gaze. As far as I knew, he had never married, and with his ability to get inside another person's head, I wondered how he even managed to get close to many people.

I know a lot of my superpowers did not have off switches, but at least my powers needed me to be near a Casino and have my coat on to work. I couldn't imagine what kind of mental screens he must

have developed if his powers worked all the time.

"Toledo Moss," I said, "meet Patty from the Horseshoe, and Samantha MacDuff, a guest there."

Samantha extended her hand and Screamer took it, gently shaking it while saying, "Nice meeting you."

Then he added, "I'm sorry about your husband. We'll find him."

I nodded. It was always a real pleasure as a superhero to see another superhero at work.

Screamer turned and took Patty's hand.

"Patty Ledgerwood," she said, smiling.

I was smiling as well. I now had her full name.

"Nice meeting you," Screamer said, his eyes lighting up at her touch.

My eyes would light up at her touch as well. I just hope Screamer didn't fall in love with her mole. I sort of felt possessive over that small spot on her neck since it had helped save me from being killed in dull-office-land.

"You're father's Alvin Ledgerwood, from the Dunes?"

"He is," Patty said.

"Tell him I said hello next time you see him. I hope his retirement is going fine. I worked many a case with him."

"He loves the free time," Patty said, "but he misses the work."

So now I knew that Patty was not only strikingly beautiful, but she was from an old-time Vegas family. No wonder she knew about ghost slots.

He let go of Patty's hand and then looked at me. "I see we have a little problem explaining what happened to Ben."

"Could you help?" I asked.

"I'd love to," Screamer said.

He again took Patty's hand, smiling at her, then reached over with his other hand toward Samantha.

"Mrs. MacDuff," Screamer said, his voice level and contained, "I'm going to show you something that Patty and The Boy here saw."

Without giving her time to say a word, he touched her arm.

She froze, her head up as if she was seeing something through the blind eyes and dark glasses.

Then, just at about the same length of time it had taken me and Patty to watch the ghost slots appear and take Ben, Screamer pulled away from both women.

Samantha shuddered, then sort of got smaller. After a moment she asked, "How did you do that?"

"It's my special gift," Screamer said. "I just took what Patty saw on that monitor and put it in your mind. I don't have the ability to alter anything."

"It felt like I was standing inside her. I know what she was thinking and seeing and feeling."

Oh, I would have loved that, but I didn't say anything.

She sort of turned her head so that if she had vision, she would have been looking at Patty. "I feel as if I invaded you. I'm sorry."

"I don't mind," Patty said, reaching across the table and untouched food and patting Samantha's arm.

"What you saw happened exactly that way," Screamer said. "If you just think about it for a second, you'll know I'm right."

Samantha shook her head and sat there for a moment. "So you're telling me you believe what you just showed me? How do I know you're not all in some sort of scam?"

Screamer smiled at me, then turned to talk directly to Samantha. "Ghost slots are not a laughing matter, and not something to be discounted. Ben was taken by ghost slots, of that I have no doubt, and these two people sitting with you are good people. You've got the best trying to help you get your husband back."

I wanted to thank Screamer for the glowing endorsement, but again I stayed silent.

"I've worked with the police a number of times over the years," Screamer said, "and would be glad to give you some names to call to confirm who I am. And trust me, Patty here has family that has been around this town almost from its old mining days."

He stayed silent about me, which I think is just fine. It's hard to explain Poker Boy, and right now Samantha was dealing with believing ghost slots. One thing at a time.

"It's just so hard to believe this happened," Samantha said, shaking her head.

"It happened," Patty said. "It's the first time I've seen it on tape, but I've been hearing about it my entire life. With the security cameras in casinos, I'm sure a lot of people have seen it. It just wouldn't be good for a casino's business to let out that this happens."

"So where is Ben?" Samantha asked. "Where did those machines take him?"

There was a long moment of silence, then I said softly, "That's what we're going to find out."

"As soon as we eat," Screamer said, leaning back and indicating that Madge should come take his order.

Madge made it over and took Screamer's order for a burger and fries, hold the onions, and I added a piece of cherry pie, since enough time had gone by that I could fit dessert around that candle-lit steak.

I suggested that Samantha eat, since she was going to need her energy to help us find Ben, and with that push she did.

I sat back and sort of studied the group as Screamer kept the two women entertained with a story about Patty's dad and a guy who had figured out a way to rob a casino of a thousand a day.

Almost every one of my adventures had a team. Very seldom did I solve a case completely alone. And from the looks of it now, this adventure had its team. A blind woman and her dog, a beautiful woman side-kick and her mole, a superhero named Screamer, and me, Poker Boy.

Those ghost slots didn't stand a chance.

Assuming, of course, we could find them. Ghosts of anything were never easy to track.

Chapter Seven

What Next?
Always a Good Question

AFTER TOLEDO MOSS, a.k.a. Screamer, finished his burger and iced tea, he looked at me. "Well? What next?"

So far the conversation over eating had been on anything but Ben and ghost slots. We had talked about the hot weather for April, I told them about the cab driver, and Samantha even told us how she got Sue a few years back for a birthday present from Ben. But I knew we had to figure out what to do next, so while the others had been talking, I had been planning.

Sitting silently and thinking is what any good poker player is good at. In fact,

in no-limit hold-em tournaments, where a player's entire buy-in could be lost in one dumb play, I liked to just toss all my hands away for the first half hour to an hour and just sit back and watch players. That way I knew how a player acted, what he was likely to do, before I went up against him with my money.

So even with the wonderful talk and Patty being so close, I still managed to do some thinking, and had an answer for Screamer.

"Can you talk to your contacts at some of the major casinos around town?" I asked Screamer. "See if there have been any reported sightings of Ben and the Saturn Slots this afternoon and evening."

He nodded and I faced Patty and those brown eyes. "Could you have the Horseshoe's security team keep a close watch on that location near the stairs where the slots took Ben. Maybe they like the place. If they come back, we want to know when and how often."

"They'll do it for me," she said.

"Good thinking, Poker Boy," Screamer said, nodding, his gaze on something not in this room. "See if we can spot a pattern, maybe figure out where the slots and Ben are going to show next."

"We can only hope," I said. "At least it's a place to start. Patty, any chance you might have tomorrow off?"

"I'll take it off," she said, smiling at me.

I kept my face and heart under control and managed to keep going. "Great, thanks. Would you help me do some research into Valley and Standard Slots. Valley owned the things during the time they were in the Horseshoe. I'm betting they are still stored somewhere."

"Good thinkin' again," Screamer said. "Two-sided attack. Always nice to work with you, Poker Boy. You always got a play." He stood and dropped too much money on the table for his meal.

"I'll also check my contacts at the police, see if anything else is going on. You staying at the Horseshoe?"

"I am," I said.

"I'll call you at seven in the morning," Screamer said.

He turned to my side-kick, Patty. "It was wonderful crawling around inside that beautiful head of yours."

Patty had the common sense to blush and say nothing at Screamer's beaming smile.

"Samantha," Screamer said to her, touching her arm gently. "Don't worry. We'll find Ben. Try to get some rest. Tomorrow's going to be a full day."

"I'll try," Samantha said.

"Thanks, Screamer," I said.

He nodded to me and turned and was out the door. The room almost felt empty without him. Only the three of us, Elvis on the jukebox, and Madge were left in the diner. Screamer had a real presence about him.

"I never thought I'd ever meet the infamous Toledo Moss," Patty said, still blushing. "I heard my dad talk about him for years. He's almost a legend around this town."

"He is at that," I said, laughing, not mentioning that he was a superhero as well.

Patty stared at me, those brown eyes digging into my very heart, lifting the lid, swishing the blood around. Luckily I am a poker player who has been stared-down by the best in the business. But it's one thing to stare into the eyes of a player trying to find out your cards, it was another to stare into Patty's big brown eyes. I hope she never took up poker.

"Yet Toledo Moss deferred to you," Patty said, smiling slightly. "Why do you think that is?"

I just hoped at that moment my reputation around Las Vegas wasn't as strong as Screamers, because he had let slip my Poker Boy name a couple of times, and if anyone would have heard of me, then I have no doubt Patty would have as well.

"I've got a few years on him is all," I said, smiling at her.

"Why did you call him Screamer?" Samantha asked, coming to my rescue before Patty managed to peal back every ounce of protection I had with those laser-brown eyes of hers.

"I'm not sure who started it," I said. "But I've heard two reasons why."

"I only heard one," Patty said. "I heard that with his special gift of getting inside people's heads he could put nightmares into a person's mind until they screamed for him to stop."

"That's one," I said, smiling at Patty. "He did that for the cops on a serial murder case about fifteen years ago. I don't think he makes it a habit."

"And the other?" Samantha asked.

"Sexually," I said, "he knows what a woman wants, what she is feeling, what she is needing, and can give it to her until she screams for him to stop."

"Oh," Patty said.

Both women sat there silently, clearly lost in their own thoughts and imaginations.

At that moment I sure wanted Screamer's superpower, and would have traded two or three of my own to get it.

Chapter Eight

Looking for a God
in all the Right Places

FOR A NUMBER OF YEARS, the World Series of Poker has been held mostly in the Horseshoe's old bingo hall on the second floor, with the cashier just inside the main door, and the tournament sign-up outside to the right in the hallway.

The World Series itself is a series of daily tournaments, with different levels of entry fees, called buy-ins, for each. I had hoped, when I arrived in town, to play in the fifteen hundred dollar buy-in, no-limit hold-em tournament that started tomorrow at noon. But now that I was helping Samantha, I would have to wait for another, later tournament.

The structure of a World Series tournament was fairly simple. You got as many tournament chips as the buy-in, then you played until only one person had all the chips. As you might imagine, that takes time, so for years the first day of every event ended when the final table, meaning the last nine players, was reached, and they started again the next day and finished off. For the last few years, they decided to just play to midnight, and everyone still left with chips came back the next day. Either way, it made for long tournaments, with the big tournament at the end of the five weeks costing ten thousand to buy-in, and lasting five days.

So, when I walked into the tournament room on the second floor of the Horseshoe, I could tell at once that there were still six tables in today's pot limit two thousand dollar buy-in hold-em tournament back in the far left corner of the room. Fifty or so players sweating to stay alive and make the top twenty to thirty positions that paid out money.

I glanced over at the electronic tournament board. Over three hundred players had started the tournament at noon and there was a first-place prize of almost two hundred thousand. There was nothing like the World Series of Poker for nice paydays. And one of those fifty players was going to pull it in.

All cash.

If I got a chance, I'd go back there later and watch a few hands.

Across the front of the room were live games with different betting limits. There were maybe forty tables of poker going at once, with a lot of people standing around talking and watching games. And across the back left of the room were satellite tournaments, where players played against each other to earn their buy-in into a bigger tournament. At the moment, there were a number of one-table events going on, with the winner on each table taking a full fifteen hundred in buy-in chips.

I liked playing satellites for warm-ups, and sometimes won my way into a big one. I planned this trip to play a bunch of what they called super-satellites until I earned my way into the ten thousand big event a month from now. Better than paying the full ten thousand out of my pocket, and more fun as well.

At first glance around the tournament room, I didn't see Stan. I didn't expect to, actually. Gambling Gods, when joining the ranks of the real players, tend to come in different shapes and sizes, and can disguise themselves very well.

"I understand you're looking for me?" a voice said from behind me as I stood near the cashier's area.

I turned around to face Stan, his long face smiling at me. He wasn't in any disguise, and was wearing his normal gray sweater and a baseball hat with no logo. His eyes were a gold and green and seemed to be able to stare right through me.

I hadn't told a person what I was going to do, yet Stan knew I was looking for him.

Scary. Damn scary.

I kept on my poker face and managed to say, "I am." I didn't ask him how he knew. "You have thirty seconds to talk privately?"

"Sure do," he said, nodding toward the small lobby outside at the top of the escalator.

The lobby was a place where deals were done, mostly between players who had no money, and people who did. The sponsors, as they were called, took a cut of a player's possible winnings in exchange for buying them into a tournament. Those arrangements were sometimes profitable for both sides, and often allowed a person who couldn't play top-level poker to ride along on the excitement with a person who could.

I led Stan over to an open spot against the wall. No one seemed to notice either of us, and I wondered if that was Stan blocking out people's attention, or just the fact that we looked like any two players trying to make a deal, which in essence, we were.

As soon as we got to a place where no one could hear us I asked him point blank, "You know what I'm working on?"

He nodded. "Trying to get a guy out of the hooks of some ghost slots." He laughed. "You always were a sucker for blind women and dogs."

"No contest there," I said, laughing with him, but not feeling that much at ease.

"And you're wondering if I have any advice on how to do what you and Screamer are trying to do?"

"Got me read in one," I said.

Stan nodded, as if thinking about how to play a hand. Then he looked directly at me. "Ghost slots are nasty things. And no one really knows how many of the things there are. They're always hungry, and they don't completely exist in the here and now. Some people say they can float through time and across distances, taking their human food with them. Once the human is drained of all energy and essence, they look for another snack."

That didn't sound good for Ben, that's for sure. "Any restrictions on the space or time they can move?"

Stan shrugged. "As far as I know, they can only travel to places where they once existed in real life, like those slots did here in the Horseshoe."

I nodded. I had figured as much, but it was good to hear him confirm that detail.

He went on. "They drive the God of Slots crazy, let me tell you. She thought she had them under control until this."

"I'll bet they get to her," I said, not feeling hopeful at all. If these things couldn't be handled by the Gambling Gods, what did a couple of superheroes like me and Screamer think we could do?

"You ever hear of anyone getting loose from them?"

"No," Stan said.

Then he stopped. I could sense that there was something he wasn't telling me. It felt odd to be reading the main God of Poker, but that was exactly what I was doing. I was putting a read on Stan.

"So what else is happening, Stan?"

Stan took a deep breath, and for a moment I thought he was going to just shake his head and say nothing. Then he glanced around.

Suddenly everyone froze. It felt as if we had moved between two moments in time.

Almost everyone around us had their mouth open, and the woman sitting at the sign-in table was in the process of adjusting her bra while looking down the hallway to her right.

Not only was everyone stopped like a statue, but Stan had shut off the sound as well, which in a casino can be very disconcerting. Casinos, the places I loved, were never completely quiet. Even in the slowest periods, slot machines made a humming noise, and often called out to customers to come play them, even though there were no customers around.

Every casino I knew had background music. Just the massive numbers of lights in casinos filled the places with a low noise. But now there wasn't a sound. Stan

and I might have well been standing in the middle of the Mojave Desert without a wind.

"Nice trick," I said to Stan, nodding.

"Didn't want anyone hearing what I am about to tell you," Stan said.

"That good, huh?" I said, turning my attention from all the frozen people around me to Stan, suddenly very worried.

"Actually, that bad," Stan said. "The case you're working isn't the only ghost slot snatch. There have been around fifty, maybe a lot more, in the last six or seven days, and today someone got a reporter from the *Sun* to go stand in a certain spot in the Mirage and watch some slots take a woman."

"Someone is doing this on purpose?" I asked, just about as stunned and surprised as I had been in years.

"Looks that way," Stan said.

I made the next jump, to the only logical reason why anyone would be doing this purposely. "They're trying to kill every casino on the planet."

Stan nodded.

We both stood there in silence, the poker players and sponsors frozen around us like statues. The ideas that casinos

were actually threatened just flat scared me beyond any monster, any killer I had ever faced. Casinos were my home, my place of power, the only reason I got up in the mornings.

Whoever was doing this was threatening me directly.

I turned to Stan. "The management has no leads on this?"

Management was what superheroes called the top gods.

"Everyone's working on it," Stan said. "I've been in two hundred casinos in the last few hours myself, looking for any clue, anything that might be a lead."

I nodded. If all the casino gods and management gods were on the case, I had no idea how Screamer and I could help. We were just a couple of lowly superheroes. And that thought came right out of my mouth next.

"So what good can I do in all this?"

Stan stared at me, and when the God of Poker stares at you, you know you've been studied, read, and put away. Never, in all my memory have I been looked at with that kind of intensity, that kind of focus, even by the best poker players in the world.

"Actually," Stan said after what seemed like the longest second I have ever survived, "you might be one of our best hopes. Burt told me this morning you were coming, would be working on this, and that I should help you where I can."

"Now I am really worried," I said.

"The managers of publicity and security have put a team together as well, a reporter and a cop. You might run into them, so help them if you can as well. All of us are after the same thing."

"Stopping these things," I said.

"Exactly," Stan said. "And soon."

I took a deep breath, glanced around at all the frozen statues of people filling the lobby at the top of the escalator, then turned back to face Stan.

"You said these ghost slots can move around when hunting, appearing and disappearing like the one I saw on that tape. Right?"

"That's what we always thought."

"So how can someone control something that can move like that?"

"You tell us that," Stan said, "and we'll know who's doing this."

I didn't really want to ask the next question, but I did. "Can it be another branch of gods, you know, the death and dying ones on some sort of strange crusade."

Stan shook his head. "No. I was there when Laverne checked with them."

Calling Lady Luck, the woman in charge of it all, by her first name, shook me. I would never have the courage to do that. Not ever. I wanted to keep playing and winning, and even though poker was a skill game, there was still that element of luck involved, and having the top of the top Herself mad at you would be a very, very bad thing.

"So we're dealing with someone who somehow has figured out a way to control ghost slots and wants casinos shut down. Some sort of anti-gambling nut-case."

"That's one of the main ways we're following as well. But my suggestion is that you track the slots to where they live here and now. Their base, their nest, their haunt, whatever you want to call it. They have to go somewhere and you never know what you might find. And don't be afraid to use your Unstuck-In-Time power to follow them if you have to."

I nodded again, not completely understanding what he meant. I didn't know I had an Unstuck-In-Time superpower, and I wasn't sure what it might be, actually. But that was no surprise. Even after twenty years I was still discovering some of my powers.

"You mean I can do this?" I asked, motioning all the people around me. "How?"

"You can," he said. "When you need it, you'll know how."

"Well, thanks, I guess," I said. "You want me to report in to you."

"No need. I'll be following your progress and helping where I can," he said.

"Thanks, Stan," I said

"No problem," he said, smiling at me. "This is something special where we all need to help each other. I'll still owe you for passing up old Betty for me. Man, you got some will power. I hear she's about as good in the sack as they come."

With a laugh and a shake of his head, he turned away and headed back for the big room as everyone around us started moving again, and the noise pounded in like a dam breaking. I had no doubt that if I followed him in there I wouldn't be able to spot him again. Gambling Gods could disappear like that.

I headed for the elevator, doing my best to not think about what might have been that Christmas Eve with Betty, and that wonderful skin and perfect body of hers. I had a blind woman's husband to rescue, the entire casino industry to save, and maybe a new superpower to use. It just wasn't the right moment for me to be thinking about wild sex.

By the time I had reached my room, I had replaced Betty's face in my mind with Patty's wonderful smile, brown hair, raspberry smell, and perfect mole.

But even her wonderful face and the memory of her smell couldn't keep the images of empty casinos, boarded up and shut down forever, from filling my thoughts.

I'd have to hang up my Poker Boy jacket and hat and go to playing poker in back rooms, bars, and Elk clubs to make a living. It wouldn't be a bad life, but it wouldn't be a great one either.

I spent most of the rest of the night on my bed, fully dressed, with my superhero uniform still on, soaking up the energy and thinking.

Chapter Nine

Too Damn Early

SCREAMER CALLED what seemed like five minutes after I had finally managed to doze off.

Somehow, I got the phone on the second, maybe third ring, and got it to the side of my face without hurting myself. Then, before I mumbled the word "Hello," he started talking.

"No luck so far, Poker Boy. But I think I got a lead. It's out in one of the old joints on the highway toward the dam. You want me to follow it?"

"Yeah," I said, fighting to get my mind focused on what he was saying and not the fading dream of spending a night with a beautiful gambling god.

"Also, this is a lot bigger than we thought," Screamer said.

That snapped me awake, remembering what Stan had talked to me about, what had kept me laying awake thinking all night.

"What do you know?"

"Looks like most of the police and the newspaper are onto this, and a lot of people have been taken, not just Ben. So far, everyone's keeping a lid on things, but I doubt, and so do others, that lid's going to hold much longer."

My stomach twisted. The last thing we needed at this point was a panic, a mass exodus away from casinos and Las Vegas.

"Heard you talked to Stan last night," Screamer said. "Did he give us any help?"

"Some," I said, surprised that Screamer knew I had met with a gambling god. Maybe Screamer had done the same thing. "Stan told me how big this problem really is, gave me a couple of warnings and a suggestion or two."

"Good," he said. "I'll chase down what leads I can, then catch up with you and Patty at the diner. How does around noon sound?"

"Perfect," I said. "Thanks, Screamer."

"No problem," he said. "You just be careful. From everything I hear these ghost slots are not something to be fooled with lightly. And I doubt that if there are people behind this mess, they are either."

"Stan said the same thing. You watch your back as well."

"Doing just that," Screamer said. "No worries, we'll tackle them together."

With that he hung up, leaving me holding the phone and very much awake. And very glad he was helping me.

The clock on the nightstand said two minutes after six in the morning. Way too early for a poker player to get up.

Poker players are, by the nature of the game, night people. I have seen six in the morning more times than I want to think about, but always from the night side, almost never from the morning side. I don't care what anyone says, getting out of bed before the sun comes up is just not natural.

Still, with Screamer's words echoing in my mind, I bid a final goodbye to the last dream-thoughts of a gambling god-dess, climbed out of bed and did all the things a person, or superhero, does to get ready for a day.

By seven in the morning, the sun was up, and I was drinking coffee and reading the morning newspaper in the diner across Front Street from the Horseshoe.

I silently thanked all the gambling gods that Madge wasn't there.

The paper had three reports of people going missing, but they were scattered and buried. Only one report mentioned the fact that the person had vanished from a casino. All three were tourists and the newspaper said the police were working at their cases. The big story was staying buried.

So far so good.

At a few minutes after eight, Samantha, her dog, Sue, and Patty joined me.

Patty somehow managed to be stunning, even early in the morning. She wore no make-up, faded jeans, and a tucked-in white blouse that gave just enough hint of the white lace-trimmed bra underneath to be alluring. Her hair seemed to shine in the diner light, and she had pulled it back exposing my favorite mole for the entire world to see.

Samantha, on the other hand, looked like she hadn't slept all night, had barely managed to get dressed this morning, and was in desperate need of coffee. Not even her black glasses could hide the rings under her eyes.

"Good morning, ladies," I said, tossing my paper aside and standing to let them join me in the booth.

Patty gave me a beaming smile and a "Good morning to you as well."

Then she helped Samantha into the booth and stepped back as Sue curled up at her master's feet.

"How was your night?" Patty asked as she slid into the booth and against the wall on my side. "You or Toledo get any leads?"

"Screamer's following one now," I said, doing my best to ignore her wonderful raspberry smell and the closeness of her arm against mine in the booth. "He's going to meet us back here at noon."

"G o o d ," Patty said.

I kept talking because it was the only way I knew to not just stare at her.

> *I kept talking because it was the only way I knew to not just stare at her.*

"I talked to a friend of mine last night up in the tournament room, called in a marker, and got a little help as well."

Patty turned sideways, moving her arm away from mine so she could look at me with a steady gaze. "Anyone I know?"

"Not unless you know some of the gambling gods," I said, smiling at her, pretending to be joking. I often figured that the best way to tell someone something they wouldn't believe, and get them to change the subject, was to flat tell them the truth.

"Oh, yeah, right," Samantha said from the other side of the booth, shaking her head in clear disgust.

Patty, on the other hand, kept staring at me, then just nodded slightly.

I was starting to gain a lot of respect for Patty. Clearly my current sidekick knew a lot more about the behind-the-scenes working of Las Vegas and the gambling world than I was giving her credit for.

Plus, she was beautiful, smelled wonderful, and had hair a person could get lost in while searching closely for a mole.

"I'm going to the police again right after breakfast," Samantha said, clearly upset, as she had every right to be. "I'm going to make them start looking for Ben if I have to stand there and just scream."

"Good idea," I said, turning my attention from the allure of my sidekick to the task at hand. "You never know when we might need their help."

I didn't tell her that I had no doubt the police were already working on finding Ben. And all of the others taken by the slots before him.

Samantha seemed a little surprised that I had agreed with her that quickly. Clearly, she still thought we were trying to run some scam on her, and had discounted the images of her husband Screamer had put into her mind last night. I didn't blame her. Believing that a person could be taken by ghost slot machines wasn't easy, even for someone like me who was used to the strange happenings.

Many, many of the people I help don't believe I can help them at first. It's an occupational hazard of being a superhero. In fact, I bet if there was ever a convention of superheroes, and we had panels and meetings about the problems we all faced, this would be one of the main topics of discussion. After all the years, I had gotten used to it, and having a person like Samantha not believe in the real problem didn't even surprise me.

"I agree," Patty said, nodding to me, then turning to talk directly to Samantha. "I'll be glad to drive you down to the main station after breakfast. I have a detective friend there that will waive the forty-eight hour waiting period for me if I ask real nice."

I'd waive anything if she asked nice, but I didn't say that out loud.

"Thank you," Samantha said, some of the anger draining from her posture. "That would be really helpful."

"Help is why we're here," I said. "Besides, they frown on people standing in the lobby of the police station screaming. It gives Las Vegas a bad image."

Patty gave me a beaming smile that reached her eyes, and Samantha actually laughed as the waitress came up to take our order.

The morning waitress wasn't a lot better than Madge in looks, but clearly younger by about twenty years, and lighter by forty pounds. Her name was Fran, her hair was bleached blonde, and her make-up heavy in the purple eye-liner department. The coffee pot in her right hand seemed to be glued there as she listened to our orders, asked the right toast and hash-brown questions, and then went off with a "Got it."

She hadn't written anything down, which seemed almost magical to me. How could she remember all that, plus have a conversation with the booth next to ours while refilling their coffee cups? Of course, what I do at a poker table looks like magic to some people, so I guess it's just where a person's focus is. And where they make their living.

Who knows, maybe Fran was a superhero in the waitressing world. Maybe she went around saving truck drivers with bad body odor with the help of the waitressing gods. I know for a fact there are such things as evil bacon, and Mexican food with a bite. So why couldn't there be superhero waitresses who rush in to save the day like we're trying to do with Ben?

"So what's the plan?" Patty asked after Fran left.

"Well," I said, "after we help Samantha get Ben officially reported as missing with the police, you and I could do some tracking. My source last night tells me the best thing to do is try to track the machines to where they live, which I assume meant where the old machines are stored."

"You think they're stored and haven't been destroyed?" Patty asked.

"I would bet just about anything on it," I said. "My source also told me they can only move around in the time frame which they existed, which means since Ben was taken yesterday, those things still exist somewhere."

"We just have to find them," Patty said, nodding. "Which means we have to figure out where the old Valley Slots graveyard is."

"Wouldn't it be owned by Standard Slots now?" I asked. "Since they bought out Valley a long time ago?"

"More than likely," Patty said. "I called my dad last night and he gave me a name to contact at Standard Slots. But he seems to think that there is still a Valley Slots graveyard somewhere."

"Graveyard?" Samantha asked, clearly not liking the sound of the term.

"It's what they call the monster warehouses in which they store the old slot machines," I said.

"Why don't they just haul them to the dump?" Samantha asked.

I shrugged. "Honestly, I'm not one hundred percent certain, but from what I've heard over the years, it has to do with their value. Some are junked, others have parts switched out to working machines, but by-and-large, they just store the things."

Now Available
from all your favorite booksellers
in trade paper and electronic editions.

"I heard it was taxes," Patty said. "And corporate valuation. A corporation just can't go throwing away assets, even though the assets have no real use any more. Plus, I think there are regs that make junking a slot machine more expensive than just renting a giant warehouse and storing them in mass."

Samantha nodded, then asked, "So how many machines are in these storage places?"

"I doubt anyone knows," I said. "I've seen basements full of the things, warehouses stacked with them, and hallways in the backs of hotels lined with the things."

"Oh," Samantha said. "And you think you're going to find four of them from more than a decade ago?"

Patty and I sat there looking at each other, not answering her. Samantha had a point. Las Vegas was a haystack made up of hundreds and hundreds of thousands of slot machines. And we weren't even looking for a needle. We were looking for a piece of hay.

A very old piece of hay.

Chapter Ten

A Nap and A Search

I TOOK A NAP right after breakfast. Yes, superheroes take naps. I know that blows the image built with decades of comic books and movies, but it is true. It's just tough for those comic book artists to draw naps, and besides, when naps are done right, they're really boring.

My nap was done perfectly.

After breakfast, Patty took Samantha down to the police station to file the missing person's report. She was going to call me in my room when she got back.

I had intended on making a few phone calls to find out what had happened to Valley Slot's slot graveyards, but it only took one call to a friend of mine at city hall to get the address of what he thought was the only Valley Slots graveyard left, owned, of course, by Standard Slots.

I sort of remember sitting there on the bed after hanging up the phone.

The soft bedspread had looked so inviting.

What would it hurt to just stretch out there and think for a few minutes?

I told myself that.

Just think.

Patty's call woke me an hour later. It was six minutes before ten in the morning.

"Any luck?" Patty asked without saying hello.

The sound of her voice had me instantly awake. "Yeah, got us an address. I'll be right down."

"Meet you in front of the main desk. I'm double-parked so don't take long."

She hung up.

I sat there for a moment wondering if I had just dreamt that call, finally convincing myself I hadn't.

I tossed a handful of water on my face, combed my hair enough so that it wouldn't look slept on, put on my hat and Poker Boy leather coat, and headed out the door.

By the time I hit the lobby, I was feeling much, much better, and ready for a day of work.

"Good nap?" Patty asked, smiling at me.

I managed to not show I was surprised at the question. "Naps are always good."

Patty laughed. "You poker players are all alike."

"A society of nappers, huh?"

"Pro nappers," she said, still laughing as she led the way out of the casino and into the warm morning air.

I could tell the day was going to be hot again. Considering it was still April, I would wager the high desert was going to be in for a really hot year.

Patty had a new model Honda, which looked a lot like most other mid-sized cars being made. It was the first half-way-plain thing I had seen about her. But even though it was a dull design, the inside of the car was clean, the air conditioning kept me comfortable, and the car had acceleration enough to get through traffic just fine.

Patty drove like a professional, smooth and direct, changing lanes when she needed to, and driving ahead, watching for problems. And she didn't tailgate. So far, even with a dull, regular car, there was nothing about this woman I didn't like.

When I gave Patty the address I had gotten from my friend in city hall, she started out what was called the Old Boulder Highway without hesitation. They've built a freeway along the same route, but Patty stayed on the old highway, going past the dozens of strip malls, old motels, and small casinos that lined every mile of the old highway.

What people think of as Las Vegas was actually made up of four medium-small cities. There was Las Vegas, North Las Vegas, Henderson, and Boulder City. There were actually a number of other smaller towns as well, but they had been pretty much swallowed by the growth of the other four.

I let Patty focus on her driving while I worked on how we were going to get into the warehouse. We sure couldn't just tell whoever was guarding the place that we were looking for the home of a ghost slot machine. Never work.

By the time Patty turned off the old highway onto a side road just south of Whitney, which is sometimes called East Las Vegas, I had us a cover story.

She pulled the car into the tumble-weed-covered parking lot of a giant warehouse and put it in park, letting the air-conditioning run on low. She looked at the huge metal building and then turned to me with a smile. "Now what?"

I could see the faded address numbers on the side of the building. It was clear that unless there was a security guard roaming the place, we weren't going to need a cover story. From the looks of this building, I doubted anyone had been around it for years. The desert sun had taken the metal to a dull gray, and the winds and sand had removed any sign that the place might have been painted at one time in the past.

"We go in, I guess," I said, shrugging. "And in case anyone stops us, we're thinking about working on a book about old slot machines, and trying to get an idea what some of them looked like."

"Good cover story," she said, nodding. "But I doubt we're going to need it here. More than likely, we're going to have to go to the Standard Slots main office and get someone to bring us back and let us in."

"Yeah," I said, shoving the door open, "but we should take a look around first."

I was hoping we wouldn't have to waste time going to the main office, and with what Stan had told me, I really didn't want anyone from Standard Slots to know we were even looking around, just in case they were involved with the kidnappings. It never hurt to be careful.

The highway noise from a few blocks over cut through the warm air as we started toward what looked to be a main door. The warehouse had four large, drive-in bay doors and a regular-sized door beside the bay door on the left.

Since I was a good block from the closest casino, I wasn't sure if my superpowers would work. Sometimes, I had what I called hold-over powers if I had spent a lot of time in a casino right before I needed the power. Spending the night in the Horseshoe might be enough, and having a small casino a block away would be a little help. At least I hoped it would, because I was going to try using a power I very seldom got to use. I called it my Open-Says-Me Power.

It worked like a charm the few times I had had to use it on locked casino doors. I had no idea if it would work on this warehouse door.

"Looks closed up tight," Patty said. "I'll bet no one has even checked on this place in six months."

"True," I said, shrugging. "But maybe we'll get lucky."

I took hold of the door knob and then, focusing my power like I was studying a guy trying to bluff me off a pair of queens, I turned the knob and heard the dead-bolt slide back. I smiled at Patty and opened the door.

The door made a scraping sound on the sidewalk as it opened, and let out cool, musty-smelling air from the dark inside.

"Looks like we got lucky," Patty said. She was shaking her head and half frowning at me. But I could see amusement in her eyes as well, and maybe a little fondness. Or maybe I just hoped to see the fondness.

"Hello!" I shouted into the warehouse as I stepped into the darkness.

The sound of my shout echoed back at me.

"No one home," Patty said, moving in to stand beside me, leaving the door open behind us. "Now that's a surprise."

"The trick is going to be finding the lights," I said.

I went left along the wall, Patty moved right. A moment later I heard a few loud clicks from Patty's direction and the warehouse flooded with light.

"Oh, my," Patty said, moving over to stand by me as I stared at what stretched out in front of us.

The place looked a lot bigger inside than it did outside, with fourteen aisles big enough to drive a forklift through. And on each side of every aisle, sometimes stacked in crates, were slot machines.

"There have to be thousands in here," Patty said.

"Easily," I said. Actually, I figured there were closer to ten thousand different slot machines facing us.

I focused my powers again, concentrating, trying to get any feeling, any of my powers to help me find the slot machines we were looking for.

Suddenly, in front of me, I could see a faint orange glow that sort of led off to the far wall and down that aisle. Superpowers still working fine it seemed. Now I'd have to come up with a name for this power.

"This way," I said, heading with the glow.

We went along the front of the big closed bay doors and then along the wall, moving past old slot machines covered in dust, some protected by either plastic wraps or tarps. All their lights were dark, their colors faded, covered in dust, or completely gone. Many had holes in their fronts from being cannibalized, many had broken arms and broken displays.

"This is damned creepy," Patty said.

"That it is," I said. "I see why they call it a graveyard."

"No kidding," Patty said.

Even with the bright overhead lights on, the canyons of old slot machines seemed to radiate old age. Though the old slots had at one time been colorful, their colors didn't seem to have made it here. Everything around us was in shades of gray.

I had the feeling as we moved along that we were walking deeper and deeper into the past. And not just because of the age of the machines around us.

It was something else.

Something very real that my Danger-Ahead Superpower was telling me wasn't good.

The orange glow stopped at a covered bank of slot machines. Under the faded black tarp loomed a shape that looked like the Saturn Slots we had seen in the security footage.

I stopped a few steps away and motioned that Patty should do the same. "Stay here."

"You think those are the ones?" Patty asked. "How would you know?"

"Just a hunch."

I moved the last few steps forward, reached up and grabbed the tarp covering the slots. Then with all my strength, I yanked.

The tarp came easily, spreading into a pile in the middle of the aisle, pushing rolling clouds of dust into the air.

I had stepped back beside Patty as I pulled, and then when the slots were exposed, we both stepped back another two steps.

What faced us couldn't be there, yet it was.

I had the feeling as we moved along that we were walking deeper and deeper into the past.

Four Saturn Slots, with four wooden chairs attached, the bright image of the planet and its rings dominating everything. We had found what we were looking for all right.

But there was a problem.

It was turned on.

Every light on the machines was working, the chrome and brass polished and shining, as if it were sitting on a casino floor just waiting for a customer.

I could feel the attraction to sit down, to just play one nickel.

And I had never once put one coin into a slot machine.

Never.

Ever.

I wasn't a gambler. I was a poker player.

Around us, the gray of the dust-filled warehouse took on colors reflecting from the machine. Every warning alarm I had in my body went off. It was as if by uncovering the thing, we were spreading its power.

"Why would someone leave it plugged in?" Patty asked, her voice almost a whisper.

"I'm fairly certain it's not plugged into anything that pretends to be electricity," I said. "It's getting its power from something else, somewhere else."

I could feel them tugging us toward them, as if they were saying *"What would it hurt to sit down and just play a nickel?"*

I took Patty's arm and pulled her a few staggering steps backward as the lights from the machine got brighter. Clearly, the machines were affecting her as much as they were trying to get to me.

Suddenly, the warehouse was filled with a man's shout, echoing through the cavernous space.

"Police! Who's in here?"

"Far aisle on the right side of the door as you come in!" I shouted. "Hurry!"

I figured the police were here for the same reason we were, and I wanted them to see these machines before they vanished, as I had a hunch they were about to do.

I pulled Patty a few more steps backward down the aisle as the machine started to pulse, its colors gaining and then losing intensity.

Behind us, I could hear the running footsteps of the police.

In front of us, the ghost slots were glowing brighter than any slot I had ever seen, filling all the old slots around them with color and light.

Then, as if I was watching a movie, I saw flashes of images flicker around the slots, different people, different casino backgrounds, clearly even different time periods.

The images came faster and faster as the pulses of light from the slot machine got brighter and brighter.

The image of Ben flashed past, the same as we had seen in the Horseshoe's security cameras.

Then the image of a middle-aged woman, then a young man and his girlfriend together, then more and more, maybe dozens of people, until suddenly the pulsing light stopped.

The Saturn Slots were gone, an empty space remaining in the rows of old slot machines.

The warehouse went back to a dirty gray, washed out by the overhead white lights.

Patty leaned against me. "Oh, my," she said softly.

I moved my arm around her waist. Having her that close to me felt right, felt nice. I just wished it were for a different reason.

"Holy shit," a woman said behind us, her voice a hoarse whisper.

I glanced around at a man and woman standing a dozen steps behind us, still staring at where the Saturn Slots had been a moment before.

The man, a Detective I knew named Johnny State, had his gun out, but it was hanging in his hand, looking very useless.

I turned back to look at the empty space where the Saturn Slots had been a moment before.

It was still empty.

The slots were out hunting.

But what happened to the people they took?

Who was controlling such an amazing monster?

And even a better question yet: What were we going to do to stop it?

Chapter Eleven

The Return from Hell

JOHNNY AND I had just finished putting the tarp back in place when the energy of the big warehouse started to change again.

I had had a lot of natural powers before becoming Poker Boy, and one of them was the ability to sense when the energy in something was changing. Usually, I used that sense in a poker game, or when someone was starting to get angry. Now I could feel it in the air around us.

I took Johnny by the arm and pulled him away from where we had been staring at the tarp being held up by empty space, moving us and Patty and the woman, Geneva, even farther away down the aisle.

Suddenly bright colors seemed to flash through the gaps in the tarp and the machines were back. I could feel the pull of them, the desire to have someone come to them and sit down.

"Those things are hungry," Patty said softly as the four of us backed even farther away.

"Let's go back to the door," I said, touching Johnny's arm to get him to move.

As I touched his skin, I got a sense of Geneva with him as well. For a second it was as if there were three of us in the same head.

I let go of Johnny's arm and glanced at him as we headed away from the machines.

"Weird, huh?" he said, shrugging.

Clearly he knew I had joined them for a moment.

Geneva had her hand on Johnny's arm. I knew at once it was touch that linked the two of them, and for some reason my touch had linked me with them for a second as well.

"How long?" I asked.

"Since we met yesterday," Johnny said.

"Doesn't work without touch?" I asked.

"Not yet," Johnny said.

We had turned the corner out of the aisle of old slots with the dangerous machines and the pull from them was almost gone.

"What are you two talking about?" Patty asked. "Include the rest of us if you would, please."

I knew Geneva had understood and been part of Johnny's side of the conversation, since the two of them were linked. But I doubted they wanted Patty to know, and if they did, they would tell her.

"Oh, sorry," I said. "Just trying to figure out who could control those monsters back there."

Geneva laughed. "It's all right if she knows, since you do, and we are all working together on this."

All four of us stopped near the front door. It was standing open and the bright light from outside was pouring in, overwhelming the warehouse lights. The inside of the warehouse seemed almost alien compared to the life, the bright light, and the distant traffic outside. I could also feel the warm air flooding in.

Geneva touched Johnny's arm as she faced Patty. "For some reason, the how or why of which we don't understand, Detective State and I have a link telepathically when we touch. We discovered this wonderful gift yesterday when we met."

Johnny was nodding.

Patty stared at Geneva for a moment, then turned to me. "And you knew this how?"

"Got a flash of it when I touched Johnny when steering us away from back there."

Patty shook her head at me. "You are sure full of surprises."

"He is at that," Johnny said, laughing. Then, without giving Patty a chance to ask any questions about what Geneva had told her, he went on. "So what next?"

I shrugged. "We found the machines and now we have more questions than we did before. I'm struggling with someone having the ability to control those things back there, if they are what they appear."

"And if they aren't, who's doing the illusions?" Patty said.

"And why?" Johnny said. "Most of the police department is on this case, tracking anti-gambling groups, religious nut-cases, and anything else they can think of. By now I'm pretty sure that even the Feds are involved, maybe the anti-terrorist bunch as well."

That all made sense to me. You just can't have fifty people or more vanish in a week from a city and not stir up everything. It was amazing that it wasn't all over the television and papers.

"For the moment, we're the only one's following these slots, right?"

Johnny nodded. "Geneva was sent to me because someone sent a note to the *Sun* to have a reporter stand at the Mirage to watch something."

"So you saw these things take someone?"

"I did," Geneva said. "The Saturn Slots sort of faded in right over a bank of slots in the Mirage, a middle-aged woman sat down, put in a nickel, and the slots and the woman vanished."

"Same thing that happened to Ben at the Horseshoe," Patty said. "We watched it on a security tape that no longer exists."

Geneva laughed. "We discovered last night that the Mirage's tape of the area shows nothing, including me standing there."

"No surprise," I said. "They are not going to use their own security tapes to condemn their own business."

"So someone's directing these things," Johnny said. "We need to figure out how, or who, or from where?"

My little voice was going off like an alarm bell. This happened all the time when I was about to make a call with a hand in a poker game that was statistically right, yet felt wrong. Once I learned to lay down the hands that my little voice told me to lay down, I started earning a lot more money.

"Back up half a step," I said. I turned to Geneva. "You said you got a note to go to a place and stand and see what happens. Right?"

Geneva nodded.

"Nothing more? Nothing about kidnapping, or ghost slots or anything?"

"That's right," she said.

"So we have a second option," I said. "Someone might not be controlling those things. They may only be predicting them."

I looked at the three puzzled faces staring at me and managed to not laugh. "Machines are machines," I said. "They are governed by programming and statistical payouts. Why wouldn't a ghost slot be working under the same basic rules? And if that's the case, it might be logical the slots are following a pattern that someone could predict."

"Possible," Johnny said. "But I'm still leaning toward someone in direct control somewhere. This entire mess has the potential of bringing down casinos all over the world. The payoff's too big to not have someone in control of it."

Geneva was clearly agreeing with Johnny, and since she was touching his arm, I knew that what Johnny had said went for both of them. Which was fine. We had a fork in the road of possibilities here. They would chase down one, Patty and I and

Screamer would chase the other one. For all I knew, it was a combination of both.

"So how long until the lid blows off this thing?" I asked Geneva.

"Not long," she said. "A day, maybe two at most. Sooner if someone besides us puts the slot machine angle firmly on the disappearances."

"Okay," I said. "Johnny, can you keep a lid on this warehouse, not even let the owners in here?"

"I can," he said. "I'll get a patrol car out here to sit and keep everyone but the four of us out." He patted his back pocket. "We have a search warrant. I'll just say we're not done searching yet."

"Make sure the cops you put on this don't come inside," I said. "Last thing we need is a cop getting taken by those things."

"Agreed," Johnny said.

I kept on talking, sort of taking control of the investigation without really giving anyone else the chance to. "Patty and I have a lunch meeting with Screamer. We'll follow up on the idea that someone might have the ability to predict a ghost slot and try to figure out who sent you that note."

"We've both got to report back in at work," Geneva said, "see if anything else has broke." She smiled. "Don't worry, not one word that we've found these things yet."

Johnny nodded his agreement.

"Thanks," I said.

I had no doubt that if the entire mess broke open, she would have to tell her boss, and write the story. And if she was as linked as I thought she was with Johnny, she would leave Patty and me out of it. That had been my deal with Johnny back when I helped him solve that murder case. He'd taken all the credit, I'd helped a guy named Brian get out of jail, and even managed to rescue a Great Dane in the process from a flash flood up in the mountains.

That had turned out to be a good trip to Vegas. Man and dog both safe and free, a new police detective as a friend, and over twenty thousand in poker winnings at the same time. A superhero can't ask for many better trips than that one had been.

> *I had no doubt that if the entire mess broke open, she would have to tell her boss, and write the story.*

"So how about we meet back here at six?" Johnny said. "Compare notes, see if we can figure out a way to study that thing back there."

"Six," I said. "I'll call you if we come up with anything quicker."

"Great," Johnny said.

With that, Patty and I headed out into the bright mid-day sun.

Johnny and Geneva shut the warehouse door behind us and got into Johnny's unmarked police car. I saw Johnny immediately pick up the mike and call for a car to come watch the warehouse.

Patty and I were back on the Boulder Highway heading into town before the air conditioning actually started to work and fight back the oven-like interior of her car. For the second day I wondered about taking off my superhero costume and then decided against it. Besides, Patty's car would eventually cool down.

We rode in silence for a few stop-lights. I was trying to wrap my mind around the fact that those machines left the warehouse, yet they never really did, since their shape could still hold up a tarp. I had seen a lot of very strange things in my days as a superhero, but nothing like that. I felt I almost needed a scientist to explain what was happening.

Or a magician if the entire thing was an illusion. I didn't think it was, but yet I couldn't exclude the chance completely.

Maybe Stan might know how that worked, or know who to ask. I'd have to find him after lunch. Besides, it might not hurt for me to check in with Stan and see if the gods of gambling were having any more luck than the police were.

"Poker Boy, huh?" Patty said as we sat waiting for the third stoplight. "Where'd that name come from?"

I glanced sideways at her. She was half-smiling, staring at the intersection, knowing that she had me pinned.

"It's just what people have called me for years," I said. "I've been thinking of changing that to Poker Man because of the gray in my hair, but so far I haven't bothered."

Patty actually had the decency to laugh and not ask anything more.

Chapter Twelve

A Quick Lunch

BY THE TIME PATTY AND I had gotten Samantha and her dog, Sue, out of her room at the Horseshoe Hotel, and the four of us had made it to the little café, it was ten before noon. Madge, the waitress, was there again, along with the woman from the breakfast shift. I managed to keep focused on Patty and her wonderful raspberry smell and avoided looking at Madge when she walked away from our table popping her gum.

Screamer joined us before we even had our drinks, sliding in beside me on one side of the booth and smiling at the two women.

"Hello again, Samantha," he said. "Police have any luck?"

"Nothing," Samantha said.

From the way she had been walking and the sound of her voice, I could tell she was tired and very down. In her situation, with a loving husband suddenly gone for no reason, I didn't blame her. Actually, I thought she was holding up very well, considering the circumstances.

"Well," I said, "now that all of us are here, let me tell you what Patty and I found out this morning. First off, we met with Detective Johnny State and reporter Geneva Gurwell from the *Sun*."

Screamer whistled softly. "You're playing with fire with Geneva. She's known as a tough reporter, maybe the best the *Sun* has."

"We know," Patty said. "And Detective State is no slouch either. The good thing for you to know, Samantha, is that just about the entire police department is working on this."

"And more than likely the FBI as well," I said.

"On Ben's disappearance?" Samantha asked, turning her head toward Patty.

"His, and a lot of other disappearances over the past week," Patty said, putting her hand gently on Samantha's. "It seems that whatever happened to Ben has happened more than fifty times this past week."

"Started nine days ago," Screamer said. "Sixty-seven people officially missing, another dozen maybes, there could be even more. And that's all I was able to get the entire morning."

I glanced at Screamer. Clearly his sources had gotten us the same basic information Patty and I got from Stan and Johnny and Geneva.

"Over seventy people?" Samantha asked, her voice soft.

"Looks that way," I said. "That's why so many people are working on this, which is a good thing."

Samantha nodded. "I guess so."

The silence filled the booth. I wasn't letting myself believe that those seventy people might be dead. Even though I had seen Ben disappear on that tape, I had to believe he was still alive somewhere. Otherwise, this was going to be one of the biggest mass-murders in modern times. But until I learned otherwise, I was going to go on the belief that we were rescuing people, not trying to stop a killer.

"We also found the Saturn Slots," Patty said. "We watched them vanish and return right up close."

"You're kidding?" Screamer said. "You saw the ghost slots where they lived?"

"That we did," I said.

"Oh, man," Screamer said, "you two have more guts than brains. Those things are monsters."

"That they are," a man's voice said from beside me at the end of the table.

All four of us turned like our heads were on the same string.

Stan was pulling up a chair to sit, moving carefully to avoid Sue on the floor.

I didn't know what to think. In all my life I had never heard of a gambling god joining someone for lunch. I supposed they had to eat, but having a god at lunch just seemed downright strange.

Besides that, the service was going to be damned slow, since everyone in the restaurant and outside the restaurant was frozen in place. Clearly Stan had moved our table into a place between moments in time. Luckily, Madge was on the other side of the café and had been coming toward us when Stan arrived.

After Stan got settled, he reached across in front of me. "Screamer, great to meet you. I've heard a lot about you."

Screamer shook his hand. "Stan, the pleasure's all mine."

"Patty," Stan said, turning to her, smiling. "It's been a while."

"Stan," Patty said, smiling back. "Nice seeing you again."

I stared at the woman I had met across the front desk at the Horseshoe like she was an alien. She clearly knew Stan better than I did, and from the smile she gave him, they had a history I wasn't sure I wanted to know about.

I am a poker player. I am supposed to be able to read people, get a clear idea of who they are, what they are going to do in any situation. Patty and Stan had just shown me my reading powers when it came to Patty were non-existent. I had met a couple of people over the years that could block my reads, but not many. Not many at all. And for some reason, I hadn't thought of Patty as one of those people. But she was. She could block my reads on her without me even knowing I was being blocked.

She was good.

Very good.

I glanced across the table at Samantha, who had a puzzled frown on her face.

"Samantha," I said, "the man who just joined us is named Stan. Stan, Samantha."

I figured there was no point in trying to tell her he was one of the gods of gambling. She had enough weird stuff to deal with as it was.

Samantha brought her hand up to shake Stan's hand and he took it.

"Very nice meeting you," he said. "Even though you aren't a gambler. But rest assured, this group can get your husband back if anyone can."

"Thank you," Samantha said. "I'm slowly starting to believe that. And I don't think I really want to know how you shut down every person and every noise around us, do I?"

"Nothing harmful, I assure you," Stan said, a smile on his face that Samantha couldn't see, but I was sure she knew was there.

She nodded and asked nothing more.

"So," Stan said, turning back to face me and Screamer. "You found the home of the ghost slots."

"Right where they were supposed to be," I said. "They sort of left and came back while we were there."

"*Sort of* is right," Patty said.

Stan looked at her, then back at me, as puzzled as I ever wanted to see a god be.

"The things were covered with a tarp when we found them," I said. "Patty and I pulled the tarp off just before they vanished. But then Geneva realized that if the things were coming and going, they couldn't have been under a tarp, so Detective State and I put the tarp back into place, showing that some invisible part of the slot machines stayed in the warehouse."

"Now that's damn weird," Screamer said.

"But you couldn't see anything that was there?" Stan asked.

"Nothing," I said. "But that heavy tarp was being held up by something in the shape of the Saturn Slots. And when the slots returned, the tarp didn't move one bit."

"And there was no person sitting in one of the chairs?" Screamer asked.

"Nothing the tarp showed in form or movement," Patty said.

"Magic trick," Samantha said. "Sounds like a magic trick Ben and I saw back before we were married at the Mirage. Those two men with white tigers did that sort of thing."

"It's a standard magic illusion," Stan said. "But there's nothing magic going on with these machines. That much I can tell you. We've checked that side out."

Screamer, Patty and I were all nodding. If a gambling god said it wasn't something, it wasn't. They had sources I didn't want to think about, and more than likely those sources had gone into the world of magic, talked to the gods that controlled magic and illusion, and got that cleared.

"So," Screamer said, "if it's not an illusion, what's powering those things?"

Stan looked at Screamer. "That's a good question. We haven't looked into that side of this yet. I will meet with Burt and Laverne as soon as we get done here to have them go after that side of things."

With the mention of Laverne's name, I wanted to almost bow my head. I could see Patty's eyes get big as well at the name. When Stan talked about Laverne, he talked about Lady Luck herself, the General Manager of all Gambling.

"Good," Screamer said, clearly as stunned as I felt at Stan's off-handed mention of Laverne.

"Stan," I said, "you mentioned there were other teams working on this."

"Sure," Stan said.

"Detective State and Geneva Gurwell are one team, right?"

"They are," Stan said. "They were given some powers to help them."

"Well," I said, "have you heard the information they have about someone pointing Geneva to a place where the slots would show up, before they showed up."

Now it was Stan's turn to stare at me, and again it felt as if I was being read by the best poker player on the planet.

"I *didn't* know that."

"Detective State and Geneva are working on the angle that someone can control the machines," Patty said. "We're going after the chance that someone can predict the things."

"Any suggestions on that?" I asked. "Who we should talk to, who might be able to predict or control ghost slots?"

"I can't imagine anyone controlling those things," Stan said. "Not even Maggie, who's in charge of slots, knows how or why those things work. They have been a thorn in the side of her department since slots were invented."

"So I want to know," Samantha said, "how machines can take my husband and all these other people? Where do the people go? Where's Ben right now?"

"We don't know that either I'm afraid," Stan said.

"If the machines are being controlled, they might be dropping the victims off in a third location," Patty said.

"But if they aren't controlled and someone is only predicting them, that's going to help us as well," I said.

"Talk to The Bookkeeper," Stan said. "He might have been the one who sent the note to the *Sun*."

I had never heard of anyone called The Bookkeeper, but clearly Patty and Screamer had from the looks of disgust on their faces.

"Where can we find this guy?" I asked.

"He's got a home out in West Las Vegas," Patty said, before Stan could answer. Her voice seemed suddenly angry and clearly disgusted. On this topic, I was having no problem at all reading her.

"Don't like the guy, huh?" I said, smiling at Patty.

"No one likes the guy," Patty said. "He's a pig."

"Amen to that," Screamer said.

"Well, at the moment, he's still our best lead," I said. Then I turned to Stan. "You're going to check on the power source question, right?"

"I am," Stan said. "I'll find you and let you know what we come up with."

"Thanks," I said.

I turned to Screamer. "Would you use your sources and find us the best old-slot technician you can find. It needs to be someone who can work on the slots as old as those Saturn Slots. And someone who can still move and get things done."

Screamer nodded. "Sure, but why?"

"If these things really are just out-of-control machines functioning on statistics and mechanics, we're going to need someone who knows what makes them tick."

"Gotcha," Screamer said. "And you and Patty get The Bookkeeper."

"Oh, yuch," Patty said.

"And what can I do to help?" Samantha asked.

I stared at Samantha for a moment. It wasn't often that someone I was trying to help asked to help in the process. In this case, I didn't blame her one bit. If I had been in her position, I would have wanted to help as well, but I had no idea what she could do at this point.

I glanced at Stan and he was smiling, staring at her.

"Let me help," Samantha said. "Anything. Sitting in that damn hotel room just waiting for something to happen is going to drive me crazy."

"Samantha," Stan said, before I could come up with some lame reason for it being important that she stay in the room. "I want you to focus on me for a moment, the sound of my voice."

Samantha turned toward Stan and nodded.

Suddenly Stan's right hand flew out as if to slap her in the face.

Samantha moved instantly, letting his open hand pass by her without touching her.

"I think she's ready to help you," Stan said, smiling at me.

"What did you do to me?" Samantha asked, clearly stunned at whatever was happening.

"I couldn't give you your sight back," Stan said, "so I just opened up your existing senses a little bit. You had already opened them a great deal since losing your vision. Now, just trust the information you are getting."

"I'm already used to doing that," she said. "Thank you, I think."

Stan laughed. "Don't mention it. It's not often I get to help someone who doesn't play poker."

Stan smiled at me. "I think she can help you now."

I nodded, believing him. After his little almost-slap demonstration, I had no doubt.

"Samantha, you come with me and Patty," I said. Then I glanced at Stan and Screamer. "We'll all meet out at the warehouse before six."

I noticed that even Stan nodded to that. I was hoping he was going to join us out there. Having a gambling god and all his powers along for the ride wouldn't hurt.

"Have a good lunch," Stan said, scooting his chair back and standing. "Nice meeting you, Samantha."

"Nice meeting you as well," Samantha said. "And thank you again, for whatever you did to me. It's amazing."

Suddenly, all the sounds of the restaurant pounded back in on the table like a wave hitting a beach. Madge moved toward us, a bubble half-popped in her mouth.

Stan was gone.

"Okay, someone tell me I'm not going completely nuts or dreaming," Samantha said.

"The gods do that to you," Screamer said, laughing. "They can drive you crazy."

"Gods?" Samantha asked.

"What can I get for you folks to eat?" Madge said, moving up and saving us from explaining to Samantha that there were levels of gods that existed that people prayed to all the time, but never really thought existed.

Madge stood close and towered over the table in a way I never wanted Madge to tower over me. It seemed as if the lights had gone dimmer in the restaurant. I looked up and could barely see Madge's forehead, her eyes, and the tip of her nose over her huge breasts.

I was in a breast eclipse. No wonder the lights had dimmed.

"Roast turkey sandwich," I said, staring at the menu instead of looking upward.

We all ordered and soon enough the light came back to the table as Madge turned and walked away.

Samantha giggled and whispered to Patty. "We're they as big as my enhanced senses told me they were?"

Patty nodded. "Bigger."

I started to glance at Madge as she walked away.

"Don't look," Screamer whispered to me.

It took every superpower I had, but I didn't.

Chapter Thirteen

The Bookkeeper

AFTER LUNCH, Samantha had taken her dog Sue for a short walk and then back to her room and left Sue there. With whatever Stan had done to Samantha's four remaining senses, she had said she wasn't going to need Sue as much.

When Samantha came walking out of the side door to the Horseshoe with her sunglasses on, but acting and moving as if she could see everything, I was a believer.

After the three of us were in Patty's car, with Patty driving, me in the front seat, and Samantha in the back, Patty asked Samantha what the new senses felt like.

"Same as before," Samantha said, laughing. "I'm still smelling, hearing, feeling and tasting like before. It's just that the first three are very heightened, and the information I'm getting from the three senses of smelling, hearing, and feeling is being put together better in my head, forming pretty good images of things."

I turned my head to look at her and ask a question, but Samantha pointed a finger at me. "There, I can tell you turned your head and are looking at me." She

reached forward and gently touched my cheek. "My combined senses even tell me exactly how far your face is from me."

"Like a computer putting data together and forming a composite," I said.

"Amazing," Patty said.

"It is," Samantha said. "This Stan person, whoever he was, did me a huge favor."

"And speaking of Stan," I said, turning to look at Patty as she headed the car out of the downtown area toward where I assumed The Bookkeeper lived. "How do you two know each other?"

She actually blushed a little.

"Oh, this might be a good story," Samantha said, laughing. "I don't need sight to tell she's blushing."

Patty actually blushed some more at that, then glanced at me, more than likely trying to get a read on how much I really wanted to know.

"Spit it out," I said, smiling at her.

"I met Stan about eighty years ago, at a club in a town called Garden City, up in Idaho. It was a gambling town on the edge of Boise at the time, full of nightclubs and card rooms and slot machines, before Idaho outlawed gambling of that type."

"Eighty years?" I said, staring at her, shocked. "That means you are one of the gods?"

"No, of course not," she said, smiling at me. "I'm at your level, only on the hotel management side. I help people who need help, just like you do."

"What do they call you?" I asked, smiling at her. "Front Desk Girl."

"Mostly just Patty," she said, laughing. "But I like that. I might use it."

"Explain the eighty years part," Samantha said from the back seat. "I have a sense you're only in your mid-thirties, not ninety or more."

"Yeah," I said. "I didn't know us superhero-types lived that long."

"No one's told you that yet, huh?" she said, smiling at me. "It's one of the benefits of the job. You're still new at this stuff. You'll learn."

The idea that I might live for a hundred years and look the same sort of stunned me. I just hadn't given getting old much thought, since in poker you get more respect if you look a little older and grizzled. I'd have to talk to Patty about this after we were done stopping the slot machines.

"So, do I even want to ask how old you really are?" Samantha said, "not that I'm going to believe any of this."

Patty smiled. "Always better to keep them guessing. Anyway, we're almost there."

"Nice avoidance on the Stan question," I said.

She just smiled at me while Samantha chuckled in the back seat.

I glanced out at the older-style ranch houses we were passing. Clearly Patty and Screamer had had dealings with this Bookkeeper person and didn't like him much.

"So who is this Bookkeeper?" Samantha asked before I could.

"He's a man who has spent his entire lifetime, and all his energy, working statistics. He sees patterns in things no one else does. He was granted longer life a hundred years back to keep studying in exchange for helping out in situations like this one."

"Everyone's not getting older," I said, shaking my head.

"I think I still am," Samantha said. "But at this point, I wouldn't even swear to that."

Both Patty and I laughed.

Then Patty said, "This guy is a real pig in just about every sense of the word. Don't let him get to you, because he enjoys that. If we stay focused on the slot machines, he'll be able to help us, I hope."

Patty stopped the car in front of a ranch-style house that needed painting and other repairs. All the windows had been boarded over from the inside, and there wasn't a live plant anywhere in the yard. The neighbors on both sides had put up tall fences to block out the sight as much as possible. Clearly, this was the one house that brought down the property values. There seemed to always be one in every neighborhood.

I couldn't talk much. I hated working on lawns and gardens more than just about anything besides going to a dentist. It was one of the reasons I lived in a double-wide mobile home in a mobile home park, where for a few extra bucks a month the owner of the park hired someone to keep the outside of my place looking at least decent.

We all climbed out into the hot afternoon. I was surprised at the intensity of the heat that hit my face after Patty's cool car. I moved to help Samantha, but it was clear she wasn't going to need my help. She got out easily, moved around the car, and expertly stepped up over the low curb and onto the sidewalk.

"This is going to be rough," Samantha said, turning to Patty and me. "I can smell this place clear out here."

All I could smell was the hot afternoon desert air.

"I can leave the car running and you can wait out here," Patty said. "If it's going to be too much for your new levels of senses."

"No, it will be fine," Samantha said. "I've got to learn to block some senses at times. Might as well be sooner than later. But I think all of us are going to need a shower after going in there."

I had a quick flash of the three of us standing naked together in a shower, then pushed the image aside. Samantha was married with a missing husband, Patty was a superhero. That sort of thing just wasn't going to happen.

"Let's get this over with," Patty said, starting up the front sidewalk that looked like it had been designed to weave in and around some sort of desert plants. But there were no plants, just gray gravel and dirt on both sides of the walk.

Samantha followed Patty and I brought up the rear.

Across the street, a neighbor peeked out of a closed curtain, and in the distance was the faint rumble of the freeway. Otherwise, this suburb was as quiet and dead as they came on a hot weekday afternoon.

Before Patty could even knock the door opened.

The man standing there was tiny, not more than five foot tall, with beady rat-eyes staring out over the tops of a thin pair of reading glasses. He had on gray, food-stained slacks and a dress shirt that might have been one color once, years before. For some reason, when Patty and Screamer had called this guy a pig, I had imagined him to be large and fat, not tiny and thin. He was bone thin, actually.

"Stan called ahead, told me you three were coming. Get in here before you let out all the cool air. Power doesn't come cheap, you know."

He turned away from the door, leaving it open for us to follow.

Patty shrugged and headed into the dark interior.

Samantha turned a little pale and followed, stumbling a little on the door step before regaining her balance.

A moment later I understood why she had stumbled. The smell coming from that open door was enough to gag a real pig. The smell was a cross between moldy cardboard, a backed-up toilet in a public restroom, and an un-emptied cat box. Samantha had been right, we were all going to need a shower after this.

I pushed the door closed and stopped waiting for my eyes to adjust to the dim light. The smell seemed to close down over me like a thick blanket. I had this instant desire to turn, open the door, and run for the street. But that wasn't an image of a superhero that I really wanted to give out. Superheroes dove in when all others ran. Patty and Samantha both were ahead of me, so I could make it as well.

With the door closed, it suddenly became very cool in the house, almost too cool. I could hear the sounds of a central air-conditioning system running from vents in the ceiling. The thing must have been turned up to full blast.

My eyes adjusted a little and I could see enough from the dim light coming from an adjacent room to tell the living room was packed to the ceiling with trash. And I do mean the ceiling, with stacks of paper, magazines, and books everywhere, forming a huge mound on both sides of the trail to the next room. I had read of a man in New York who had an apartment filled like this and a mound had collapsed on him and trapped him for two days.

I moved quickly down the canyon between walls of stacked paper, hoping against hope that I would brush nothing, that no stack would tumble onto me. Having Patty and a blind woman rescue me from a stack of paper might be more than my ego could handle.

I finally made it into the light area that must have been a dining room at one point. Now the entire room was filled with computers, monitors, and other electronic equipment. A big orange cat lay on the top of one computer, its tail flicking back and forth as it stared at me. So the cat explained one of the smells, the stacked paper and high air-conditioning explained the mold smell. That left the backed-up toilet smell which I had no intention of investigating.

The Bookkeeper was already in the high-backed chair in front of the computer, his fingers working over the keys as fast as I had ever seen anyone type. There were no other chairs, no place to even lean in the clutter, so the three of us just stood and watched him.

Actually, two of us watched him and Samantha did her other-senses thing.

After a long moment of typing he said, "I was wondering when you people would come talk to me. I had something like this happening projected years ago."

The man's voice was high and shrill, and even though he had said nothing really annoying, I felt annoyed at him anyway.

"You sent the note to the *Sun*?" I asked.

"Yeah," he said, still typing. "Had to get some of you idiots on the right track."

"And exactly what is the *right* track?" Patty asked, her voice low and very pointed.

Right at that moment, I decided I never wanted her angry at me. Not only did I have no idea what superpowers she had, the feeling of anger in her voice was enough to freeze this already cold house.

"Ghost slots," the little man said.

"We already knew that," I said. "We've already seen them in their home warehouse. What more can you help us with?"

"Well good for you," the little guy said, still typing while he looked up with a sneer on his rat-like face. Then, without looking he hit one key and pushed back. A moment later a high-speed printer spit out two sheets of paper. The little man handed the sheets to Patty.

"The exact times and locations the machines will appear over the next two days. That help?" He stared at me, daring me to say something.

I nodded at him, holding his gaze with mine. "A lot. So tell me, are there patterns in who these machines have been taking?"

"No," he said. "I've plugged in sixty-three names, including the name of this woman's husband."

He pointed to Samantha, then went on.

"No patterns in the victims."

"No one controlling them?" Patty asked.

The little man flicked the papers Patty was holding. "If there was outside control could I tell you when and where they were going to appear?"

"Not unless you knew who was controlling them."

"You're a funny man," he said, staring at me, his tiny black eyes seeming to dig right under my skin. "No one controls ghost slots, but they are machines and their actions can be predicted. If you aren't smart enough to stop them with that, I can't help you. Show yourselves out and close the door behind you tightly."

With that, he turned back to the computer screen and started typing.

"Contact Stan if you come up with something more," I said.

"There is nothing more."

Without another word, I led the way back through the towering stacks of paper and garbage to the front door.

Outside, I was hit in the face with a blast of hot, clean-smelling air. In all the years of being in and out of Las Vegas, I never thought I'd hear myself say I was glad to breathe the air there. But at that moment, any air besides the putrid cold air inside that house seemed like a drink from a mountain stream.

As Patty closed the door Samantha said, "Now I wish I had waited in the car."

Patty took her elbow and led her down the sidewalk toward the car.

"You going to be all right?" I asked as she slid into the back seat.

"If I don't throw up on the back of your head going into town, I'll be fine," she said.

Patty looked worried and Samantha just sat in the back seat looking green. I sat beside Patty, holding the two sheets of paper and staring at the locations of the future appearances of the ghost slots, not having a clue what to do next. I always figured that superheroes always came up with a plan after discovering important information.

I was plan-less.

At least I had another superhero beside me that might bail me out.

Halfway back to town I broke the silence and asked her. She had no idea what would be the best thing to do with the information either, besides giving it to the police.

Two plan-less superheroes and a nauseated blind woman. Not exactly the best team to save the entire casino industry and a whole bunch of people's lives.

Chapter Fourteen

The Troops are Gathered

I COULDN'T REMEMBER a shower that had felt so good. It was as if the smell from The Bookkeeper's house had stuck to me like a paste. I could almost see the water washing the smell off, sweeping it down the drain in a thick, gooey mess.

I stuffed the clothes I had been wearing into a plastic bag for hotel cleaning, and after I got out of the shower I called the front desk to come pick the bag up. I couldn't imagine leaving those clothes in my room.

I ran a wet wash cloth over my Poker Boy leather coat to clean it off both inside and out, then switched to a different hat, leaving the first one to air out beside the window. I still needed my superhero uniform for my powers to work, and no smell was going to stop that.

On the way down the elevator to the front desk area, I had this intense desire to just hit the second floor button, get off and go play some poker. I had come to Las Vegas for the tournament and hadn't done much more so far than just walk through the tournament area a few times.

Of course, I couldn't let the ghost slots keep taking people. I had the location of where they were going to show up next, and if The Bookkeeper was right, we could now at least save anyone new from getting taken.

Was Samantha's husband and the others who were taken still alive? Could these monsters be stopped? Those two questions alone were enough to get me right on past the World Series of Poker tournament area and down to the lobby.

I guess I was a superhero first, a poker player second.

Patty and Samantha were both standing near the front desk. Patty looked refreshingly clean, her skin almost glowing, the smile back on her fantastic face. She had her wet hair pulled back off her head, exposing my favorite mole. She had changed into black dress slacks and a Horseshoe employee's shirt that she had tucked in, shaping every wonderful thing about her body.

Her raspberry smell was strong enough to greet me like a hug as I joined them. She had said she was going to use the employee locker room to clean up. Clearly, she must have stashed a bottle of her favorite shampoo in her locker. Either that or the raspberry smell was just her natural smell. I was fine with either way.

Samantha also looked clean and freshly dressed in a tan blouse and skirt and sandals. She had on her black glasses, but none of her movements indicated she was blind in any respect. Stan's help with her other senses had given her back her freedom of movement completely.

"Feeling better?" I asked her.

"Still a touch green around the gills," she said. "But getting better by the moment."

"So it's proven," Patty said as we all turned and headed out the door and into the warm afternoon heat. "Men do take longer in showers. I even had time to make copies of the list we got."

She handed me a copy.

"I didn't know it was a race," I said, giving her my best disarming smile. "But under the right kind of pressure I can be pretty darned fast with a bar of soap."

Samantha snorted, but Patty just smiled at me and said nothing. I had no idea what she was thinking at that moment. She was impossible for me to read in any fashion.

Right at that moment, I would have traded a bunch of my superpowers for Johnny and Geneva's ability to be hooked up to Patty in thought. I could only hope that Patty was thinking of me in the shower, in a *nice* way.

The image of Patty in the shower with me, handing me the soap with that smile of hers made me trip over the curb and stumble.

"You all right?" Patty asked as she moved around her car.

I nodded, not trusting myself to say anything at that moment. Every time I turned around, this wonderful woman was surprising me, making me stumble, making me have wonderfully rude thoughts about her. I couldn't remember the last time a woman had had this kind of effect on me.

Maybe it was the raspberry.

Maybe it was one of her superpowers. I sure hoped to find out at some point, after all this was over.

With me in the co-pilot seat and Samantha in the back, Patty expertly drove her car out the old Boulder Highway toward the warehouse where the ghost slots lived. The next location The Bookkeeper said the slots would show was in an old casino out on the same highway at a little after seven this evening.

I planned on giving a copy of the list to Johnny so that he could have the area in that casino guarded to keep anyone else from being taken. But I really hoped to find a way to stop the machines before then.

We rode in silence through a few stop lights, then Samantha asked, "Do you think Ben is still alive?"

Patty glanced up into the rearview mirror, then at me.

I turned as much as my seat belt would let me turn to face Samantha. "I don't honestly know," I said. "What does your gut tell you?"

"That he is," Samantha said.

"Trust that feeling," Patty said.

A car-sick superhero wasn't going to be much good to anyone.

"I agree," I said. "There're a lot of things in this world that happen and are not easily explained. One is the connection between a couple in love. It's as powerful a sense as the ones you are using to *see* without your eyes. Let that feeling come forward and you'll know your answer."

Samantha was nodding, clearly lost inside her own head.

"The connection is real," Patty said. "If you know he's still alive, then he is."

"Thank you," Samantha said, her voice quivering a little. "And thank you both for helping me."

"It's what we do," Patty said as she accelerated the car away from a stop light, weaving through traffic like an expert.

I turned back around to watch the road ahead. The last thing I needed at this point was to get motion sickness. A carsick superhero wasn't going to be much good to anyone. Facing backward in a car always made me carsick, even one being driven as smoothly as Patty was driving.

The clock on Patty's dashboard said ten minutes until five. We were going to be an hour early for the six o'clock gathering. I hoped Stan and Screamer would both show up early as well. The information they had gone after was going to be critical in how we stopped these machines. We needed to get the machines to spit back out the people it had taken, or find where they had been taken to, then figure out what was powering the slots, and how to turn them off.

I had no clear idea how any of this was going to work, but my sense was to trust the team and it would all come together.

In the warehouse parking lot the only car was a marked police car sitting directly in front of the door. When Patty pulled up and stopped, one of the officers climbed out and walked toward the car.

Patty put her window down, letting in a blast of warm air. She smiled at the officer. "I'm Patty Ledgerwood."

She indicated me, then Samantha. "This is Conway Moore, and Samantha MacDuff."

The officer nodded. "Detective State says you have clearance to go in. He's on his way here. Should be arriving in less than ten minutes."

Patty glanced at me, then smiled at the officer. "We'll wait for him out here."

"I'll tell him," the officer said, then turned and headed back for his car as Patty slid up her window and turned up the air conditioning to cool the car quickly.

"Nice in here," Stan said from the back seat.

"Cripes!" Samantha said as Patty and I spun around to see Stan sitting next to Samantha in the back seat.

"Ring a bell or something next time," Samantha said, both her hands on her chest. "Not sure if my heart can handle that again."

Stan laughed. "Sorry about that."

For the first time, I actually thought that moving up the ranks to one of the gods might be a good idea. Stan's ability to pop in and out and move around without cars and planes would sure save a lot of time and money. I could play in the World Series and sleep at nights in my own bed. But I doubted the trade-off would be worth the politics and infighting that went on among the gods.

"How are the enhanced senses working for you?" Stan asked Samantha

"Perfectly," Samantha said. "I hope you're not going to take them away after we solve all this."

Stan laughed. "Of course not. But we may ask you to help us once in a while in trade."

"That's a deal I can live with," Samantha said.

"Power?" I asked Stan. "Any idea what is powering those ghost slots?"

"Nothing from this plain of existence," Stan said. "Bernie in maintenance tried to trace the power from the things in there, but couldn't do it. It's like the power circles back in from inside."

Bernie was the gambling god in charge of casino maintenance and operations. I had heard his nickname was Back-up Bernie.

"So shutting the power off to those things from the outside isn't an option," Patty said.

"Afraid not," Stan said.

"Something about that circling thing," I said, releasing my seat belt so I could turn and face Stan in the back. "Any chance the power is coming from the people it has taken."

"You mean like the myth says?" Patty asked.

I nodded.

"Possible," Stan said. "Bernie couldn't find any yes or no on that either. This has got him as stumped as the rest of us."

I hated it when gods said they were stumped. It made me feel even less capable of saving Samantha's husband and all the rest. What could a minor superhero do that the gods couldn't do?

"Sorry I couldn't be of more help," Stan said. "Good luck in there."

"You're not coming in with us?" I asked, but by the time my question reached the back seat, Stan was gone.

"Someone's got to put a bell on him," Samantha said. "So he can warn us when he's coming and going."

"So the gods are as clueless as we are at this point," Patty said, turning to look at me with those big brown eyes of hers. "Any ideas?"

"A few," I said.

I didn't add that all my really great ideas concerned her naked in a shower and me holding the soap.

I didn't have a clue what to do about the ghost slot machines, saving over seventy lives, and stopping the ruin of the entire gambling industry.

"Great," she said. "Because I sure don't."

At that moment, Johnny and Geneva drove up beside Patty's car and stopped, followed closely by Screamer's car. It seemed it was time to get to work and do some superhero-type deeds, if I could just figure out which deeds we needed to do.

Chapter Fifteen

A (sort of) Plan Forms

ALL SEVEN OF US moved into the warehouse and stood just inside the door in a large circle, surrounded by thousands of dead slot machines.

The place was warm, but not as hot as outside, and it echoed, giving all of our voices a feedback quality. The warehouse smelled of dry dust with a faint burnt electrical odor over everything. The big space would have given me the creeps even without the ghost slot machines living back along the side wall.

Patty stood beside me on my right, Samantha on my left.

Johnny and Geneva stood across from me. Both had occasional looks in their eyes as if listening to something in the distance. They weren't touching, but if I had my guess, their power to hear each others thoughts didn't need touch anymore.

Screamer stood to Patty's right with a grunge-looking man with long hair black pulled back, a nose ring, and tattoos showing on most areas of bare skin, including a naked woman along his neck that twisted and moved every time the guy turned his head. He wore jeans and a loose shirt and looked like he hadn't had a good meal in years. He carried a beat-up blue backpack in one hand and an unlit cigarette in the other.

Screamer had introduced him as Brian, but said everyone just called him Tech, since he was so good with computers and machines.

I had expected Screamer to bring an older man, someone who had actually worked on the old-style slot machines back before everything went computers. But if Screamer thought this guy could do the job, then he could do it.

I started off by asking Johnny and Geneva what they had discovered. They gave a quick rundown of how they had eliminated any last thoughts of this being a magic trick, then told us about their meeting with Rees, a major magician, often finishing each other's sentences as they spoke.

"Wow," Tech said, staring at Geneva and Johnny. "You actually talked with Rees "The Mechanic" in his home?"

"Yeah," Johnny said, clearly half-disgusted at the question.

"He's the best there is, man," Tech said.

"So anything come of the meeting with him?"

"Just that he was surprised about the people being taken when the machine is showing a jackpot," Geneva said.

"Real surprised," Johnny said.

"You sure on that jackpot part?" Tech asked Geneva.

Both her head and Johnny's nodded like they were being pulled by the same string.

"Rees said that being taken, actually losing on jackpots just isn't the way the machines work."

"What's that mean?" Screamer asked Tech about a half second before I could ask him the same question. The security tape we saw of the machine taking Ben out of the Horseshoe wasn't set at such an angle that we could see the reels on the face of the machine Ben was playing.

"Man, it means that someone got inside those old things and reset a half-dozen different settings on the reel board."

"So someone is behind this after all?" Johnny asked.

"No kidding," Tech said. "No other way a machine can get set like that. Can't happen accidentally that's for sure."

"Why's that?" I asked, wanting to be very sure.

Tech stared at me for a moment. "There's a solenoid on the reel board that works like a switch to determine jackpots. I don't even think a normal solenoid in one of these old sixties machines has a setting for full payout every time. There wouldn't be enough coins in the machine for one, and second there would be no reason to even have such a setting designed in. No, this is special work here by someone."

I wasn't sure I understood exactly what he meant, but I nodded and let it go for the moment.

Johnny indicated we should hold on a second, then pulled out his cell phone and made a quick call. When someone answered he identified himself, asked for a Captain Walk, then said, "Captain, I've got a lead on the disappearances. I need someone to get the records from Standard Slots on anyone granted access to the old Valley Slots graveyard warehouse."

He listened for a moment, then said, "Just the last month should be enough. Thanks."

I nodded to him as he clicked his cell phone shut, then turned back to Tech. "So how do we change those settings back?"

"And get my husband out of that thing," Samantha said. "If that's where he's at."

Tech shrugged, causing the naked woman on his neck to contort into a very unnatural posture. "I figure we first got to check out what's powering the whole mess, shut that off. Do that and I can open up the machine and reset everything, maybe replace that faulty solenoid."

I stared at him. I had seen those machines come and go, once on a tape, once up close. I couldn't imagine anyone simply walking up to one of them and opening the front.

"Are we going to need a key to open the things?" Screamer asked.

Tech held up his old backpack. "Got that, buddy."

"In case we can't stop these things quickly," Patty said to Johnny, "You need to get some people at these locations at these times."

Now Available
from all your favorite booksellers in trade paper and electronic editions.

She handed Johnny a copy of the sheets that The Bookkeeper had given us showing where the machines were going to appear next.

"You found out who is controlling these things?" Geneva asked, glancing at the paper in Johnny's hand as he read it.

"No," Patty said, "but we know who sent your newspaper that first note. A guy called The Bookkeeper who uses math to predict these things."

"And you are sure he has nothing to do with this?" Johnny asked.

"Completely," I said.

Johnny nodded. "So we have about two hours until the machines shift, if this is to be believed. So what do we do next?"

"I suppose we see if Tech and I can get the face of one of those things open."

At that moment Johnny's cell phone rang and he answered it, listening for a moment before saying, "You're sure?"

He listened again for a short moment, with the rest of us standing there in the warehouse staring at him.

Then he said "Thanks."

He clicked his phone closed and shook his head. "The last man to be in this warehouse was almost three weeks ago. A guy named Harry Timmer."

"Oh, man," Tech said. "Old Harry's been missing for three weeks."

"That's what my Captain just said."

"You know him?" Screamer asked.

"Sure," Tech said. "Everyone in the business knows old Harry. He's a retired slot tech from the days before computers took over the machines. He liked working on the old mechanicals, fixing them up and selling them as novelty items. He was always scrounging for parts. Made some good money doing it too."

"So he'd know how to reset the slots?" Johnny asked.

Tech laughed. "He could make those old machines dance if he wanted. But, man, if you're thinkin' he's behind all this, you've flat lost it. Old Harry wouldn't hurt a fly, let alone use the machines he loved for something like taking people."

"Maybe he was forced to," Johnny said.

Tech shook his head, making the woman on his neck dance the twist. "I can't see him doing this."

"So let's go take a look at these things," I said. "Johnny, you and I will take off the tarp. Tech, you see what you can see, but don't touch them just yet."

"Got you it in one on that," Tech said.

I led the group to the far aisle and down toward the ghost slots. I could see faint colors coming from under the tarp, pulsing like a warning light. And the closer we got, the closer I wanted to get, as their unnatural attraction was pulled at me even through the tarp.

Patty, Geneva, Samantha and Screamer stopped about twenty paces from the machines, leaving Johnny and me and Tech walking slowly at the machines like three old-west marshals headed toward a gunfight.

I could feel the pull of the things getting stronger with every step. A little voice in my head was telling me to sit down, just play a little.

What could it hurt?

Tech stopped across the aisle facing the slots and stood waiting as I went to the far side of the machines and carefully grabbed the tarp without touching any metal.

Johnny did the same on his side and then nodded at me.

"Now," I said.

We both yanked at the same time, pulling the tarp down and away.

The entire warehouse again lit up with the rainbow of colors coming off the glowing Saturn Slots. The things seemed to have so much energy that they were pulsing.

"Oh, man," Tech said, stepping back.

"Cripes," Screamer said.

The moment the tarp was gone the pull to sit down and play was fantastically stronger. I could feel myself struggling with the desire. And I had no doubt I wasn't the only one feeling it as Geneva stepped forward and took hold of Johnny's arm and drew him a few steps back.

Over the years as Poker Boy I had run into my share of things I wanted to just run away from. But as a superhero, I just had never done that. I guess running scared just wasn't part of the job description. But that said, right at that moment, I wanted to run as fast and as far from those machines as I could get. However, I think I was so scared my feet didn't want to move.

So I just stared at the machines, at the blinking lights, at the bright colors, at the incredible image of Saturn and its rings dominating the area over the machines and the four wooden chairs.

I took a deep breath and dug down deep into what made me a good poker player. I had been stared-down by the best players in the world, bluffed and intimidated, yet I had always remained cool and level, no matter how much money had been at stake.

Now there was something a lot more than money at stake. People's lives. This was not the time for Poker Boy to break.

So I stared back at the four machines, daring them to take me down, daring them to get to me or anyone else around me.

After a moment, I realized I had won. My mind had done its trick of putting things into compartments, just like it did with the fear I felt on the final tables of big tournaments. The force the machines were using to try to draw me to them was now trapped off to one side of my mind. It was still there, but it wasn't going to affect what I did, how I played this hand.

Maybe being able to do that was also one of my superpowers. If it was I was going to have to figure out a name for it. Something like my Fear-Away Power.

I glanced around at the others.

Johnny and Geneva were also doing fine it seemed, keeping each other level.

Screamer had a confused look on his face, like he was hearing something in the distance. I had no idea how the pull on these machines would affect his power.

Patty tried a half-smile at me. It was enough to show me she was fine as well. As Front Desk Girl, I was sure she had dealt with more angry people than I had. More than likely, she had a way of compartmentalizing this type of energy like I had. Maybe her own special superpower.

Tech was still standing facing the machines, but his look had changed from fear and shock to curiosity. It seemed the fearlessness of youth was serving him well.

"Ben's in there," Samantha said, moving toward the machines like she was a zombie in a bad movie. "I can sense him. He's trapped in there."

I stepped across the front of the machines and took her by the shoulders, stopping her five paces from the machines beside Johnny and Geneva. "What do you mean you can sense him?"

"He's in there," she said.

Everything about her seemed locked on the machines. She clearly wasn't aware of where she was at the moment for some reason. She half struggled against me, but I wouldn't let her take another step toward those monsters.

"How do you know?" Johnny asked her, stepping up and blocking her from the machines.

With that she seemed to come back to the warehouse, back to a presence in her own body.

She turned to face me. "My new senses," she said, clearly checking in with herself.

"New senses?" Johnny asked.

"She's blind," I said to Johnny, "so Stan at lunch gave her other senses, some extra power so that she could help us out. She's just getting used to them."

"Stan?" Geneva asked.

"Long story," I said, not wanting to waste time right at that point explaining gambling gods to someone who wasn't going to understand. "Just believe that like you two, she has some special senses."

Both Geneva and Johnny again nodded as one.

"So what did you sense?" I asked Samantha.

"Still sensing," she said. "Ben is close. He's in that machine and very much alive. I can tell he's confused and a little angry and getting slowly tired."

"Is his energy being drained?" Patty asked. She had moved up to stand beside Samantha.

Samantha nodded slowly. "Maybe. He's getting tired."

Patty glanced at me. "The myth."

I nodded, agreeing. The power was more than likely coming from the people inside. And for the first time in some time I had an idea on how to solve this problem. Samantha held the solution to what we were facing. If she could somehow link to her husband and transfer that information to me, I might be able to figure out what to do next.

"Screamer," I said, motioning for him to come up beside us.

"Samantha, you know how Screamer put the images of what Patty saw into your mind?"

"You want him to put what I'm sensing into yours?" Samantha said.

"If you don't mind."

"Anything to help Ben get out of there," she said, the strength in her voice clear and strong, now that she believed her husband was alive.

I glanced at Screamer and he nodded his agreement. He touched my arm, then Samantha's arm.

For a moment everything went black, as if someone had turned out the lights in a windowless room. Then I realized what I was experiencing was Samantha's blindness.

I opened my mind up to the other senses, amazed at how the warehouse around me came back into focus in sort of an overlay with what I was seeing with my own eyes, only vastly enhanced.

I could see the heat of each person, smell them, hear even their stomach's rumbling. And all the thousands of sensory inputs were coming together to form a picture without color, yet very clear and accurate.

I also suddenly knew Samantha's memories, her fears, everything about her, and I had no doubt she knew everything about me.

"Can you hear him?" Samantha asked.

"Yes," Screamer said.

I realized there was a person, a presence I didn't recognize from my own world, yet was very, very familiar to

Samantha. I could see what she meant by sensing him. He was there, inside the machine.

Ben was alive.

All the people that had been taken were alive. I could sense that as well. They were existing in the wires, in the circuits of that machine. To them it felt like white corridors, forever twisting around on each other, with no exit. Most of them seemed to be walking those white corridors, getting more and more tired.

Of the four machines, it seemed that only the one on the right had been taking people. They were all in there. I somehow just knew that fact.

"Can you communicate with Ben?" Johnny asked from a place that seemed outside the world I was focused on. Part of my mind was in the white spaces of the circuits of the machine, part of my mind was still aware of the warehouse, with Samantha's heightened senses as an overlay.

I felt Samantha try to contact her husband. I felt her mind call out to him.

But Ben didn't respond, didn't hear her.

Screamer let go of both of us, breaking the image of the white place where the people were trapped.

Breaking my contact with Samantha's enhanced hearing and smells and feelings. It was as if I had suddenly gone from a full color movie to a black-and-white one. It was shocking the difference in attention to other senses rounded out the world around a person.

"You all right?" Screamer asked Samantha.

She nodded. "Ben can't hear us. But he's in there. All of the people are."

I glanced at Screamer and he nodded in agreement.

"Can you talk to him," Johnny asked. "Get those inside to shut down the machine?"

"No," I said.

That way was a dead-end. But I was getting a glimmering of a plan.

"Tech," I said, "anything you can do to open those things up?"

"I don't see why not," he said. "But I'd be afraid to do anything unless I was completely sure what I was doing would kick those people out of there."

"I agree with you there," I said. "Your friend Harry seems to be the first to have disappeared in there. If you could talk to him, you think the two of you might come up with something?"

"Him on the inside, me out here?" Tech said. "Sure."

I nodded and turned to look at Johnny.

"I'll do it," both Johnny and Geneva said at the exact same moment.

"Do what?" Samantha asked.

"Stick a nickel in that thing and go inside to find Harry," I said.

"That's bug-nuts crazy," Tech said.

"Oh, no," Samantha said.

Patty just looked pale.

Screamer shook his head.

The silence in the warehouse was smothering.

Chapter Sixteen

Contact at Twenty-Four Volts

I STARED AT JOHNNY as he watched through Geneva's eyes what was happening in the casino with the ghost slots. At one point he had shouted "Get her out of there!"

Then he had laughed and explained to all of us standing there staring at him, worried, that an old woman had sat down at the ghost slots. He said that Patty and Geneva and a cop had managed to stop the woman before she got a coin into the slot. His laughing and shaking his head cut the tension a little in the warehouse among the five of us.

Screamer and I stood next to Johnny, ready to help him in any way we could under the circumstances.

"Geneva's sitting down at the machine," he said.

Suddenly he was very serious again and I could hear the worry in his voice and see it on his face. He didn't like this, and I didn't much like it either, but it had come to be our best choice.

And our only plan.

Tech was afraid to touch the machine for fear he would do something that would kill all the people inside. He wanted the help of the old guy I was betting had reset the slots in the first place, Harry Timmer. But Harry was inside the slots, and had been from the start. So someone had to go in and talk to old Harry and relay the information out to Tech.

The connection between Geneva and Johnny made one of them a natural for the job. I didn't like it, but none of us could come up with another way of trying to rescue all those people inside there.

As Geneva said to one of my objections, "You often have to jump into water and endanger yourself to rescue a drowning person."

She was right. I knew she was right. I just didn't much like the pool she was jumping into. And neither did anyone else.

"She's put a coin in and pulled the handle," Johnny said.

Suddenly he grabbed his head and bent forward, as if he had a bad hangover.

Screamer was about to grab him to hold him up, but I waived him off. Whatever was happening to Geneva and Johnny, I didn't want Screamer feeling it as well.

Johnny moaned a few seconds later, but remained standing, bent over, his hands grabbing the sides of his head like he was trying to hold his skull together.

Then he screamed.

It was like no scream I could have ever imagined coming from a big, powerful detective. It sounded like a combination of him and Geneva, high and sharp at the same time as low and guttural. It sent chills up my spine.

The scream echoed through the warehouse, then Johnny tipped forward onto his hands and knees on the concrete.

"Help him!" Samantha said.

"Don't touch him yet," I said, waiving everyone away. "We need his connection with Geneva clear."

A moment later the slots shimmered into view, bringing back with them the intense desire to go sit down and just try my luck. But of course, putting a nickel in that slot machine at this point wouldn't have much luck involved. Just stupidity, which was how I often felt about playing slot machines even when they weren't ghost slots.

Around us, the gray of the warehouse had changed back to reflected colors and energy from the lights on the machine. Every face, every old slot machine covered in gray dust now had multiple colors as the image of Saturn glowed brighter than any light in the warehouse.

Being careful to not touch any of Johnny's skin to jeopardize his connection with Geneva, I bent down and he let me help him to his feet.

"What happened?" Screamer asked.

Johnny took a deep breath. "The shock and the pain knocked her out."

"Shock shouldn't have been that bad," Tech said. "Those machines are run on twenty-four volts."

"You all right?" I asked. I could feel his shoulders shaking a little, but with each passing second he seemed to be gaining control.

He nodded slowly. "I think so, but I'm betting on one hell of a headache."

"Is Geneva all right?" Samantha asked.

Again he nodded slowly. "I think so. She's knocked out, but I can still hear her thoughts under her dreams."

"Okay, now that's got to be real weird," Tech said.

I had to agree with Tech on that one. Listening to a person's dreaming mind must seem like watching a bad psychedelic movie while being very drunk.

"Actually, at the moment, she's dreaming she's swimming to the surface of a pool," Johnny said, his eyes staring off into the distance. "Very peaceful, no panic or worries. Hang on. I see what she's doing. She's trying to reach the surface and wake up."

We all stared at him until he finally nodded and turned to look at me. "She's all right. She's awake and she's in there."

He pointed to the ghost slot machine.

"Oh, wow, cool," Tech said. "What's it look like?"

"White corridors," Johnny said. "Everything is shades of white, including her clothing, hair and skin. All the colors are gone from everything. She feels normal-sized and very lost in the maze of corridors. Nothing seems to have any corners either, including the corridors. They're more like round tubes that twist and move off in different directions."

It was like no scream I could have ever imagined coming from a big, powerful detective.

"I'll bet she's in the electrical wiring," Tech said. "Have her move until she finds a junction area and then describe it."

"She agreed," Johnny said.

"Is she meeting some of the others in there?"

"She is," Johnny said. "And she's already asking for Harry."

We all stood silent for a moment watching Johnny, who was with Geneva inside the ghost slots. After a moment, Johnny said, "It's weird, because I'm in there with her, and she's out here with me at the same time. It's helping her stay calm being here through my eyes. Also weird that everyone in there that she meets somehow knows they are inside a machine."

I had no idea how people trapped as energy inside the wiring of a machine could know where they were. I couldn't imagine there being windows out of the side of the wiring. But at this point, nothing about ghost slots would surprise me.

"Tech, she's at an intersection," Johnny said. "One corridor into a wide triangle area, three corridors out side-by-side."

Tech seemed to think for a minute, then said, "I'm betting she's at the electrical junction sending power to the wheels.

SMITH'S Monthly

You need to have her turn around and go back the way she came."

"You think you might know where Harry is at?" I asked Tech, surprised at how definite he sounded.

"If I was stuck in there, and knew where I was, I'd be at the solenoid on the reel board."

"Solenoid?" Patty asked as she came back toward us down the rows of dead slot machines. "Sounds like she's in there and just fine."

"She is," I said.

The relief on Patty's face was clear.

I was very happy to see her back from the casino. I felt more comfortable with her beside me on this problem. It was as if I got a "balance energy" from her, keeping my mind clear. Next time I made the final table of a big tournament, I might ask her to come and watch from the stands, just for that energy boost.

"The solenoid is an electric coil used as a control and switching devise," Tech said. "Its purpose is setting payouts on the machines built in this period. It's located on what they called the reel board, the electrical panel area that controls the three reels of the machine."

Patty stopped right beside me as I asked Tech the next logical question. "Is that one of the things that would have had to have been changed to make the machines hit jackpots all the time?"

"The main thing," Tech said.

"Hang on," Johnny said, holding his hands up. "Someone Geneva just ran into knows Harry."

There was a pause as we all waited for Johnny's next statement. Then he smiled at me. "Says he's been trying to help Harry figure out a way to escape. He's taking Geneva to Harry now."

"Great!" I said.

I turned to Screamer. "I'm going to need you to hook up Tech and Johnny, so Tech can talk directly to Harry. Make sure he gets everything right. Can you do that?"

"Easy," Screamer said.

"Hang on," Tech said, "you're saying that I can talk through Johnny, then through Geneva, to Harry who is inside that machine?"

"Actually, through me first," Screamer said, smiling at the young guy with all the tattoos.

"A conversation through three heads," Tech said. "I'm going to be lucky to not need counseling after this is finished."

I agreed with him on that. Running around in Samantha's head earlier had left me unsettled. I knew way too many things about her that I wanted to forget. Too much about her dreams, her fights with her husband, her sexual pleasures. And she knew the same stuff about me, which I didn't really want to think about.

I wasn't sure how Johnny and Geneva had made a constant connection between them work so quickly over the last day, but after my short romp with Samantha's mind, I now knew that I didn't want to see what Patty was thinking, or even know how she felt about me. And I didn't want her seeing my daydreams about her in the shower and me with a bar of raspberry soap. It was going to be a lot better learning about her slowly, blindly, one question at a time, one nude shower at a time.

More fun, too.

"She's almost to where Harry is at," Johnny said.

"Ready?" I asked Screamer.

"As I'll ever be."

I motioned for Tech to come over closer to Johnny while Screamer placed

132

himself between the two. Samantha and I and Patty stepped back out of the way.

"Here we go," Screamer said, winking at me.

Then he reached out and first touched Tech's arm, right below a tattoo of an eagle, then touched Johnny's arm.

Tech's worry left his face as his eyes sort of glazed over. Clearly he wasn't seeing the aisle of the old slot machine warehouse anymore. He was inside the slots, inside Geneva's mind.

Screamer looked at me, clearly in his eyes and reported what he was seeing. "Harry's sitting down in there. He seems very, very tired and old. I think the energy drain caused by the machine is almost too much for him.

"Yeah, it's me, Harry," Tech said out loud.

Screamer smiled and sort of rolled his eyes, making it clear to us that he thought it funny that some people had to talk when thinking to another person.

"Don't ask," Tech said. "I don't even understand how this works."

All of us smiled at that.

"I've been feeling that same way," Samantha whispered to Patty.

"So what did you do?" Tech asked the unseen Harry.

A moment later Tech said, "Oh, shit."

None of us smiled at that.

Screamer almost whispered to us, "Harry said he was the one that caused this all to happen, and he's very sorry."

"You're kidding?" Tech said. "You know how much pain and worry and fear you've caused."

A long pause followed that.

"So any idea exactly how many people are in here?" Tech asked.

Pause.

"So what's going to reverse this?"

Nothing for a moment. Screamer seemed to be listening and had stopped reporting to us the other side of the conversation.

"If it's that easy, how come you haven't done it before now?" Tech asked.

A very long pause that seemed to make the silence of the warehouse grow in intensity and power.

"Oh," Tech said.

"Oh, shit," Screamer said. He looked like he was about to be very sick.

"Impossible," Johnny said, shaking his head, the look of worry and fear very strong in his face.

"I'll be back," Tech said, then pulled his arm away from Screamer and staggered a few paces away.

Screamer let go of Johnny and turned to walk a few paces away.

Johnny just slumped to the concrete floor and put his head in his hands.

I glanced at the very worried look on Patty's face, then stepped forward toward Tech. "What happened. What was that all about?"

"No problem reversing the process Harry started," Tech said, staring at the floor without looking up at me. "Harry got sucked into these ghost slots while scrounging in here for parts. He figured he could reconfigure the machines from the inside to spit him back out, but he missed a setting, reversed a few things, and got the machines taking more people on jackpots."

"So he's the reason this has all happened?" I asked.

"Yeah, Harry trying to save himself caused all this," Screamer said, turning back to face me. "No wonder no one could figure out what was going on, or who was behind it."

Tech nodded. "He's feeling damn bad about it, too. And he has since figured out how to solve the problem and set the machines from in there to spit out everyone."

"So why hasn't he done that?" Samantha asked, moving up beside me. "Why hasn't he let my Ben out of there?"

"One chair," Patty said.

I turned and glanced at her, then at the one old wooden chair attached to the front of the Saturn slot machine that held everyone. She was right. Where would the people go?

"One chair," Screamer said, agreeing. "There are one hundred and three people in that machine right now counting Geneva and Harry. They would all appear in that chair, reformed in their bodies, like coins dropping out of a pay-out chute. About three per second."

"Not possible," Samantha said.

"That's right," Johnny said from where he sat on the floor. "They would all be killed, their bodies materialized together in a massive pile of flesh and bones."

"And there's no way to slow it down?" Samantha demanded.

"There is no setting in the machine that regulates the rate of payout," Tech said. "Just the amount."

"So get Harry to set the payout at one," I said.

Again Tech shook his head. "That's what Harry has been working on, but again, there are no single unit payouts on this machine, and nothing goes that low in any setting he can find. And if he can't find it from in there, it doesn't exist.

"How many is the minimum?" Patty asked.

"Three," Tech said.

"Three, two, one-hundred," Tech said. "It's not going to matter.

I stared at the single chair in front of the old slot machine and tried to imagine three human bodies appearing there in one second. Tech was right. Three or one hundred. They would all die.

And die horribly.

Chapter Seventeen

Two Superheroes, No Soap

THE SILENCE in the big warehouse became intense as we all were lost in our own thoughts. It was as if we were sitting in a big, neon-lit tomb, the gray and dust of the place pushed back and barely held at bay by the bright colors of the enemy machines.

The pull from the ghost slots was still strong, but I had put the feeling off to one side and was ignoring it, and it seemed the rest were dealing with it as well, although none of us got within four paces of the things.

Over one hundred people were trapped in that one ghost slot machine, and there was no way to get them out safely. That fact was enough to depress just about anyone. And I couldn't even imagine how Johnny was feeling. He shared his mind with Geneva, and she was going to die with him inside her head. More than likely it would kill him as well, or do so much damage as to never let him function normally again.

I couldn't let that happen. There had to be a way to save them. There had to be.

We just had to find it.

I glanced around at the team. Johnny was sitting on the concrete floor. He was the closest to the machine, staring at it, clearly in contact with Geneva.

Samantha sat cross-legged a few feet behind him, her back against a tarp-covered machine.

Screamer was pacing up and down and up and down the aisle, his steps silent on the concrete floor.

Tech had walked twenty feet away and now stood with his back to everyone, not moving.

Patty stood beside me, her beautiful head tipped back as if she were studying something up near the roof of the big warehouse.

I moved over beside Johnny and knelt down. "How long does Geneva think they have in there?"

"Harry's been in there the longest and he's very weak," Johnny said. "There are a few others like him."

"Thanks," I said, standing and letting Johnny and Geneva go back to being together in their minds.

Not only was the town about to explode with the news of all the missing people, but if Harry died in there, drained of energy by the machine, there would be no chance at all of any rescue without sending Tech or someone else inside to set the machine.

I moved back over beside Patty and tapped her shoulder. She looked at me with those big brown eyes of hers and I almost forgot that I wanted to talk to her. I indicated that she should follow me toward the warehouse door. She nodded and without a word to any of the others we moved away.

I didn't exactly know what I wanted to talk to her about. She was a superhero like I was, had been around a lot longer than I had been, and she kept me balanced. If I was going to think out loud about this project, it made sense to think out loud to her. And right now, I really needed to do some out-loud thinking.

On really tough cases, like this one, I usually went back to my room, paced and talked to myself, trying to work out a solution. Granted, that wasn't the way I did things on a poker table, where I solved problems silently, without even showing emotion on my face unless I wanted the emotion shown. But this was a lot more serious than a poker tournament. Lives were at stake and I didn't need to keep my emotions hidden.

From the light coming in the open door, it was clear that the sun was starting to set. I could feel that the heat outside was still pretty intense from the way it poured in the open door. More than likely the heat wouldn't fade until closer to midnight.

Patty and I stopped and faced each other near the door. At that moment, as if I were playing a hand I was unsure of and was suddenly convinced my play was right, I knew what to say.

"Time," I said. "Time is our problem."

Patty nodded. "Three people per second materializing into the same space. It doesn't give us enough time to get each person out of the way before the next person starts to appear."

"Exactly," I said, now seeing one possible solution. "So we stop time between each person."

Patty stared at me like I had said something really silly, then slowly smiled. "Can you do that?"

I shrugged. "Stan told me I could do it when I needed to do it. But I have never needed to try, to be honest. And he can do it as well."

Patty sort of looked off into space for a second, then said, "I have the ability to stretch time for myself," she said. "It doesn't really stop, but it stretches for me so I can get a lot of paperwork done for customers and make it seem fast to them."

"Can you control that?"

"Sort of," she said. "Normally, it just sort of clicks-in, if you know what I mean."

"I do," I said. "Most of my powers are the same way. Sometimes I can bring them on with really intense focus, but usually they are just there when I need them."

"Me too," Patty said.

"Well, we need them now," I said. "Can you stretch time with me included?"

She looked worried, the first time I had ever seen a worried look on her face. "I can try."

She reached out and took my hand. For a moment I thought I heard the Hallelujah Chorus sung by a one-hundred member choir with me singing the lead. Her skin was as soft, as firm, and wonderful as I had imagined it would be. The image of her holding my hand while we stood naked in a shower flashed over my mind and I let myself go with the image for a moment before I realized what I was doing.

Somehow, I dropped the bar of raspberry soap, pushed the thoughts back, took a deep breath, and focused on the situation. Luckily I had that kind of control as a poker player, otherwise I might have pulled her into my arms and kissed her right there.

But I had control.

Control.

Control.

I repeated the word a few times more and was solidly back in the warehouse holding Patty's hand as she tried to slow down time around us.

"I think it's working," she said, smiling at me.

I glanced around. Where we were at near the door there was no way of telling.

Nothing was moving in the slot machine graveyard.

"Can you hold it until we get back near the others?"

"I think so," she said. "Just don't let go of my hand. You're giving me energy I don't normally feel."

I didn't tell her what energy she was giving me. I figured that would be more appropriate later, after we rescued everyone.

Hand-in-hand, like two school kids, we walked back to the aisle with the ghost slots and the rest of the team. No one there seemed to be moving, but they hadn't been moving much before we left either.

Then Patty pointed at Screamer and smiled.

I could see what she was pointing at. He was in mid-stride, and as we watched his foot came slowly down. What would have taken less than a second now took a full five seconds.

I could feel the hope for the people inside that machine flood back into me.

Suddenly everyone moved around us.

"Slipped," Patty said, sighing.

"What slipped?" Screamer asked, glancing at us.

"How did you—?" Samantha was looking up at us clearly surprised that we had suddenly appeared in front of her without her new senses alerting her to us.

All the hope I had felt a moment ago drained out like someone had pulled the plug. "Does it slip often?"

She shrugged, looking very upset. "I don't know."

I didn't tell her what energy she was giving me.

She had the same type of control over her powers that I did over mine. They were there at times, at other times they didn't show, and it often made no sense. Before now I was just happy when any of my weird powers showed up to help me out of a situation. It had never been an issue before to have a power be consistent and controlled completely. And clearly, that had been the same for Patty.

Patty looked at me with an apologetic look on her face, as if she had let me down. She and I both knew we couldn't depend on just her power to get those people out of there. Too much chance things would slip at the wrong moment and people would die. So we would use it only as a last resort.

"Can your power back-up my power?" she asked, still holding my hand.

"Never hurts to try," I said.

Keeping a firm grip on Patty's hand, I took a deep breath of the musty-smelling warehouse air, then focused on slipping between two upcoming seconds. That's what it had felt like when Stan had taken me between time, and I tried to bring that feeling back.

"It worked," Patty said, laughing.

I glanced around. Screamer had his mouth open, about to ask a question. Tech had started walking back toward the group, and was now in mid-stride.

I felt immediately proud. I had actually managed to stop time around me. What a cool superpower this one was.

Then just as quickly I realized this wasn't really that useful in this situation unless I could do it with split-second timing.

None of my superpowers had ever been that on-demand and in my control, and I had no doubt this one was either.

Patty pulled me to a place on the other side of Screamer. "Take us back into normal time."

"Done," I said.

And low and behold Screamer started into his question and stopped since to him we had vanished.

"What the—" Screamer said, turning around to stare at us. "You two can really get on a person's nerves."

"Again," Patty said softly to me, squeezing my hand and giving me balance."

I focused on between seconds and again time stopped around us.

She pulled us around behind Screamer again. "Let it go, then do it again as quickly as you can."

"Practice?" I asked, seeing what she was doing.

"Practice," she said. "We'll work on your power for a few times, then on mine, then see if we can combine them in some fashion to get some safety margins."

Now I saw what she was intending. Her power wasn't safe enough to use alone. And mine wasn't quick enough, but between the two of us, we might get the chances down to acceptable risks for the people coming out of the machine.

I started to feel hope again.

"Here goes," I said. "In and out a few times as quickly as I can make it work."

"Ready," she said, squeezing my hand softly.

I took a deep breath, pushing back the wonderful feeling of having her holding my hand, and focused on what I was about to try. I was going to flick on-and-off a superpower like it was a light switch. I had never tried that before.

I dropped us back into normal time.

"Back here," Patty said to Screamer's back.

I switched us back between seconds.

We moved down the aisle to a position behind where Tech was walking, then I dropped us out again.

Screamer wasn't halfway through his turn when we appeared.

"Sorry, Tech," Patty said. "Just practicing."

Tech jerked and started to whirl around as I took us back between seconds.

This would have been a great party trick if the situation wasn't so serious and so many lives were at stake.

I took us in and out five more times, then stopped with us standing in the middle of a very confused group.

"Stay put for one second," Screamer said.

"That was very weird," Samantha said.

"How did you do that?" Tech asked.

Johnny just sat on the floor and shook his head in amazement.

"Sorry guys," I said, smiling at Patty. "We are just practicing a little to see if we can come up with a way to slow down time enough to get Geneva and Ben and the rest out of there."

"You actually think you can do it?" Johnny asked, climbing to his feet.

"That's what we're trying to figure out," Patty said. "Poker Boy here can stop time. But so far, the best was four seconds apart. I can slow down time, but I can't always hold it."

"So pardon us while we practice a little more," I said. Then I took Patty and me between time, stopping the questions from the others for a moment.

She smiled at me with that wonderful smile of hers, then squeezed my hand. "You're getting pretty good at this."

"But not good enough," I said. "Do you see any way we can combine our two powers to make this safe enough for people coming out? I clearly can't stop and start time three times in one second."

"I think there's a way," Patty said. "But I need to practice my slowing of time, try to figure out if I can sense when my power is about to slip."

I nodded, seeing where she was heading. "If you can tell when your power is about to slip, you can signal me and I can stop time until you can get reset."

"That's what I'm thinking," she said.

"Okay," I said. "Let's practice."

I dropped us back into real time, letting Johnny complete his last step toward the group.

"Who has a measured step?" I asked before anyone could react to Patty and me being in different positions. "We need someone walking a timed pace down the aisle so we can do some tests."

"I'll walk," Screamer said, moving back into a position like he was a racer at a starting line.

"I've got a stop-watch function on my watch," Johnny said. "Will that help?"

"It will," Patty said.

"Five seconds and stop," I said.

A moment later Johnny clicked his watch and said "Go."

Screamer paced out like he was a businessman in a hurry to get to a meeting. About eight paces away from the group Johnny said, "Stop."

Screamer stopped and turned around.

"Good," I said. "Repeat that when I say go. Johnny, time him again."

I glanced at Patty and she nodded that she was ready.

"Go."

Patty slowed time just as Screamer lifted his leg to take his first step and a fraction of a second after Johnny clicked his watch. We moved carefully away from Johnny and Samantha and Tech and off to one side of the aisle.

Slowly Screamer walked back toward us, very slowly. Patty seemed focused inward and I said nothing as Screamer finished his first step.

Then what seemed like an eternity later his second. His third. His fourth. His fifth. He was on his sixth step when Patty squeezed my hand. "It's slipping."

I focused and stopped time right in the middle of Screamer's sixth step.

Patty took a couple of deep breaths.

"You all right?"

"I am," she said. "But it takes focus for me to tell when the power is starting to slip."

"I understand that," I said. "But now comes the part I've been worrying about since we came up with this idea. Can your power work now that time is stopped so I can let go?"

"Let's find out," she said. "Ready?"

"Ready," I said.

"Now," she said.

I let go and let time come back to normal, but time wasn't normal. Screamer was still moving in his slow motion way. I watched as he took his last two steps and then stopped as Johnny's thumb slowly clicked his watch.

"Slipping," Patty said.

"Let it go," I said.

She did and everything came back to normal pace as the group turned to face where we had moved.

"That is so weird," Samantha said again, shaking her head.

"Well," Johnny said.

"I think we can make this work," I said. "We need a little more practice. But one thing we can't test is if we'll be able to pull people out of the chair and maintain our focus on holding time at bay."

Patty nodded. "I don't think I can safely do that."

"I'm afraid I'll get distracted," I said.

"So you're going to need some help," Screamer said. He turned to Johnny. "Think you can sit in that chair without touching that machine?"

Screamer pointed to the ghost slot machine that had everyone and the wooden chair attached to it.

Johnny nodded, took a deep breath and moved to the slot machine.

Screamer took up a position right behind him. "I'm thinking you are touching me, doing your time thing and including me. When someone shows I shove them out of the chair sideways like this."

Fairly gently he pushed Johnny sideways and away from the face of the ghost slots. Johnny managed to stumble but not fall to the concrete.

I nodded and glanced at Patty as both Johnny and Screamer moved a few more paces away from the slot machines. She was nodding also, as if it just might work.

"Tech," I said, turning to the stunned kid standing out of the way to one side next to Samantha. "That machine's lowest payout is three, right?"

Tech nodded.

"How is it triggered?" I asked. I was afraid one of us was going to have to pull the handle and I didn't much like that idea at all.

"Harry can trigger it to pay out from in there," Tech said.

Johnny nodded. "Geneva just asked him and he agreed."

"Can he space the payouts two minutes apart?" Patty asked, slightly ahead of where I was going with my questions. She and I were both thinking we were go-

ing to need rest between each use of our powers.

"He can," Tech said.

"He can," Johnny said a moment later.

I looked into Patty's deep brown eyes. I could see worry there, but also a lot of confidence and power. I wouldn't want to try to do this alone, but with her holding my hand, I felt we just might have a chance.

"Okay then," I said, glancing at everyone. "Let's get ready. Johnny, I need you to get some ambulances and police here to help with those coming out. How much longer do we have before these monsters jump again?"

Johnny pulled the sheet of paper we got from The Bookkeeper out of his pocket and stared at it. "Six in the morning."

"Let's hope these things are long dead by then," I said.

I also hoped we didn't have a bunch of dead people at that point as well. It was all a matter of time. And how well Patty and I worked together controlling it.

Chapter Eighteen

The Draining of a Machine

I MADE PATTY and me and Screamer practice just enough to be sure we had the routine down, yet not enough to get us tired. I didn't feel too drained from using my newest-found superpower, but that didn't mean that I wouldn't get tired an hour from now. With two-minute breaks, three people at a time, over one hundred people in the machine, an hour still wouldn't be enough time to have everyone out.

Finally, it seemed as if there was nothing left for us to practice, nothing left for us to do but start the process. I could tell Patty was nervous, and there was no doubt I was scared to death. I was trusting a strange superpower I didn't know I had twenty-four hours ago to save hundreds of people.

I kept thinking I should just call a halt and go get Stan or one of the other gods to help us. Yet another part of me knew that Stan and the gambling gods were watching, and if they didn't think we could do this, they would step in and help. There was a lot at stake for their world as well. That thought gave me a little more confidence.

Not much, but a little.

I did one more quick check of everything we had done to get ready. Johnny and Tech had gone around the warehouse and gotten a number of tarps off of old slot machines. Using those tarps, they had built up a "landing pad" on the concrete floor where people were going to hit when Screamer pushed them out of the chair. I figured it was better than having people sprawl out face-first on concrete.

Johnny had given the police orders to not come into the warehouse. I had asked him to do that because I didn't want to take any chances of a lot of people coming in over the next hour and distracting Patty's and my concentration.

Johnny and Samantha and Tech would help the rescued people to the door of the warehouse. And as Johnny pointed out, Ben and Geneva would soon be with them to help as well.

I hoped he was right. There were so many things that could go wrong.

Ghost slots had taken a lot of people over the years. No one had ever escaped from one before, and we didn't even know if it was going to be possible for that to happen. The people in that machine were just energy in wires. Could they even be reformed into human bodies?

I mentioned that worry to Patty while we had time stopped in one of our practice sessions. She just squeezed my hand in that wonderful way she had of squeezing and said, "There are a lot of things in this world we don't understand and need to just trust. Let's trust this one to work."

"Think Stan and the rest of the gods would show up here and stop us if this was a bad idea?" I asked her.

"I'm betting on it," she had said, smiling that wonderful smile of hers that reached and filled her brown eyes. Then before my mind could drift to my holding a bar of raspberry-smelling soap and her naked in a shower, she had directed me to get focused on practicing again.

I actually managed to stay focused and not think of her. That's how important this was.

"Ambulance and police are here and ready and standing by outside," Johnny said, coming down the aisle from the direction of the entrance.

Tech held up Johnny's watch. "Timer ready."

I nodded. I had had Johnny give him the watch because I had a hunch that when Geneva came out it was going to be painful to Johnny again. Keeping exact timing on this was going to be critical.

Samantha was standing beside the pile of tarps where we hoped people would land after Screamer pushed them out of the chair. She was ready to help, and looking just about as scared and nervous as a person could look. I didn't blame her. Her husband's life was at stake. If this didn't work, he was going to die an ugly death right in front of her.

Screamer moved over and stood behind the old wooden chair that people were going to materialize in. His job actually was going to be the hardest. He needed to push each person out of the way after they had materialized, but before the next person showed up. That was going to be a very physical and rough thing to do, and he was going to have to do it with exact timing.

I moved over to stand beside Screamer facing the colorful slot machines. The image of Saturn dominated everything, demanding that I sit down and just play. The blinking colors, the bright lights were very, very strong draws.

Patty moved up to my left and took my hand. The feel of her wonderful skin against mine allowed me to push the attraction of the machines back into a corner of my mind and away from any bother. Now, instead of looming over me, they were just old machines with a nice design. The feel of Patty's skin against mine was the focus for me.

I reached out with my right hand and grabbed the thin black belt that Screamer was wearing, holding on squarely in the middle of his back. It was the best way to keep in contract with him without restricting his movements in any way.

"Ready?" I asked Patty.

"Ready," she said, squeezing my hand.

"Ready Screamer?"

"As I'll ever be," he said.

"Johnny, tell Geneva we're set to go."

Johnny nodded. Then a moment later he said, "Now."

"Clock started!" Tech said.

I focused on my power as Patty slowed time around us. I needed to be ready to stop time completely if Patty signaled her power was slipping in any fashion.

The next three seconds slid by very, very slowly in Patty's control. Tech and Samantha and Johnny were all outside Patty's influence and moving like a bad slow-motion video.

Slowly Johnny's hands went to his head, as if he had felt a very sharp pain.

Then, in front of Screamer the air started to shimmer.

A vague outline of Geneva started to form, filling in moment by moment in what seemed a very quick time in our slowed-down universe.

Then she was there, fully. Her back was to Screamer, sitting just as she had been when she had gone into the machine.

Screamer, reacting as fast as he could, took her by the shoulders and tipped her out of the chair and onto the tarps. She fell slowly, just as another shimmering started in the chair.

That was close.

Very, very close.

If Screamer had hesitated at all the next person would have started to form where Geneva sat.

I glanced at Patty. She wasn't watching, but instead had her head tipped back and her eyes closed. Her grasp on my hand was firm and solid.

A middle-aged woman shimmered into shape and the instant it was clear that she was all there, Screamer shoved her sideways and out of the chair.

She was barely out of the way and hadn't yet landed on Geneva when the shimmering started again.

Three people in less than one second was almost too fast for even Patty's slowed time. It was very lucky for us that Screamer was reacting as quickly as he was.

Ben, the man Patty and I had watched disappear on the Horseshoe surveillance

Coming in June
**from all your favorite booksellers
in trade paper and electronic editions.**

tapes shimmered into place. Screamer took no chances and shoved him instantly out of the chair and onto the pile of tarps with the two women.

"Slipping," Patty said, squeezing my hand.

I froze time and then said, "Clear."

Patty took a deep breath and looked around at me, then at Screamer and the three people twisted and frozen in place on the pile of tarps. They looked like a twister game gone terribly wrong.

"We got them?" she asked.

"We got them," I said. "But I wanted to have us stay in control of time to make sure no one else was coming."

Screamer nodded. "Make sure the three-payout setting was right. Good thinking."

"Good work on your part," I said to Screamer. "Even with time slowed they appeared faster than I expected them to."

"Me too," Screamer said.

Patty took another couple of deep breaths, then said, "I'm ready."

I wanted us to go another five or so seconds to make sure no one else was coming, so when Patty nodded, tipped her head back and closed her eyes, I slipped us out of between time.

On the mat the three people there were still moving and reacting to being shoved and tangled together, just very, very slowly. It would have made a really funny home video on one of those stupid television programs that made money out of people making fools of themselves.

I had also gotten just a glimpse inside each of their heads as Screamer pushed them aside, but I ignored that.

But the good thing was that all three were awake and alive and moving. And slowly Johnny and Samantha were bending down to help them.

The look on both Johnny and Samantha's faces was something else. Now I can honestly say I have seen pure joy.

Slow motion joy, but still pure.

No one else was materializing into the chair, so I finally squeezed Patty's hand. "We're clear."

She let us slip back into real time.

"Tech, watch that time closely," I said.

Screamer, Patty, and I stayed in positions as Johnny picked up Geneva and hugged her like I had never seen anyone hug before. She was going to be lucky to not have a few cracked ribs.

Samantha seemed to do the same for Ben, holding him and crying.

The other woman, clearly the tourist Geneva had seen being taken from the Mirage, sort of sat there on the tarps watching the scene around her, then glanced up at the Saturn Slot Machines with a look of horror. "Was I in there?"

"You were," Screamer said. "But you're safe now."

The woman scrambled off the tarps and away from the machine.

"Welcome back, Geneva," I said after letting them hug for a few more seconds. "How are you feeling?"

"Headache will pass," she said. "And I know what to do to help."

Samantha let go of her husband and turned to us. "Everyone, this is Ben."

The poor man sort of nodded, then glanced at the machines and stepped back in horror, just as the woman on the tarps had done when she moved away from the machines. I was betting that the people who had been taken were never going to sit down at a slot machine again.

"How long?" Patty asked Tech.

"Seventy seconds," he said.

"Johnny, get this woman out to the ambulances to be checked and then get back here," I said. "Samantha, you want to take Ben out as well?"

"I'm fine," Ben said, "What can I do to help?"

Samantha gave her husband a hug and a huge smile.

"Help Samantha and Johnny and Geneva get the people who are coming out of the machine to the ambulances and police."

"Understood," he said.

Johnny took the frightened tourist by the arm and headed her away from the ghost slots toward the door to the warehouse, introducing himself as he went.

Geneva, Samantha, and Ben stayed.

"Thirty seconds," Tech said.

I turned to face Patty, who was smiling all the way through her eyes. That smile of hers melted me every time, and it started to do it again when Tech said, "Fifteen seconds."

The melt of my very soul froze and I asked her, "You ready for another three?"

Patty took a deep breath and nodded.

"Ten seconds," Tech said."

Patty squeezed my hand, took a deep breath, and tilted her head back and closed her eyes.

"Five seconds," Tech said. Then as we had practiced, he started counting down.

At three seconds Patty slowed time again.

What seemed like a long three seconds later a shimmering started in the chair, right on time.

Three out, almost a hundred left to rescue. It was going to be a long, long grind, and we didn't dare slip even for an instant. If we did, someone would die.

Chapter Nineteen

No Going Down with the Slot

I DON'T REMEMBER ever being so tired.

Over one hour of real time had passed, but with my stopping time on a half dozen different occasions, and Patty's slow time, I wagered Patty and I and Screamer had been at this for almost three or four hours.

So far so good.

The closest call we had was when a very large man showed up in the chair first in a group of three. Screamer had to almost throw himself with the big guy to the mat to get the man's bulk out of the chair. I somehow managed to hold on to Screamer's belt with one hand and Patty's hand with the other, but for an instant I thought the problem would make Patty lose control.

Somehow I froze time far faster than I ever thought I could, almost like a reaction to the situation. Good to know I could do it that fast, but I hoped to not test it again.

With time frozen all three of us moved around, together, never losing touch of each other, and got the big man's legs out of the way.

Then we got back into position and Patty took over control again and the next two people in that group made it out just fine.

From there the process just went on, two minutes of break followed by slowed time and a feeling of near panic as three people appeared very quickly.

About ten groups ago the man getting off the tarp had told us that Harry was now all alone in the main room. He had been the last one in there helping the old guy stay on his feet.

That worried us all, especially after Geneva had told us how tired and worn out Harry had been. But the next group, and then the next had appeared on time, so it looked like old Harry was hanging on.

Over the last few groups, Patty was having more and more problems, and I had had to stop time twice in both groups to give her a rest. She was getting tired, and I was getting very worried at both of our abilities to keep using our superpower in such a sustained way.

"How many left in there?" I asked Geneva as Tech gave us the sixty second warning.

"If our count is right," Geneva said, "And Harry's count was right, Harry should be the second one out on this next group and that should be it."

"You're kidding?" Patty said. I could hear the relief in her voice.

"We're close," I said, squeezing her hand slightly.

She straightened her back and nodded. "Let's do this."

Tech counted us down just as he had done every time before and Patty slowed time just as she had done so much over the entire rescue operation. Screamer stood ready to push just two more people out of that chair.

But nothing happened.

"Slipping," Patty said.

"Clear," I said as I focused and froze time and let her take a few deep breaths.

"What happened?" Screamer asked. "It's been too long."

I knew that as well. Patty had held that last time slowing a good five seconds longer than what it should have taken to get anyone out of the machine. Harry had

been so perfectly on time with everyone before this one.

"We need to keep in slow time and ready," Patty said, "in case he's running just a little late."

I agreed. "Tell me when you are ready."

She tipped her head back and said, "Okay."

I let us come out of between instants of time and Patty had control. This time she held it for twelve real-world seconds, which seemed like an eternity to me as no one appeared in the chair.

"Slipping," she said.

"I got it," I said, again taking us between time.

Near the pile of tarps Ben, Samantha, Tech, and Geneva were looking very worried, their frowns frozen for the moment.

"Not good," Screamer said.

"Harry must have passed out and can't trigger the last group," Patty said.

"Or he died in there," I said.

Patty took a few more deep breaths and said "I'm ready again. "Let's give him ten more seconds before we give up. He'll know not to trigger the payout without exact timing."

I waited until she squeezed my hand to let me know she had it and again took us out of between moments of time and let Patty control.

Ten more seconds and nothing appeared in the chair.

"Slipping," Patty said.

"Let it go," I said.

An instant later we were back functioning in real time.

"I was afraid this might happen," Geneva said. "Harry was so weak."

"Actually," Tech said, "I'll wager the machine needs three to pay out."

"Three minimum?" Johnny asked. "So there's not enough people in there is what you're saying?"

Tech nodded. "Machines don't pay out less than the full amount. Most of these old machines just froze if there wasn't enough to pay a jackpot. An attendant had to be called and the machine refilled."

"Oh, great," Geneva said, "and we're the attendants to a ghost slot machine?"

She had a good point there. We were the ones running this thing, sort of. Actually Harry was the attendant from inside the thing. And now he and some other person were trapped in there.

"I'll go in and get him," Tech said.

I stared at the kid. I hated the idea of him doing that. Hated it.

"You can't," Geneva said. "No communication with anyone out here. I have to go back in."

"Or I do," Johnny said as he strolled down the corridor toward the group. He had been taking the last person of the last group out to the waiting police and ambulances, although so far no one had been hurt beyond being very tired and headachey.

"No, I do," Tech said. "If Harry's too weak to trigger the payout you need someone to do that."

"You can do it through Geneva to me," Johnny said.

"Or through Johnny to me," Geneva said.

I couldn't believe that they were having an argument over who was going to get taken by a ghost slot machine. I had no idea how two people who could hear each other's thoughts could even argue. That would seem to take all the fun out of fighting. Or maybe make it worse. Either way I didn't really want to find out.

"We can set the timing with back-ups if I go in," Tech said.

All three of them were willing to risk their lives to save the two people in there. It sure showed how really brave the people I was working with were. This was one amazing team that had come together to solve this problem.

Tech, Geneva, and Johnny sort of stared at each other for a moment, then turned to me. They wanted me to decide who would risk their life, maybe lose their life, in trying to rescue the last two people inside that machine. This kind of decision was a lot rougher than trying to decide to lay down pocket kings when an ace hit the board. Or shove all my money into the center of the table on one hand that might get beat and knock me out of the tournament. Those decisions seemed stressful, but nothing like this one.

This one the stakes were human lives, both inside the machine and facing me.

I took a deep breath, reached over and touched Patty's hand and then took the two of us between moments of time.

"Any suggestions on this one?" I asked her, relishing the feel of her skin against mine.

"None," she said, "other than I think it has to be either Geneva or Johnny. We need the contact with the people inside in case something doesn't work out the way we think it's going to."

"Agreed," I said, sort of knowing now who I would pick. Just talking to Patty gave me the strength to act.

I dropped us back into real time and without hesitating said, "Johnny, it would be best if you gave it a try."

"Why?" both Tech and Geneva asked at the same moment.

"Tech, we need the contact in there in case there's something wrong we don't know about, not counting the timing issue. Geneva, you've been through that once already and seem fine. But I don't want to push it twice."

Johnny nodded. "I agree, Poker Boy. "Should I go in here, or wait until the machine jumps in the morning and go in at the casino?"

"Harry's too weak to wait," Geneva said. "I'm afraid he might not last until morning."

"Right here," I said, sounding a lot more sure of myself than I felt. "Let's do this and get this finished."

Johnny bent down and kissed Geneva hard and fast, then turned toward the machine holding up a nickel. "I'll be right back."

As the rest of us moved a few more steps away from the machine, Johnny sat down in the same chair that Screamer had been knocking people out of, dropped the nickel into the machine, and pulled the handle, almost in one motion. It was as if he slowed down and thought about what he was doing he wouldn't be able to do it.

Over the years I had learned that jumping in fast and quick was often the best way to do something unpleasant. Of course, acting like that in a hand of poker had sometimes cost me a tournament. But other times it had won me tournaments. I hoped this time it would be a winner for all of us.

As the first reel on the machine clicked to a stop showing a Saturn, Johnny seemed to jerk, as if getting shocked.

Geneva bent over and grabbed her head.

Ben and Samantha were beside her but not touching her. There was nothing they could do to help her or Johnny at this point.

The second reel clicked to a stop showing a Saturn.

Johnny jerked hard in the chair, not letting go of the machine's handle.

The third wheel clanged to a stop with a sound that seemed to echo throughout the warehouse.

Saturn.

Johnny sort of leaned forward into the machines.

Geneva screamed in pain.

Then Johnny and the ghost slot machines shimmered and disappeared, leaving the warehouse gray and much darker than a moment before.

I stared at the blank place where the slot machines had been, not believing what I was seeing, or *not seeing* as the case might be. The old row of slot machines that filled the wall looked like a row of perfect teeth with a front tooth missing.

"Where did they go?" Tech asked.

Geneva was on her knees staring open-mouthed at the empty place in the row of old, dead slots.

"Geneva," I said, using my most commanding voice, "do you sense Johnny?"

She slowly shook her head.

Then she looked up at me with the most horrific empty look I have ever seen. "He's gone."

Chapter Twenty

Math Doesn't Work

I DON'T THINK anything had ever shocked me, at any time in my life, as much as the machines vanishing had done. Yet I knew that's what happened every time a person was taken by a machine.

Why would this time be any different?

Yet I hadn't expected it and I should have.

Now the connection between Johnny and Geneva had been broken, and who knew where the slot machine had jumped to.

Or if it was even coming back.

I needed answers and I needed them fast.

I moved quickly to the pile of tarps, grabbed the top one and swung it around and up over the space where the ghost slots had been. It settled over their form there, just as the tarp that had been over them originally had. We couldn't see anything in that spot, but the part of those evil machines were still right here in the warehouse.

"They're coming back," Patty said.

"That they are," I said as I yanked off the tarp and tossed it back on the pile. "But if my guess is correct, they need a person to jump."

"Not necessarily," Tech said. "They jumped out of here without a person."

I stared at the kid. He was right. They had.

"Where were they headed in the morning?" I asked.

"Johnny's got the paper," Geneva said.

"Circus Circus," Patty said without hesitation, staring at me. "Back wall of the main casino on the far right."

I must have had a very puzzled look on my face because she said, "I know exactly where and when. I memorized the list. Part of my skills."

I had no doubt that was only a minor part of her skills, and I was looking forward to learning a lot more of them, but I didn't let myself go down that road of thought. The ghost slots were loose again and we still had people to save.

"Patty, get on the phone to The Bookkeeper and tell him what happened. Ask him if that changes things on his projections."

She nodded and grabbed her cell phone, stepping away.

"Samantha, Ben, Tech, stay here. Geneva, Screamer, come with me. We've got to get the police to the Circus Circus if they aren't already there."

Geneva, Screamer, and I had taken no more than a dozen steps down the aisle between all the old slot machines when from behind us Samantha said, "Too late."

The three of us spun around like someone had pulled on the same rope. The shimmering of colored lights pushed the gray of the old warehouse away as the ghost slots came back.

And with them the intense desire to sit down and lose myself in their power.

"Johnny," Geneva said softly beside me.

"You two back in touch?"

"We are," she said, nodding and smiling at the same time. "Thank god."

"Is he all right?" Screamer asked.

"He's fine," Geneva said, beaming like a kid given a long sought-after toy at Christmas. "He just found Harry."

"How is Harry?" Tech asked.

"Weak and very tired, but still alive."

"Fantastic," Screamer said.

"Thanks," Patty said, turning back toward us and snapping her cell phone closed in disgust. The super-powered woman I was in lust with had a lot of emotions, and I sure didn't want the one she was showing right now directed at me.

"The Bookkeeper his old charming self?" Screamer asked.

"He said we're all idiots," she said, clearly disgusted.

"We know that," I said, trying to lighten her mood a little. "But did he say if the machine would stay on the pattern he worked out."

Patty smiled at me and nodded. "It went to Circus Circus and stayed until it got someone, then came back. It's next trip out, unless we feed it someone else, isn't until tomorrow at a few minutes after noon. It will go back to the Horseshoe then, same spot near the stairs."

"And if we feed it again," I asked.

She looked at me with a very funny look on her face. "It will jump to the Horseshoe early is all. But why would we do that?"

I pointed at the machine. "Because right now there are four people in there."

"Oh," Tech said, his voice hushed yet. "The math doesn't work."

"Exactly," I said.

"Oh, no," Samantha said.

Patty just stared at me, her wonderful brown eyes wide. She knew, without a doubt, just as I did, that we were going to have to feed more people to the beast before we had any hopes of saving everyone. Two more people to be exact. One here and one at the Horseshoe.

I glanced around at the shocked team.

Patty and I and Screamer couldn't go in, since we were the rescue team needed to get everyone out. Geneva had to stay out as well since she was the contact with Johnny and Harry inside. That left Tech, Samantha, and Ben. And Ben had already been in the thing once before. I don't think we dared stress him with twice through a ghost slot machine.

"I'll go," Tech said, stepping forward.

"So will I," Samantha said.

"No, I will," Ben said.

"Get Ben to do what I was doing and let me take a crack at it," Screamer said.

In all my years of helping people, I had never seen a braver bunch of people in one room. At that moment I was very, very proud to be working with them.

"Ben," Patty said, "we don't dare send you back inside. We don't know what twice through that thing would do to a person."

"We don't even know the long-term ramifications of once through," I said. "And Screamer, we need your practiced quickness and knowledge of when to get people out of that chair. I don't want to take a chance on someone new at this point."

Screamer nodded. He knew I was right, just as I knew he had to offer to go inside.

Ben started to open his mouth to protest, but Samantha took his hand and squeezed it lightly, some sort of private signal between them that he shouldn't say anything.

I glanced at Patty and she nodded, understanding and agreement in her wonderful brown eyes.

"Geneva, Patty, Tech, Screamer, the four of you go out and convince Johnny's partner out there that he has to take Tech to the Horseshoe. Ben, go with Tech to the Horseshoe and show him exactly where the machines appear. Tech, when you are in position and ready, call Patty."

"I'm going in here?" Samantha asked, her voice firm.

I nodded.

"Now wait," Ben said.

"It's all right," Samantha said, turning to face her husband. "These people rescued you and all those others. They'll get me out as well, along with everyone still inside there. You need to help Tech make sure he's in position so we do this right."

Ben nodded after a moment, then bent down and kissed his wife. Then he said, "I'll be waiting here when you come out."

"Actually," I said, smiling at him. "We plan on having all of them out of there before you can get back here from the Horseshoe. So she'll be waiting for you."

Ben stared at me for a long moment, then nodded.

"Let's go," Patty said. She, Geneva, Tech, Screamer, and Ben headed for the door to the warehouse.

"Looks like all we have to do now is wait," Samantha said.

"The really fun part," I said.

Samantha eased herself down onto the pile of tarps and I sat down beside her. The things were a lot firmer than I had thought they were. More than likely a few of the people we had rescued were going to be very bruised and sore from being tossed on this pile.

"This is a brave thing you are offering to do," I said. "You know we can find another volunteer from the police outside."

"No," Samantha said. "I'm going to do it. I got all these sensory powers from your friend Stan so that I could help. You saved my husband, it's the least I can do in helping the others still trapped in that monster. If this is how I can help, then this is what I'm going to do."

I nodded, gave Samantha a quick hug around the shoulders, then stood, moving over and leaning against an old quarter slot machine across from Samantha. The silence of the big warehouse became heavier with each passing second. The bright lights and colors of the four Saturn Slot machines seemed to call to me, like a bully who just wouldn't give up.

There were four people inside that machine under that giant image of Saturn. Two more of my team were going to willingly go in there to try to save them, under my direction. I just hoped I was making the right decision in letting them.

In all my years as Poker Boy, I had never lost someone who tried to help me. But in all the years, I had never sent anyone into such danger before. Normally I went into the danger myself, making sure the others helping me were safe.

This time, I needed to stay outside of the danger and let friends put themselves purposely at risk so that I could help rescue them and others. Patty and I and Screamer were the superheroes here, yet we really weren't taking any risks.

That didn't feel right.

In fact, it felt just plain wrong. But for the life of me, I couldn't see another way.

And that didn't feel right either.

Chapter Twenty-one

Death and the Machine

AFTER WHAT SEEMED like the longest time, Patty and Screamer and Geneva came back inside the warehouse, moving toward Samantha and myself at a quick pace.

"All set," Patty said. "Tech and Ben have a police escort to the Horseshoe."

"Good," I said, moving away from the machine I had been leaning against and facing Patty. "How are you feeling?"

She shrugged. "Tired, but fine."

"How about one more quick practice before we send anyone else in there?"

I didn't want to tell her that I had gotten more and more worried about my powers fading. I often had powers for a time outside of a casino, sometimes a few hours, sometimes half a day depending on how long I had been in the casino and charged them up. So I was getting a little worried.

She smiled, her brown eyes taking me in clearly. "I was going to suggest the same thing. You reading my mind now?"

"Not yet," I said. "But there's still hope."

She laughed at my lame joke and then reached out and took my hand.

Again the feel of her skin against mine gave me sensations I never wanted to let go of. Little shivers up my back, along with a warmth inside my gut. It was amazing I had been able to concentrate as much as I had so far.

I pushed the hope of helping her shower with a fresh bar of raspberry soap away and replaced it with the image of my friends dying in front of my eyes because I screwed up. That kind of image will shut down just about any erotic and fancy-filled thoughts, and that's exactly what it did.

"Ready?" I asked, looking into her eyes.

She nodded, tipped her head back, closed her eyes, and slowed time down around us.

"You got it," I said. "Now, let me see if I can still make this work."

She squeezed my hand and said nothing.

I focused on taking the two of us between seconds. For a fraction of a second I couldn't feel anything different, then suddenly it worked, just as it had all evening.

"Got it," I said.

Maybe being around all the old slot machines was like being in a casino. Or maybe Stan had increased my powers like he had with Samantha. Either way, Poker Boy was still in full force and I was damned glad of that.

"Letting go," she said.

She did and opened her eyes. She glanced around at the frozen time and then smiled at me. "I think we're ready."

"I do too," I said, letting us drop back into real time.

"Problems?" Screamer asked.

"None," Patty said.

I regretfully let go of her hand and moved back to the quarter slot I had been leaning against a few minutes before. Samantha looked nervous sitting on the tarps and finally climbed to her feet and started pacing.

Patty watched her for a moment, then moved over to Geneva. "Are Johnny and Harry all right in there?"

"They are," Geneva said. "And Harry completely agrees on the problem with a three person payout. He was afraid that might be a problem, and was hoping we could figure out a way around it. He thinks we're nuts for doing it the way we're doing it, but is thankful we are at the same time."

Since Geneva was connected clearly to Johnny, and he was with Harry, I had a question I had been worrying about. "Did Harry notice anything when the machine took Johnny and jumped? And then when it took the other person at Circus Circus and jumped back?"

"Nothing," Geneva said, relaying Harry's answer through Johnny.

"Good," Patty said. "I had been wondering about that as well? Samantha's and Tech's jumps won't bother anyone then."

"Nope," Geneva said.

Again, the big warehouse went deathly silent as we waited.

There was nothing worse than waiting, and nothing worse than the silence of a bunch of dead, dust-covered machines that once had been active. Only the ghost slot looked alive, its colorful lights filling the space between the rows of dead slots.

I wondered how many other ghost slots were functioning in this building, maybe not active now, but waiting for a little bit of energy, a little bit of attention like Harry had given these Saturn Slots.

Harry's mistake in trying to save himself by getting the machine to pay him back out was the only thing that might end up saving him. His mistake had caused the ghost to keep hunting and take lots of people, even though it had him inside.

And it was the sudden large amount of people going missing that had led us to this place, this moment. Thankfully, most of those people were now safe and back with their loved ones. Only four more to save, but to do that, we had to risk two others to get the total right so that the machine would work.

Patty's phone rang with a Mozart tune that seemed very out of place.

Samantha froze and turned to face Patty.

Patty pulled the phone from her pocket and answered it with a simple, "Yes."

"Good," she said. "You're near the top of the restaurant stairs?"

"Okay," she said, "here it comes."

She clicked the phone off and turned to face me. "Police in position, have the area blocked off completely. Only Ben and Tech are there."

I turned to Samantha. "You ready?"

"One problem," she said.

"What?" I asked, suddenly getting very worried about her.

"Can I borrow a nickel?"

She smiled at our shocked faces, then turned to Screamer who was digging in his pocket.

He handed her a coin. "Safe trip. See you shortly."

Samantha took the coin. Then, with a quick adjustment of her sunglasses,

153

moved over to the machine and sat down, her back to all of us.

"The machines seem very intense, radiating energy in a number of spectrums," she said, fumbling with the coin for a moment before putting it into the coin slot.

"Coin and machine noises are very loud," she said, reporting the experience to us and more than likely keeping herself as calm as possible under the circumstances.

She reached out and pulled down on the metal arm.

"Noises even louder now," she said, turning her head slightly as if listening to the wheels of the slot machine spin. "Almost like voices calling to—"

The first wheel locked down onto Saturn and she jerked with the electrical shock going through her arm.

The second wheel locked down onto Saturn and she jerked again.

The third wheel stopped on Saturn and she slumped forward toward the machine as it took her and vanished.

"I hope I never have to see that again," Screamer said, his voice low and angry.

I felt the same way. I was angry that we had to put Samantha through that.

And scared for her as well.

"You in contact with Johnny?" Patty asked.

Geneva shook her head, the empty and scared look back in her eyes.

"Deep breaths you two," Patty said, turning to face me and Screamer. "There are some brave people risking a lot right now. We are shortly going to have work to do."

Patty smiled at Screamer, then at me. Whatever calming superpower Front Desk girl was using at that moment, sure worked on me. I smiled back at her.

"Ready," Screamer said.

"Ready," I said.

"Now all we need is a ghost slot machine," Patty said, taking my hand.

The three of us stood there, waiting, facing the empty hole in the row of old slot machines, waiting for the ghost slots to come home.

Three superheroes with nothing to do until the enemy showed itself.

Five long seconds later it did exactly that, shimmering back into place, very much alive and radiating light and energy.

The three of us, like a military unit, stepped forward and into position behind the seats of the four slot machines, with my left hand in Patty's right hand and my right hand holding onto Screamer's belt.

"Tell Johnny to tell Harry we're ready," I said to Geneva after getting a slight hand-squeeze from Patty.

"They're ready," Geneva said. "Two minute intervals just like before. I'm timing you. Just say the word."

Patty leaned her head back and squeezed my hand that she was ready.

"Now," I said.

"Triggering payout now," Geneva said.

Patty slowed time as I stood ready to stop time completely for the three of us.

A long few seconds later a shape started to form in the chair in front of Screamer. Just as before, Screamer waited until the very instant Tech was all there, then shoved him out of the chair and onto the tarps as Samantha's form started to take shape.

Samantha was suddenly fully there and again Screamer got her out of the way just in time for a man's shape to start to appear. This was the guy taken at Circus Circus before we could stop it from happening.

Screamer got him out of the chair and onto the tarp with the other two as we waited.

No one else. At least yet.

"We're clear," I said.

Patty let the slowed time drop and the three of us rushed to help Geneva get the people off the tarp.

Tech was still out cold, but breathing well.

Samantha was moaning and holding her head, but she also seemed all right. The man from Circus Circus just looked confused. He was clearly a tourist. He had on a bright red shirt and Bermuda shorts, with white tube socks and black leather shoes. His hair was thinning and his skin was slightly burnt from too much time in the sun on his first day in town.

"Stand over there and don't move," I told the guy, using my best authority voice.

He meekly nodded and backed to a position against the opposite side of the aisle, his eyes wide.

"How much time?" Patty asked.

"Forty-five seconds," Geneva said.

"Here we go," I said.

I turned to Patty. "You ready for one more group?"

"I am," she said.

This time I reached out and took her hand as we moved into position behind the old wooden chairs of the Saturn Slots.

"Ten seconds," Geneva said. "Johnny wants to know if you're ready?"

"We're ready," Patty said, tilting her head back and starting to concentrate.

Geneva counted it down just as Tech had done. "Now."

Patty closed her eyes and took us into slowed-down time.

A second later Johnny's form started to appear in the chair. I could feel

Screamer brace his feet and the moment Johnny was fully there, Screamer shoved the big detective hard toward the tarps, barely getting the man out of the way before a young woman started to appear.

This woman had been in the slots almost as long as Harry, and the moment she appeared she was like a wet rag being shoved from the chair.

Then finally, one last form started to take shape.

The Saturn Slots started to hum, the noise even louder in slow time, climbing quickly to a high-pitched sound that made me want to put my hands over my ears. I managed to not do that, keeping a firm hold on Patty's hand and Screamer's belt.

I could feel the pavement shaking under my feet as the ghost slot fought to keep its last source of energy.

Finally, the figure of an older man I assumed was Harry appeared completely in the chair.

Screamer knocked him sideways and onto the tarp with Johnny and the young woman.

He moaned and lay there, breathing.

He was alive.

We had got them all out alive.

In front of us, the ghost slots sat, dark and very silent.

The pull to sit down and play that had been a constant was gone.

"We're clear," I said to Patty, squeezing her hand lightly. "And we're finished."

She opened her eyes and let us slide into normal time.

"It's dead," she said, staring at the machine, her voice sounding almost shocked that we had actually beaten the thing.

"Very, very dead," Screamer said.

I just stared at the ghost slot.

A few moments ago, it had been a dangerous monster. Now it was just four old, worn-out slot machines. Still dangerous, I would bet, but as long as no one played the things, they couldn't harm anyone.

They had no energy, no human to feed them and drive them to take and take and take.

I glanced down the row at all the other old machines sitting along the wall, stacked in rows in the huge warehouse. How many of these slots had taken the life force from someone in the past and now just waited to be fed again?

I suddenly very much wanted to be out of this graveyard and back in the bright lights and activity of a poker room. I very much wanted to be risking tournament chips instead of people's lives.

The Saturn Slots sat there, staring at me with the three reels showing small Saturn jackpots.

I stared back, knowing that this time we had beaten the machine.

This time.

But as anyone will tell you in Las Vegas, you can't beat the machines over the long haul.

And I didn't even want to try.

Chapter Twenty-two

A Happy Ending (with Food)

AFTER STARING at the dead slot machines for the longest time, Patty put her arms around me and gave me the biggest, most wonderful hug I ever remembered getting.

That hug broke my deep thoughts about slot machines and the nature of life, and took me right to wonderful daydreams about showers and bars of raspberry soap.

Screamer suggested a few moments later, after Patty stopped her hug and let me take a breath, that everyone meet at the diner off Fremont Street. He said he would go ahead and make sure Madge kept the place open for them.

Everyone agreed, but Johnny and Geneva weren't sure they were going to make it. Johnny had a lot of work ahead of him and Geneva had to report in to her boss Adam, although Geneva said there was no chance she was writing about what actually happened.

Johnny and I and Patty and Geneva had a quick huddle and agreed that no slot machines should be officially mentioned, that the case of all the missing people would just remain an unsolved mystery in the files of the police.

Johnny asked just how he should explain where all the missing people came from. Patty just smiled and said, "Tell them you found them in the warehouse, and if anyone pushes the point, tell them to ask the kidnapped victims where they were, see if anyone believes that."

I had no doubt all this would be the main topic of gossip around town. And Johnny would again be a hero on the force.

Once again, I got him to agree to not mention my name in any fashion. Patty asked for the same thing, and he and Geneva both agreed.

I had never felt such fantastic relief as I left that warehouse and followed Patty quickly to her car, avoiding any talk with any of the police.

One hour later, after a quick shower alone in my own room, I joined Patty and Screamer and Ben and Samantha and

Tech at the diner across the street and around the corner from the Horseshoe.

We were the only customers in the place, and the closed sign was in the window. They had pulled a couple of tables together to make a large one right in the center of the place. Madge was waiting on them and was even smiling as she popped her gum and brought everyone drinks and food. I had no idea what Screamer had offered her to keep the diner open late for us, but whatever it was, she liked it.

I slid into a chair beside Patty and she gave me a big smile and a squeeze of my hand.

Her eyes lit up with the smile and the touch of her skin lit me up.

Everyone was laughing and talking and enjoying the moment. After all, it wasn't often you got to celebrate saving the lives of over a hundred people.

Twenty minutes later, to all of our surprise, Johnny and Geneva showed up, walking in hand-in-hand and smiling from ear-to-ear.

"How did you two escape?" Screamer asked before I could as the two pulled out chairs and sat down.

I couldn't imagine how much paperwork Johnny was going to have to do with solving this many kidnappings behind him.

"Dinner break," Johnny said.

Geneva laughed. "We gave them no choice. And it's past the morning edition deadline. Adam wants to take his time on how we come at this one."

"Don't blame him on that," I said.

I could just imagine how bad any decent newspaper would do if they printed a story about ghost slot machines. They'd be the laughing stock of the industry, no matter how much proof they tried to offer. And besides, this was Las Vegas,

and the *Sun* was the main newspaper. No smart newspaper would print something that would kill the golden goose. I can see why Adam wanted to be careful and not rush into print with anything.

Suddenly, I felt the now very familiar feeling of time stopping around the table. Madge was on her way across the room, frozen in mid-step. The sound of an old Buddy Holly song was gone.

"Great work, people," Stan said. "You are an amazing bunch, let me tell you. Laverne and all the gang working the casinos sent me to thank you all."

Screamer and I and Patty and Samantha just sat there. I know I was stunned, and by the way Patty's mouth was hanging slightly open, I would have bet she was as well.

Tech, Ben, Johnny, and Geneva just looked confused. They had no idea who this person was who had just stopped time and walked up to the table.

They had no idea who Laverne was.

Lady Luck herself had sent her thanks. I had no idea what that meant, but I sure had my hopes.

"I want to thank you, Stan," Samantha said, "for what you gave me."

"You earned it," Stan said. "I hope you and your husband decide to move back here. The security forces of some of these casinos could sure use your special powers, as could those I work with once in a while."

"We were actually talking about that on the way here," Samantha said, smiling at the shocked look Ben was giving Stan.

"Great," Stan said.

Stan then turned and looked directly at me, his gaze cutting through every thought I had.

"Poker Boy, I still owe you for that Christmas thing. Now I owe you for this as well. Don't forget to collect if you need to."

"I won't," I said.

Stan took Patty's hand and kissed the back of it lightly. "A pleasure, as always. I owe you as well, and look forward to your collecting."

Patty had the decency to just blush and say nothing.

Stan then pointed to Screamer. "No rest for the weary."

"What's going on?" Screamer asked, pushing his chair back and standing.

"Police just caught a guy they think buried his wife alive somewhere out in the desert," Stan said. "Sorry to take you from the party, but they need to find out where he buried her and try to get to her to see if she's still alive."

"That's it for me," Screamer said, smiling to the group as he moved to stand beside Stan. "Next time, everyone. And Poker Boy, tell Madge I'll make it up to her later."

He gave me a smile that let me know I didn't want to ask exactly what he was going to make up to Madge.

"Thanks, Screamer," I said.

"Yes, thank you," Samantha said. "For helping bring Ben back to me."

"I'll see you around I'm sure," he said to Samantha. "Maybe we can even work together on a case some time."

"I'd love that," Samantha said.

"Again, congratulations, everyone," Stan said. "And thank you from us all."

With that, the Buddy Holly song started back up, Madge kept coming toward us, and Stan and Screamer were gone.

Patty and I spent most of dinner, between wonderful laughing and bad jokes about old slot machines, explaining who the gambling gods were to Ben, Samantha, Johnny, Geneva, and Tech,

and why it was so special to have Lady Luck herself thank us.

It was somewhere in the middle of my mixed-berry pie that Patty reached over and put her hand on my leg under the table.

Oh, at that moment I felt better than if I had won the entire World Series of Poker. So many thoughts, so many emotions were going through me that I just about had a melt-down right there.

Patty leaned over, her hand firmly on my thigh, and whispered softly in my ear. "Don't eat too much dessert."

I wanted to ask her why, but just barely managed to turn and look into her eyes instead.

"I've got a very special dessert for you back at my place," she whispered. "It includes a long hot shower and a bar of raspberry soap."

She pulled back slightly so I could look into those wonderful brown eyes of hers. I could tell instantly that she was very, very serious.

I started to ask her how she knew about the soap and shower of my dreams, then realized that she was a superhero. She was Front Desk Girl. More than likely, one of her special powers was to sense someone's wants and needs. Over the time we had been together, I had been giving off a lot of clues. Even the most rank of poker players could have read me and my emotions when it concerned her. No doubt her superpowers had me read right from the start.

I pushed the remainder of my pie away with a firm push that sent it into the middle of the table.

She laughed. "I take that as a yes?" she asked.

I put my hand on top of hers and squeezed, then with a smile I turned in my chair to face where Madge was standing and shouted, "Check!"

Later that night, I practiced my new superpower ability to stop time, making the shower and the wonderful-smelling bar of soap last a very, very long time.

The next morning, Patty went back to work, with a promise of a very special late dinner after the tournament was over.

I signed up and played in the three-thousand-dollar-pot-limit hold-em tournament. I got knocked out a little after eleven that evening, after my pair of black sevens caught another seven on the flop to make a set. I got all my chips in and was ahead in the hand until the guy who had called me with a pair of fives caught runner-runner hearts to make a heart flush.

So much for doing favors for Lady Luck.

But that night, staring into Front Desk Girl's wonderful brown eyes, I knew right then and there that I was the luckiest person alive, and sometimes there was more to life than winning a poker tournament.

~

FICTION RIVER: YEAR ONE

Missed a volume from Fiction River's first year?

No problem. Buy individual volumes anytime from your favorite bookseller.

See why *Adventures Fantastic* calls *Fiction River* "one of the best and most exciting publications in the field today."

FICTION RIVER: YEAR TWO

A subscription to Fiction River saves you money and ensures you receive the very best short fiction from some of today's best authors. Subscriptions are available in electronic and trade paper formats and begin with the very next volume.

Don't wait!
Subscribe today at www.FictionRiver.com.

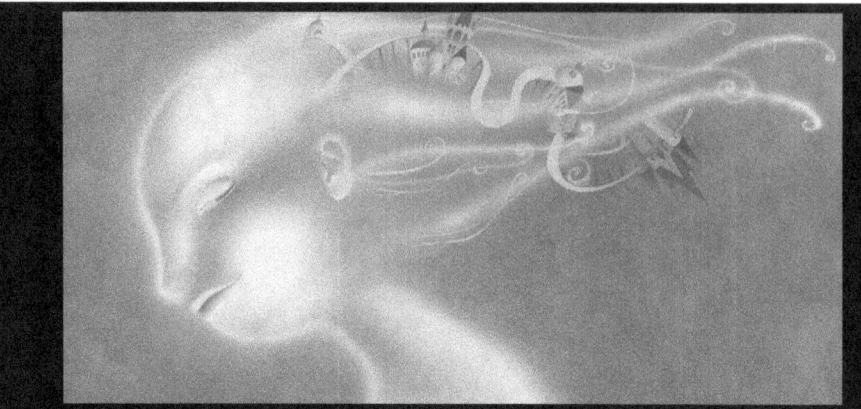

Poems by Dean Wesley Smith

My Farts Cry

You died bringing me a son,
he died with you.
I was angry at you, at the world, at myself,
for you leaving, and taking him. I missed you.

I started drinking, lost my job,
eventually all my friends and yours gave up.
I moved to a new city, cheap old apartment,
where nothing would remind me of you.

It didn't work, I couldn't hold work,
I ate cans of pork and beans and drank beer,
your face, your smile, your absence
always around me.

My apartment now smells like a stopped-up toilet,
old newspapers scattered to the wind.
I open a can, wipe off a spoon,
and drip tears in the beans as I eat.

A swig of beer, a mouthful of beans,
I have no reason to go on.
Even my farts cry
for you.

www.ingramcontent.com/pod-product-compliance
Lightning Source LLC
Chambersburg PA
CBHW081150170626
46813CB00009B/3143